Secrets of the Blue Moon

Jan Heidrich-Rice

NDY Press

Copyright © 2024 by Jan Heidrich-Rice

This novel is a work of fiction. Any references to historical events, real people, or real locales are used fictitiously. Other names, characters, places, and incidents are the product of the author's imagination, and any resemblance to actual events or locales or persons, living or dead, is coincidental.

All rights to reproduction of this work are reserved. No part of this book may be reproduced in any form or by any means (electronic, mechanical, photocopying, recording or otherwise) means, without permission in writing from the copyright owner, except by reviewers, who may quote brief passages in a review. Thank you for respecting the copyright. For permission or information on foreign, audio, or other rights, contact the author at jan@janheidrichrice.com.

First edition | Fall 2024 ~ Paperback ISBN: 979-8-9909771-1-2 and 979-8-9909771-2-9 ~ Digital e-pub ISBN: 979-8-9909771-0-5 ~ LCCN: 2024913432

Cover by Elizabeth Mackey ~ Edited by Misha Carlstedt at Verity Ink Editorial ~ Proofread by Cynthia Houston

SECRETS OF THE BLUE MOON ! Published by NDY Press ~ Printed in the United States of America

For my family.
I love you all to the Blue Moon and back.

"Every man is a moon and has a side which he turns toward nobody; you have to slip around behind if you want to see it."
Mark Twain

A blue moon is the second full moon in a calendar month.
One falls on Halloween only every nineteen years.

Contents

Content Note	XI
1. Chapter 1	1
2. Chapter 2	6
3. Chapter 3	12
4. Chapter 4	18
The Diana Homestead	24
5. Chapter 5	26
6. Chapter 6	32
The Lake Gardner Mill	39
7. Chapter 7	41
8. Chapter 8	47
9. Chapter 9	54
10. Chapter 10	61
11. Chapter 11	67
12. Chapter 12	73
Andre's Chop House	81

13.	Chapter 13	83
14.	Chapter 14	89
15.	Chapter 15	96
	The Dalton Creek Bridge	104
16.	Chapter 16	106
17.	Chapter 17	110
18.	Chapter 18	116
19.	Chapter 19	121
20.	Chapter 20	129
21.	Chapter 21	135
22.	Chapter 22	141
23.	Chapter 23	147
24.	Chapter 24	154
	Reader Note	165
25.	Chapter 25	166
26.	Chapter 26	173
27.	Chapter 27	179
28.	Chapter 28	187
29.	Chapter 29	194
30.	Chapter 30	201
31.	Chapter 31	208
32.	Chapter 32	214

33.	Chapter 33	219
34.	Chapter 34	226
35.	Chapter 35	231
36.	Chapter 36	237
37.	Chapter 37	244
38.	Chapter 38	249
39.	Chapter 39	255
40.	Chapter 40	260
41.	Chapter 41	266
42.	Chapter 42	272
43.	Chapter 43	277
44.	Chapter 44	281
45.	Chapter 45	285
	Author's Notes	291
	About the Author	293

Content Note

This book was created to be an uplifting story of hope, resilience, and redemption. However, it does contain sections that deal with issues of loss, self-harm, and death.

If you find yourself triggered, or if you are in crisis and need help, please reach out to someone you trust for support or call 988.

No one should ever have to be alone.

Chapter 1

LAKE GARDNER, GEORGIA – OCTOBER 2020

On the main drag, a pop-up banner for a haunted walking tour dared: "Meet the Spirits of The Diana Homestead." As Marnie drove past it, her lips twitched. She'd come to Lake Gardner to exorcise her own ghosts. Only now was the irony of her decision sinking in.

The GPS directed her onto Amani Way, and she squinted, looking for house number nine-one-one. Or maybe nine-eleven? Either way, it sounded menacing. The road led to the lake, which reflected a waxing moon. Along the way, the beams of her headlights bounced off ghoulish shadows. A small shape darted in front of her vehicle. She jammed on her brakes, then let out a relieved sigh. Hitting a black cat the week of Halloween wouldn't bode well.

She opened her windows and inhaled the piney night. Edging forward, she spotted her destination—an early 1900s farmhouse dwarfed by a splendid magnolia tree. A custom nameplate hung askew from the porch railing: The Diana Homestead.

Marnie studied the well-lit porch. With its pumpkins and potted mums and rustic rocking chairs, it reminded her of her childhood home in north Georgia. It looked cozy. Not haunted. Steeling herself, she parked, walked up the porch steps, and rang the bell.

The door creaked open, revealing a striking woman dressed in black. The woman's eyes flickered, the same soft silver as her hair, which angled at her chin in a bob. Very senior chic.

"Ah," she said, "you must be Marnie Putnam. Please come in."

Before Marnie could take a step, a hulking man stormed up the porch.

"Willow!" He shoved a goldenrod-colored sheet of paper at the older woman. "This house is no place for your witchy voodoo-hoodoo crap. And if I hear you're charging for these bonfires—on my property—I'll take your ass to court."

Willow peered at the flyer, then waved dismissively.

"This is from the 14th." She touched his arm lightly. "I'm sorry you missed it. We celebrated the waning crescent moon, which was lovely. Free and open to all."

Red-faced, the man balled his fists and huffed back down the walk. He climbed into a golf cart parked at the curb and drove off, all hotheaded.

Willow motioned her inside. "Please forgive our impetuous mayor."

The mayor? Interesting. The mayor's wife, Kate Remington, was the one who'd hired Marnie—sight unseen—to record oral histories on the town's ghostlore. She hadn't mentioned witches or voodoo.

Marnie stepped inside. Even with indoor lighting, this woman didn't look like a witch.

"Your room is upstairs." Willow pointed. "Down the hall to the back. Help yourself to anything you'd like in the kitchen, including breakfast in the morning if I'm not here."

Marnie lugged her bags up to her room, grateful Willow hadn't forced small talk. She flipped on the light and flopped down on the brass bed, not bothering to remove its white lace coverlet. Scrolling on her phone, she looked to see if Lee had posted anything to Insta or TikTok. Of course he had. He'd posed for a selfie on the links beneath clear skies. Shared his score card. (Three over par on eighteen holes.) Typical Lee. No signs his life had veered into the rough.

Should she text him to check in? She thought better of that and called him instead.

"Hey, babe," he answered after one ring, his voice warm. "You on your way home?"

"Hey, yourself." She rose and strolled across the room, sitting on the edge of the bay window seat, waiting to see if he'd laugh off his question as a joke. When he didn't, she reminded him, "You know I'm going to be gone for three weeks."

His voice lost its warmth. "We never agreed you should take this assignment."

True, Marnie had nabbed it before fully vetting it with Lee. She'd learned about it while checking out the graduate writing program at the nearby university. While she wasn't eligible to register for classes without graduate school test scores in hand, the school just had a student bail on the oral history project, which offered room and board in Lake Gardner with a small stipend. Plus class credit if she ended up going back to get her master's.

She closed her eyes now. "I thought you understood I needed—"

"Babe," he cut in. "Hang on. I need to take this other call."

Biting back frustration, she further inspected the room. Its farmhouse décor provided rustic but clean refuge, with plenty of windows, a private bath, and a white pitcher of flowers on a writer's desk. Lee returned to the phone as she checked out the ample closet.

"Sorry, Marn," he said. "I'd just like to have you back home. Sleep on it, okay?"

Lee was finished talking, whether she was or not, and he ended the call with a brisk goodnight. She checked her email, then hopped into the shower. As she dressed for bed, her mind swam with thoughts of Halloween. She sure had chosen the perfect place to spend it. Adding even more eeriness, this year's All Hallows' Eve coincided with a blue moon for the first time in almost two decades. But the silly distractions—the black cat, the blue moon, the pop-up banner for a haunted house—did nothing to dwarf the dread of facing her dying marriage.

Lying in bed, she focused on the coolness of her pillow, the crisp sheets enveloping her. Breathing in the pillow's vanilla and lavender scents, she closed her eyes and tried to pray. Instead, her mind jumped back to the mayor on the porch, overheating into a snit at the mention of witchcraft and bonfires.

Were witch hunts *really* still happening here in Georgia in 2020? Surely not.

Turning on her side, she made herself recite the twenty-third Psalm, even though her faith had grown more precarious after her second miscarriage.

"The Lord is my shepherd..." she chanted in her mind. Finally, she fell asleep.

Marnie jolted upright, sweating, unsure of her surroundings. Moonlight slipped through the cracks where the blinds met the windows, breaking the blackness. Her phone shined: 3:34 a.m. Leaning back on the pillow, she remembered. She'd had a dream. Vivid, but just a dream.

In it, she gathered chicory for tea with her mom, Patsy. They sang a hymn to pass time, harmonizing like a church choir. "*Oh, sister, let's go down...*" They moved to the rhythm of crickets, inhaling the earthy smell of the river. Butterflies flitted from milkweed to sunflowers, then on to spiderwort.

Hugging her covers, Marnie tried to shut out the next part. The part where the singing stopped, where her mother cried out that one of the lambs had broken loose. But the dream had continued. Her heart burned as she ran to help. Her head throbbed, desperate to shut out the mournful wails and the burble of rushing water. Tears blinded her, but she kept on running. When she fell, all went still.

Awake now, she rubbed her eyes and squinted to get her bearings in the dark. To ground herself, she stared up toward the ceiling fan, telling herself everything was all right.

Except something *wasn't* right. The fan blades moved slowly, then stopped. They moved again. From the attic portal beside the fan, something—someone?—stared down at her.

"Mom?" She sat upright, partly hoping but also dreading that maybe her mother's spirit had come to call.

She drew her covers closer, unnerved by a translucent flame that now flickered and spat from the portal, emitting a playful, sparkler-like sound. It smelled of cinnamon, its essence strong but sweet. Marnie tried to identify what else she heard. Shuffling feet. Sobs. Or maybe giggles?

When an intense energy yanked the covers from her, she stiffened.

Three sharp clapping sounds came from the portal.

Thwack. Thwack. Thwack.

Then they stopped. So did the giggly sobs.

The flame, larger now, continued to flicker in the quiet and smelled more pungent, like a cinnamon-laced whisky.

Was it the same flame?

Like it even mattered. This was ridiculous.

Marnie clutched the covers back around her and squeezed her eyes shut. *Please be a dream.* Yet when she opened them, the flame still glowed.

"Who are you?" She tried to sound brave, even though she was scared shitless.

The flame blinked.

She tried one more time. "What do you want?"

The flame flickered large, and Marnie feared her heart might stop.

She held her breath, waiting.

But then a gust of wind whipped through the room, and the flame snuffed out.

Chapter 2

It wasn't like she'd never seen a ghost before. Her mother's spirit had become a strange kind of normal in the early years following her death. But seeing a ghost that was *not* her mother? That left Marnie unglued.

Her mind still rankled from the early dawn encounter as she descended the stairs into the kitchen. Her pulse thrummed in her ears against the emptiness of the old farmhouse. She poured a cup of coffee and sipped it, waiting for the caffeine to kick in. A whiteboard on the wall contained two notes, the first a menu for tonight's dinner.

Monday, Oct. 26 - Antipasto salad ~ fresh bread ~ brownies.

The second note, in the same neat scroll, addressed her personally.

Marnie – Come have breakfast at the farmer's market at Melrose Farm Park. ~W~

No need to twist her arm. She was ready for some space from The Diana. Not to mention she needed to track down Kate Remington to learn more about her assignment.

She drove into town, following the signs to the farmer's market across the tracks. Old brick structures towered on both sides of the crossing. Signage on the right beckoned the public to stop by the Lake Gardner Mill: "Come, have a cold one with the ghost of Isabella!"

Well, Halloween *was* right around the corner. Marnie always celebrated with harvest décor, like corn stalks and uncarved pumpkins. Apparently, Lake Gardner preferred witches and ghosts.

She followed the town's seasonal theme into Melrose Farm Park, which sprawled for acres. Scarecrows trumped ghosts here, and pumpkins lay tucked among asters and mums in the landscape. A large pond anchored the park's center, a walking track looping around it.

The sun warmed her as she exited her Outback and approached the market activity. A light breeze ruffled the gold-and-purple petals on the pansies one vendor displayed. Her stomach growled as the scent of apples, sugar, and spices teased the air. She checked out the goods—vegetables, eggs and cheese, honey, pottery and art—some splayed out in truck beds, most on tables. She recognized Willow, selling crystals and herbs, offering samples of iced lavender tea.

"Hey, you." Willow waved her over amiably.

Willow was dressed in dark blue today, her steel-gray protective mask imprinted with crescent moons, dragonflies, and feathers. She handed Marnie a sample of tea, the sunlight catching the ornate silver rings on her slender fingers and a tattoo on her left forearm—a Celtic cross intersecting the four elements.

"Listen," Marnie said, accepting the tea, "something weird happened to me back at the house." She fumbled for her money, but Willow waved her off.

"I don't doubt it. Old houses are full of magic and mystery, aren't they?"

Willow tilted her head toward one booth over, where loaves of bread and muffins and scones lay showcased against vibrant flowers made from papier mâché. "The tea pairs well with Lindsay's scones."

Um, okay? Willow was either blowing her off or flaky as hell. Time would tell.

Marnie approached the dark-haired Lindsay, whose brown eyes flickered in the sunlight as she nodded a greeting. She looked extremely young.

"You live in Lake Gardner?" She offered a generous sample of scone.

"For three weeks," Marnie replied. "I'm here to write some of the town's oral histories."

"Ahhh, yes. The ghost book."

A shaky little voice piped up from behind them. "I don't like ghosts, Mommy."

Startled, Marnie whirled around to see a small girl staring through big hazel eyes up at her mother, who stood nearby.

"Oh, sweetie." Lindsay crouched down to hand the girl a purple flower, its crepe bloom as big as a grapefruit. "Don't be afraid. Ghosts aren't real."

Willow piped in. "Besides, your fears have no clue how strong you really are."

The little girl's eyes shimmered with delight as Willow placed a plastic light-up star necklace around her neck. Marnie smiled, too, but her lips turned down some when she recognized the beefy man driving a golf cart down the middle of the market.

Mayor Remington wore a chamber-of-commerce-approved grin today as he slowed the golf cart to a stop in front of Lindsay's booth. A petite woman beside him—his wife, Marnie presumed—tousled her caramel-blond hair over the shoulder of her cream-colored satin top.

"You're Marnie Putnam." The woman beamed, offering her hand once they stopped.

Flustered, Marnie murmured, "Yes, ma'am."

The pandemic now edged into its eighth month, and safety protocols ebbed and flowed and exhausted. Marnie still chose to share a feeble nod rather than a handshake.

"I recognize you from LinkedIn." The woman's laugh sounded like music. "I'm Kate Remington. And this is Dutch." She pointed to the man, who bobbed his head politely.

"I'm Mr. Kate Remington." He had an easygoing manner today. "Aka the mayor."

If he had a clue Marnie had witnessed last night's tantrum, he didn't let on.

Kate rubbed her hands together, delighted, as Dutch hopped out of the cart. "I'm so glad I caught you here, Marnie. How 'bout I drive you by the sites we want covered in the book?"

"Great plan." Dutch clasped Marnie's hand before she could stop him. "Pleased to have you on board. Now if you'll excuse me..."

He had already moved on, ready to schmooze somewhere he'd be more appreciated, as Marnie found herself perched inside the golf cart, preparing to ride shotgun.

Kate took the wheel and restarted the engine, letting her colorful protective mask hang under her face like a necklace.

"I'm so tired of all this social distancing nonsense," she muttered.

Marnie, too, had grown weary of the pandemic. The protective mask-wearing *did* get old. Still, she tucked her own mask over her nose and mouth. Kate gave her a happy thumbs-up. Mask-free, she appeared to have no qualms with whatever Marnie chose to do for herself.

Blond waves blowing in the wind, Kate drove northbound, where the houses grew statelier. A mix of shotguns and painted ladies lined the street, along with some rebuilt Craftsmen bungalows.

"Some of these homes date back to the 1860s," Kate said. They passed an old red brick elementary school. "Dutch and I had hoped to convert that old school into a bed-and-breakfast. But so far, the red tape's been too much." Kate kept driving. "Up ahead"—she nodded toward an expansive Victorian, its trim a mix of purples and pinks and oranges—"is the Joy Sass Grace Place. It's a social enterprise that supports victims of domestic violence. During the war of Northern Aggression, it was a residence and a makeshift hospital." Kate slowed down.

Marnie shivered thinking of all the Civil War spirits that likely walked the streets of this town. But none were trying to flag her down. At least not here in the light of day.

"I'd love you to write up a history on The Joy Sass Grace Place," Kate said, stopping the cart. "But Dutch thinks your schedule will run too tight. He'd rather have you cover the Dalton Creek Bridge instead. It's several miles down that way." She gestured toward the tree-lined road.

Great. Marnie couldn't even navigate her own marriage. Now she was supposed to referee the Remingtons'?

Kate started the cart again, veering left and across the tracks. The houses ran smaller here, their yards unkempt and dotted with items more suited for trash than décor.

"Not our most vibrant postcard picture here, but there are even worse areas near certain parts of the lake." Kate mouthed *meth labs*. "Not that you need to see those."

She turned left again. The homes began to look more like what Marnie had seen earlier—ranch style on neater lots, newly built, perched among some older homes, not so old as to be charming, but just not new.

"So how many places will be covered in this project?" Marnie asked.

"Five. There's the Dalton Creek Bridge...or the painted lady. The Diana makes two, and Dutch and my place makes three. We're right up the street from Willow—easy for you to find."

Kate turned left onto a side street, passing two art galleries and a spa before reaching the main drag. Despite the pandemic, a fair number of people moseyed the streets. Kate pointed to where a couple lingered in front of a sign for Andre's Chop House.

"Andre's is the fourth venue. It was quite the spot back in the Roaring Twenties."

As the cart cobbled over the tracks alongside the Lake Gardner Mill, Kate gestured.

"And the mill here is your last spot. The Lightners can tell you its history."

She drove into the Melrose Farm Park lot, and Marnie pointed to her Outback. When Kate stopped the cart, she pulled a thumb drive from her purse and handed it to Marnie.

"Here are some project files." Her lips curled up almost shyly as she added, "I hope this won't sound silly, Marnie, but I hope you and I can become friends."

Marnie nodded, unsure how else to respond. There was a catch in her heart at Kate's tone. Because beneath all that kick-ass style and confidence, Marnie sensed a lonely lady.

Chapter 3

Back at The Diana, Marnie studied her room and the attic portal closely. While she'd accepted this gig for several reasons, she couldn't deny the ghost angle had been a draw. Sort of a love-hate attraction, so to speak.

"Mom?" she whispered now, waiting for some kind of response.

But nothing. Nada. Zip. She exhaled slowly.

Eleven years ago, after her mother, Patsy's, death, a shining opal orb that smelled of her mom's pear perfume first appeared to Marnie as she lay in bed. The presence, light as a bubble, came and went for years, communicating only through lights and scents, not words. It even followed her from the family orchard to her apartment when she returned to college.

One time Patsy's essence dimmed gray as a cloud after Marnie had a particularly bad date. It was as if her mom was telling her, *oh, hell no*. Marnie had laughed. In better times, the orb shone like a luminous gem to show pleasure.

Marnie first told herself the orb's visits were just her imagination, a sort of magical thinking on her part. Over time, as she truly came to believe the orb was her mother's spirit, she fretted about what her presence meant. What did her mother want, really? Sometimes Marnie had felt Patsy was tormenting her for causing her to die before her time. Yet when her mother's visits stopped right after her father died, Marnie was more devastated than relieved.

So had she really expected her mother's spirit to appear here today? Maybe a little. She'd been sensing some sort of ghostly presence recently—different from before yet still familiar.

Pushing thoughts of her mother aside, Marnie popped the thumb drive Kate had given her into her laptop. When its list of folders appeared on screen, she leaned in, trying to figure out how they pertained to her project. They looked more like Kate and Dutch's personal folders. She told herself not to invade. But one folder beckoned. One titled *Wedding Photos*.

Unable to help herself, Marnie clicked into the folder. Big mistake. She felt an immediate twinge of longing, seeing Kate on her father's arm, aglow in her strapless white satin dress, a tiara tucked neatly into her graceful updo. For a moment, Marnie had to look away.

But something about the picture of Kate with her dad drew her back in. When Lee had proposed, he suggested an elegant Buckhead venue much like the one in Kate's picture. Marnie hadn't wanted a fancy classic wedding, though, not if her dad wasn't there to give her away.

The venue challenge continued. Her sister-in-law, Amanda, suggested she marry back home at the orchard, where her brother RJ could give her away. Marnie begged off, stating Lee had other ideas in mind. In truth, she couldn't bear the thought of a wedding near the spot where she'd caused her own mother's death. Not to mention, she'd turned her back on her brother there, too, during their father's final days.

Amanda, not understanding how Marnie could marry without warm connections to family all around her, sent her the blue silk handkerchief Patsy had carried on her own wedding day, the one she then passed on to Amanda. Marnie thanked her sister-in-law but tucked it away in a drawer. That part of her life was over. She didn't need a reminder.

With a sigh, Marnie clicked on a couple more pictures on the screen in front of her. Guests posing for each other in front of disposable cameras. A closeup of Kate and Dutch looking into each other's eyes, their love so real she could almost taste it.

Enough. She ejected the thumb drive and rose to stretch her legs. Walking to the window, she scanned out back, seeking a distraction. Yet all she could see in her mind was Kate and Dutch, so in love on their wedding day. Were they still? If so, then why did Kate seem so lonely?

Watching the dead leaves fall, Marnie's heart tightened. Never mind Kate and Dutch. What was happening with her and Lee?

From the very start—a blind date eight whopping years ago—he drew her in with his confident charm. He introduced her to escargot, oysters, and fine wine. She got him to try candied bacon and Irish Car Bombs. *Real* apple pie. Teaching was her calling, she told him. He said he found that *sweet*. They were an odd match. She doubted they would last.

But a weekend in Savannah, where room service delivered champagne and chocolate-covered strawberries, sealed the deal. Marnie was nervous. She'd only ever been with one other man. Lee was tender, though. He told her he was falling in love with her. Before long, Marnie was ready to tell him she loved him, too. He was established and responsible and made her feel safe—something she desperately craved after losing both of her parents.

They were married after the end of the school year. In Vegas. Per her wishes, not his.

A sharp knocking interrupted her thoughts. She whipped her attention back to the portal. There was no sign of a flame, but the sharp scent of cinnamon whisky overwhelmed her.

"What do you want from me?" she snapped.

She sensed this spirit's displeasure with her company. Well, the feeling was mutual. Then the cinnamon smell dissolved in a huff, and Marnie no longer felt the otherworldly presence. Good riddance.

As she gazed back out at The Diana's gardens, there was a heightened sense of emptiness. Why had she never told Lee—her husband, her safe haven—about her mother's ghost? Then again, why would she have? Patsy's ghost had dissipated long before she and Lee met.

Recently, though, after the miscarriages, the opal orb had returned, enhanced by a glittery pink dot of light on the right and blue on the left. It was like her mother had come back to her, lost babies in tow. Except Patsy's spirit no longer communicated, not even through cryptic light signals. If the visits were intended to comfort Marnie, they weren't working.

Marnie wished she could talk to Lee about them, but she couldn't. Not after all this time.

Another rapping sound cut the air, and she jumped, jerking to look up toward the portal.

But it was Willow, peeking in through the door. "There's someone here to see you."

"Oh?"

A smile toyed at the corner of Willow's lips. Biting her own lip, Marnie followed her down the stairs. Through the open front door, she saw the familiar Lexus parked at the curb. Her heart quickened as she recognized the man peeking through the doorway, a bouquet of hot-pink spider mums in his hand.

"Lee?" She had expected him to call, not to make the ninety-minute drive.

"Let me put these in water for you." Willow reached for the flowers and disappeared.

Marnie joined Lee on the porch, where he leaned against the rail. A striking man, tall and sinewy and sandy-haired, he still had a tan in late fall. "I missed you," he said. "And I felt bad we didn't have more time to talk. The way you wanted."

Her mouth was dry. She pointed to a willow rocker, then sat in the one next to it.

"Let me get your bags." Lee didn't move from the porch rail. "Let me take you home."

Marnie tensed. "You said you wanted to talk."

"I do." He scanned the porch. "But I'd prefer somewhere more private."

She flushed. "You want to come up to my room?"

"Marnie." He laughed. "Come home. Then we can talk all night if you'd like."

She relaxed a little at the way his eyes sparkled and the pleasing quality in his voice. It reminded her of the old Lee, the one she'd fallen in love with all those years ago.

"We don't need all night," she said. "I just appreciate your hearing me out."

"Of course." He still didn't move from the porch railing.

She searched for the words to reach him. "I know it seemed impetuous to you when I accepted this gig. But it wasn't just a whim. I need something of my own."

Marnie looked past him, searching for how to explain.

"I mean, you have your career," she said. "Your hobbies. Your guys' weekends."

His eyes lit up at that. "Hey, why don't you and Tecia do a weekend in the mountains? A week, even?"

She shook her head. Her best friend, Tecia, had a job and twin daughters to work around these days. She barely had time for texts or phone calls anymore.

Marnie didn't need Lee to fill up her calendar for the sake of busyness. Rather, she craved his empathy. She wanted to know he understood how much she mourned losing her teaching job on top of all of life's other wildness.

Lee just didn't get it. His eyes sparked again.

"I know." He had another idea. "Why don't you come with me to Charlotte later this week? I have a two-day business trip, but we could extend it."

Marnie studied him, trying to understand why they weren't communicating.

"I can't do the baby thing anymore," he said softly. "I'm sorry. I just don't have it in me to do the up-and-down thing, getting excited and then deflated over and over again."

Ah. Maybe Lee had processed more than she was ready to hear.

She stared out at the massive magnolia. *He* didn't have it in him? Funny, she thought *her* body carried the onus of pregnancy—and loss. Not to mention, she did have it in herself, to check out fertility options, to keep on trying. She choked back her frustration.

Did he always do this—cut off the conversation whenever her needs arose?

"I need more, Lee." She rocked the chair mechanically, still hoping to help him understand. "I need to reframe my life and do something that...matters."

His eyes flashed. Out of hurt? No, he was angry.

"I don't understand you, Marnie. I just don't. Is being my wife not enough?"

Her heart stung as badly as if he had slapped her. "That's not fair."

"Well, that's how you make me feel. Like I'm not enough."

"Because you're not." She squeezed her fists and blurted it out.

Shit, shit, shit. Her heart pounded, but she couldn't retract it. Not to mention, she shouldn't have to. She would never ask him whether being her spouse was enough or whether he wanted more. Why couldn't he get that?

He hung his head, defeated. "I'm going home." He took a couple steps, then turned to face her before leaving. "You can come if you want, but..."

She waited, her face growing warmer. "But what?"

His eyes lost their sparkle. He turned and walked away without finishing his sentence.

Chapter 4

Marnie clenched her fists, watching the Lexus disappear.

Part of her wanted to chase after Lee, to holler, "You don't just get to walk away!" But her pride wouldn't allow it. Neither would her anger—at him for refusing to hear her out, but also with herself for her inability to make him understand.

What did it say about their marriage if standing up to him made her fear she'd lose him?

The front screen door squeaked and Willow appeared. "How about some lemon balm tea?" She gestured toward the kitchen. "I've got some steeping."

Marnie faked what she hoped was a happy face, not trusting her voice to hold steady. She followed Willow, who poured their tea and suggested they go out back, where a couple of Adirondack chairs rested near the house. They sat, and Marnie's tension eased in the sunlight that glimmered off the garden squares and beyond.

"I sensed you could use a breather," Willow said. "Or even a friendly ear."

Marnie fidgeted with her mug and inhaled the lemony scent. She'd rather not share her woes with a stranger. Then again, she had no one else, and there might be something to say for the fact Willow didn't know her. What did it matter if Marnie spilled a secret, an embarrassing confession, even? Who would Willow tell?

Marnie took a sip of tea before letting out a long sigh. "You're not married."

"I'm a widow." Willow smoothed her hair, the silver rings on her fingers catching the afternoon sun. "Married for forty-five years."

Marnie felt foolish for the way she had opened the conversation. Her own parents' marriage had been long, too—much longer and wiser than her and Lee's seven years.

Willow stared into the back lot. "We had a good run. Far from perfect, but marriage is hard." She glanced at Marnie. "Just about anything worth having is."

Such a trite statement. But true, too.

"We struggled with infertility for years." Willow's voice softened.

Marnie's skin tingled. Had Willow been eavesdropping on her and Lee on the porch?

"We eventually had a beautiful daughter." Willow still scrutinized the orchard. "And years and years of good times. When we lost her..." Her voice caught, but just for a second. "All I can say is, I wouldn't give back the pain if it meant never experiencing the joy."

Willow *had* been listening. But how could Marnie be angry with this woman who shared her own struggles with loss and renewed hope in order to ease Marnie's burdens?

"I'm sorry for your loss," she whispered.

"Thank you." Willow cocked her head. "But back to you. I suspect you're pondering which challenges you'd rather tackle, the ones back home, or the ones here?"

"Are you psychic or something?" Marnie's words came out in a soft laugh.

"Oh, butterfly." Willow laughed lightly, too.

Marnie liked how this woman didn't care much about how others saw her. She approached matters in a straightforward manner. But she was kind. Then again, maybe Marnie just liked how Willow called her *butterfly*. She wasn't sure why Willow did it, but it sparked warm memories of the way her own mother used to call her *marshmallow*.

"You know," Willow continued, "we all have psychic abilities."

"I don't think I do." If Marnie did, she would read Lee's mind to know exactly how to reach him and help the two of them connect again.

"We all have spiritual gifts," Willow insisted. "Some of us are just more tuned in than others." She looked at Marnie, her eyes gleaming. "Walk with me?"

They strode in silence among the property's garden squares, sixteen of them.

"You garden?" Willow asked.

"I grew up on an orchard."

Marnie hadn't noticed the pumpkins before, but there they were out back, their vines an intrusive, snarly mess. Yet among the vines rested the fruit, plump and orange, ready for harvest.

"I love the beauty of a garden," Willow said. "Being among the plants and earth and animals." Her eyes crinkled at the corners. "The Divine is in nature, don't you think?"

Hmmm. Marnie pictured her Buckhead garden, a pretty Pinterest-inspired mix of flowers and vegetables planted to promote healing. Yet she and Lee just seemed to reap anger.

At the next garden square, Willow stopped, pulled a towel and shears from her apron pocket, and bent to snip some greens. She wrapped the greens and handed the shears to Marnie, pointing toward a clump of rosemary sprigs. Marnie clipped a couple, lifting them to her nose and inhaling their piney essence. They walked again, back toward the house.

Marnie spoke delicately. "Something strange is going on here. Up in my room."

Willow kept walking. "Tell me about it."

She thought back to last night. "I saw a flame. It smelled like cinnamon. I heard what might have been crying. Or giggling. And then something—some kind of force—pulled the covers off me." Marnie's heart quickened, remembering. "I couldn't move."

Willow nodded. "Sleep paralysis." Perhaps reacting to Marnie's puzzlement, she added, "It's a time between wakefulness and sleep. The sleeper is aware, but they can't move."

Marnie got that part. "But what do you think I saw?"

Willow shrugged. "Only the Divine knows."

For some reason, that comment irritated Marnie.

Willow must have sensed it. "Sorry. I wasn't trying to blow you off with a bullshit answer, if that's what you think."

The older woman continued walking toward the house, and Marnie followed her into the kitchen, where Willow laid the produce on the counter.

"It sounds like spirits visited you," she said.

Marnie's heart pulsed in her throat. She hadn't expected her to state it with such a matter-of-fact tone. At Willow's prompting, they left the kitchen and walked down a hall, past a utility closet and a powder room. They stopped at an area outside a study where Marnie guessed Willow saw her life-coaching clients. Willow studied her with her silver-gray eyes.

"Does that frighten you—the idea that spirits may have visited?"

"I'd like to say no. But maybe a little." Marnie stared at a nearby table topped with stones, candles, oils, and herbs. "I respect the spirit world," she clarified. "Which is different than fearing it." She looked at Willow.

They stood in the quiet, and then Willow pointed up to the oval-framed photo on the wall above the table. "That's Roxy and CeCe." When Marnie tilted her head, confused, Willow added, "The mother and daughter who died here in 2012."

In the photo, a round-faced older woman beamed from what appeared to be The Diana's front porch. She cradled the back of a rocker where a younger woman sat, one with the same full face and expression. But instead of her mother's silver-white hair, CeCe's was golden. And instead of Roxy's crinkled eyes that smiled downward, CeCe's almond-shaped eyes slanted upward. Her neck was short, and the features on her face flat.

"CeCe had Down syndrome," Marnie surmised. "How did they die?"

"Double murder?" Willow straightened a candle, askew in its holder on the table. "The case never got solved. But some people claim they've seen Roxy's ghost searching the house, calling out CeCe's name."

There was disdain in the woman's tone. "You don't believe them?"

Willow's lips twitched downward. "I don't think it's my place to deny those stories, even if they do come across as cartoonish pap. I mean, an older lady in a dither, wringing her hands and crying for her daughter. Kind of cliché, don't you think?" She looked at Marnie earnestly. "But who knows? Spirits probably show themselves in different ways to different people at different times."

Marnie looked away. "Have you ever seen them?" she asked.

"Roxy and CeCe?" Willow's expression softened. "No. But I used to see signs they'd visited. Spilled flour and sugar and cinnamon in the kitchen in the morning. Muddy tracks from the back door." She straightened the frame on the wall. "I found this picture of them in a box in the basement. And I got to thinking. What if they just wanted to know we remember them?"

"Have you seen signs of them since you hung the picture?"

"No." Willow's eyes probed Marnie's. "But I don't think the dead continue to haunt us unless they think we can help them." She paused. "Do you?"

Without waiting for an answer, Willow stepped away, into her office, where there was a shuffling of papers. When the older woman returned, she thrust something into Marnie's hands.

Marnie studied the brochure for *Lake Gardner's 2020 Walking Ghost Tour.*

"Read this," Willow said. "At least the part about The Diana. Even if it makes you mad."

Marnie stared down at the brochure, a chill running the length of her spine.

"There's a reason you're here," Willow said. "I can sense it." She turned back toward the kitchen. "Dinner's at six. We can talk more then."

The Diana Homestead

Lake Gardner's 2020 Walking Ghost Tour

With its well-tended gardens and its tidy, refurbished structure, it's difficult to believe The Diana Homestead is the site of Lake Gardner's most heinous crime—the Blue Moon murders of August 31, 2012.

The deaths were not discovered until three days later, when on Monday, September 3, 2012, a neighbor, concerned that newspapers were piling in The Diana's driveway, requested that law officials perform a welfare check. Upon arriving, deputies discovered the bodies of Roxane (Roxy) Tripp, age 73, and her daughter Cecelia (CeCe), age 35, dead at the scene.

Authorities would not provide details except to confirm the women died on the night of August 31, a date that marked a rare occurrence—the second full moon within a one-month period, commonly known as a Blue Moon. The law officials' silence spawned rumors.

Some Lake Gardner residents speculate the deaths resulted from a murder-suicide. Others believe a double murder remains unsolved to this day, possibly tied to a coven of witches gathered at the nearby old Dalton Creek Bridge for a Blue Moon cleansing ceremony.

Meanwhile, periodic visitors and residents of The Diana have reported seeing a distressed woman searching the house. Dressed in a pink bathrobe and blue slippers, she wanders up and down the stairs, into every room.

According to current owner Dutch Remington, "Some boarders have claimed to hear her crying out in search of her daughter, CeCe. Personally, I haven't encountered that. But who am I to say? Just because I haven't seen or heard her ghost doesn't mean it doesn't exist."

Chapter 5

Shortly before six, Marnie returned downstairs. From the foot of the stairwell, she could see into the kitchen, where Willow visited with another woman. Willow glanced her way and beckoned with a wave.

"Marnie," she called out, "come meet my dear friend, Vanita Patel."

The other woman shared an amiable nod. She appeared to be of Asian-Indian descent and, like Willow, perhaps in her mid- to late-sixties, although Marnie couldn't be sure. Her father used to joke he could never tell a woman's age as she matured, because unlike men, women's hair never changed color. Whether enhanced or natural, Vanita wore her shiny blue-black hair in a pixie with side-swept bangs. Smart and sassy.

"Let's sit on the sun porch." Willow pointed to an extended area of the kitchen, where she had set a table with three place settings. She pulled a couple of dishes from the refrigerator, and Vanita picked up a basket of heavenly smelling bread, already sliced.

Marnie followed the women and sat at the open place. Willow poured them each wine from a ceramic jug before asking for a moment of silence. Afterward, Marnie accepted a piece of bread and served herself from the huge salad bowl laden with cheeses, olives, peppers, and tomatoes. She added some meat from the separate plate of cured ham, salami, and pepperoni.

"Most of the produce is from the gardens here on The Diana," Willow said. "Vanita often joins me for dinner. I prepare it, we eat together, and she leads cleanup duty. You're welcome to join us with that arrangement if you'd like?" Willow paused. "Unless you like to cook."

"I'm fine with your cooking," Marnie said.

"Works for me, too." Vanita took a healthy bite of salad.

"So what can you all tell me?" Marnie stabbed an olive with her fork. "About this house? And the Remingtons'?"

Vanita swallowed quickly. "For starters, some people claim The Diana is haunted."

"As described in the brochure Willow gave me." Marnie already knew this much.

Willow's lips thinned into a stern line. "I hate to think Roxy's and CeCe's memories are going to be dragged through the mud again with the ghost tours. And the book you're working on." She turned quickly to Marnie. "Don't get me wrong. I'd love to have answers. But they seem at peace now. I worry that stirring up past energy might change that."

Marnie stuck with her questions. "Do you believe their deaths were a double murder?"

"Probably," Vanita said. "Especially if it's true someone beat them to death with a hammer and slit their throats ear to ear."

Marnie shuddered. Those details hadn't made it into the brochure.

"Those were just rumors." Willow scowled. "Along with the severing of CeCe's pinkie. But authorities only ever confirmed one thing. The women died on the night of August 31."

"During a Blue Moon." Vanita drew out *blue* and *moon*, wiggling her fingers to feign a sense of eeriness.

"Some folks tried to tie the deaths to a lunar Wiccan ritual," Willow said. "Or, as some called it, a satanic ceremony."

Vanita gestured again, her eyes big. Marnie wondered who she mocked, the alleged Wiccan worshipers or the townies who pointed blaming fingers their way.

"Roxy and CeCe were reclusive," Willow continued, ignoring Vanita. "They had no family, except for Roxy's foster son, Jack. He'd aged out of the system, but he stayed in touch. Which is probably why he became the lead suspect."

Marnie sensed Willow didn't buy this theory. "Was he arrested?"

"Yes," Willow replied. "But the judge ended the trial before it went into jury deliberations due to insufficient evidence."

"Do you think he did it?" Marnie pressed.

"We'll probably never know," Vanita said. "Jack died last year. From a brain aneurysm."

Willow's eyes clouded. "The police weren't exactly transparent during the investigation. The more vague they got, the more folks jumped to fill in the gaps with their own imaginations."

People did tend to do that. Marnie understood the longing for answers.

"You'll need to know more for your book." Willow patted her hand. "Lucky for you, Vanita works at the library." She rose to clear the leftover food.

"I'll be happy to give you a tour of our archives and share the passwords to some databases," Vanita said.

Willow returned to the table with a plate of brownies.

Vanita grinned at her. "Are these brownies…um…special?"

"You're full of sass tonight, V." Willow shot her a half-wink.

Willow's response didn't exactly answer Vanita's question. Still, when both women helped themselves to a brownie, Marnie did likewise.

"I am feeling extra irreverent tonight," Vanita admitted between bites.

"You brought up the Remingtons." Willow smiled balefully at Marnie. "Thinking and talking about Dutch can get Vanita's blood boiling."

Marnie made a silent note of that and used the comment as a springboard. "So, what can you all tell me about Dutch and Kate?"

Willow stared off. "They came to Lake Gardner in the early 2000s, before my time here. I understand they bought their house up the street when it was undergoing foreclosure."

"Dutch's background is in the building industry," Vanita added. "Kate's is in interior design. So they started buying and flipping houses." She cut off another sliver of brownie. "When Dutch got frustrated with how long building approvals took, he ran for city council. Then mayor. Some say he brought this town back from the economic ashes."

"Kate certainly seems to think so," Marnie said between nibbles on her brownie. "But what's with the ghost obsession?"

"Plenty of locals enjoy celebrating the town's ghostlore," Vanita said. "Especially at Halloween." Then she added with a laugh, "Same could be said about the town's witches."

Marnie choked back a laugh herself. "Dutch doesn't seem too keen on witches."

Willow shifted her weight, probably remembering the same thing Marnie did—his verbal outburst on the porch the night before.

Vanita spelled things out with more clarity. "Dutch thinks Willow is a witch."

This time when Marnie choked, it wasn't to hold back a chuckle.

"I work as a life coach," Willow piggybacked on what Vanita said. "It sometimes involves helping people through their struggles to deal with death and grief. Their own or those of their loved ones."

Marnie understood those struggles all too well. But she wasn't sure what they had to do with witches.

Willow added, "Dutch is just uncomfortable exploring outside his beliefs."

Vanita made a face but then relaxed it and held her hand to her heart. "Exactly. Take me, for example. I'm Sikh." She pronounced it with a short I, *sick*, not *seek* as Marnie had always heard it. "Dutch can't even wrap his head around the fact that I don't eat meat. It's not in his fiber to grasp why I might not see heaven as the endpoint or Jesus as the only way."

Ah, yes. Plenty of people had trouble seeing other people's faiths as valid options.

"I'm kind of surprised the man believes in ghosts at all then," Marnie mused.

Vanita burst out laughing. "Oh, honey. He doesn't need to believe to capitalize on them. Especially The Diana's story."

Willow stood. "I'm a little disappointed in Kate, though. She didn't used to be so flip about life after death." She walked to the sink and filled a kettle with water for the stove.

Marnie rose to collect their silverware.

"So how do you feel about ghosts, Vanita?" she asked. "Do you believe in them?"

Vanita flashed Marnie a sheepish grin. "I'm not sure I believe in them." She paused for just a beat. "But I do know they frighten me."

Marnie let out a soundless laugh.

The tea kettle whistled, and Willow removed it from the burner.

"Tea?" Vanita asked, reaching into the cupboard for mugs.

Marnie declined and moved to the sink to rinse dishes.

Willow waved her off while filling the tea mugs with steaming water.

"We'll cover cleanup tonight, butterfly."

"Yes," Vanita added. "Why don't you go finish unpacking?"

As Marnie dressed for bed, a rap on her door caused her to jump. Holding her hand to her heart, she opened the door to Willow.

"Sorry to frighten you," the older woman said, noting Marnie's frazzled reaction.

"It's okay." But she couldn't help think, by the time she left The Diana, she would be one strong warrior. That, or she'd never leave. She'd be dead. From heart failure.

Upon invitation, Willow carried in a handful of items, including a large seashell, which she set on the writing desk. From it, she retrieved several bunches of herbs and sticks tied together.

"White California sage smudge sticks," she explained. "I use them for energy clearing, but word on the street is they also ward off spirits."

She winked, but Marnie sensed a seriousness in what she said.

"Now," Willow continued, "if you want a repeat of last night, don't burn the sage." She set a lighter beside the shell. "Or...if you do light it and the scent's too much, I can bring you some blue sage. It's also good for cleansings and meditation, but it's less bracing."

"This is fine." Marnie dipped her chin, grateful. "Thank you."

Willow's eyes bore into her. "Just remember, it's only a stop gap. Kind of like your escape here to The Diana. A nice reprieve, until you're ready to face what you're *really* running from."

Marnie had to break away from Willow's scrutiny.

"If the spirits truly want to find you," Willow said, "they will. Eventually."

"Thank you for that," Marnie deadpanned.

Willow glanced around the room, then directly at Marnie. "Sleep well," she said warmly.

Once alone, Marnie lit the sage and braced herself for a harsh astringent scent. She found it more woodsy and herbal than she'd expected.

For a bit, she lay in the dark, tuned into the smoldering sage. She needed a good night's sleep, and if burning sage presented an avenue to help her get that, so be it.

Wrapped in the soft white quilting, she recalled the words from a wall plaque Willow had hanging in the kitchen. They weren't from the twenty-third Psalm, but Marnie repeated them now anyway.

"I am here, I am now. I am safe, I am well."

Chapter 6

The next morning, Marnie poured herself a cup of fresh coffee from the carafe still steaming on the warmer. The sage had worked blessedly well, keeping the spirits at bay through the night. She wanted to thank Willow, but Willow was scarce.

Placing some bread in the toaster, Marnie thought back to when she first suspected her mother's spirit *truly* visited her. With no one to ask about this mysterious otherworld, Marnie had researched ghosts on her own. The web turned up shit-tons of information. *Ghosts appear and behave as they did in life,* one source stated. *They manifest as orbs,* another asserted. Hands-down, the most offensive claim: *Individuals who say they see ghosts are often experiencing the early signs of schizophrenia.*

That one pissed her off. Like anyone seeing spirits couldn't possibly be of the right mind.

Her toast popped, and she jumped. Then she laughed. Clearly, she *wasn't* of the right mind, but she didn't think mental health issues were the reason.

As she doctored her toast with apple butter, she remembered something else from her info dives. *Ghosts are non-believers who have no way into heaven.* That gem had ended her research completely, shaking her faith, which filled her with guilt. But if her mom didn't deserve a divine afterlife, that didn't say much for the God Marnie had grown up worshiping.

Standing at the counter, she ate her toast and studied Willow's *I am here, I am now* plaque. Her new roommate puzzled but didn't frighten her. That was more than Marnie could say for the house's spirits, who were new and strange and might indeed mean her harm.

There's a reason you're here. I can sense it.

Marnie had pushed Willow's comment out of mind yesterday, uninterested in messing with the afterlife. Clearing her breakfast dishes now, she reconsidered. Her run-ins with her mother had always been elusive. She'd come to accept that. But maybe she could control her ghostly encounters more than she'd ever imagined. Like last night. With the sage.

Rinsing and stacking her dishes, she had another thought. What if the *reason* Marnie was here had nothing to do with spirits? What if it had more to do with saving her marriage? Or, to pose an even more disturbing question, with whether she wanted to save it or not?

That thought hit her hard. Marriage was a lifetime commitment. She'd always believed that. But as she wiped down the kitchen counter, she reminded herself she accepted this project to give herself time and space. To grieve, yes. But also to revisit her sense of self and purpose. That included thoughts on faith and love. And marriage. Because she did have options.

She brooded on that as she walked up the Remingtons' porch steps after breakfast. Kate sprung from her seat on the steps but stopped short on hearing she'd shared the wrong files.

"Where have I put my brain?" Her laugh mixed with the wind chimes twinkling in the morning breeze, and she added, "Wait here."

Marnie sat on the steps, watching the porch ferns sway, the dew on their leaves sparkling in the sun. When Kate returned, she handed over a new thumb drive and sat beside Marnie.

"I'm glad your husband let you take on this assignment," she said.

Marnie stiffened. "I don't think it's Lee's place to *let* me do anything."

Kate brushed at the air dismissively. "Oh, you know what I mean. If he's anything like Dutch, I'm sure he likes to have his say. And get his way."

"Well, who doesn't?" Marnie glanced at Kate sideways.

Kate laughed that musical laugh of hers. "Dutch has always liked to pull the strings, even mine." She dipped her chin. "He dotes on me in so many ways. What does it hurt if he handles me, as long as it's subtle and I'm aware of it?"

Marnie chafed. She didn't consider Lee expressing his wishes as handling her.

"I suppose if I could do things over," Kate said, "I'd acquiesce less."

Marnie picked up a chocolate cookie smell. A whiff of cinnamon, too. She jerked her head to see where it came from. In the ferns, a playful flame now bounced among the lights.

Kate didn't seem to notice. She kept on talking.

"At first I *didn't* see it," she told Marnie. "Dutch would just drop clues that he *liked* something, and then he'd grow frustrated when I didn't pick up that he meant he *wanted* it."

Marnie waited.

"This house, for instance." Kate gestured around them. "Dutch hinted he admired the property. But he wouldn't come straight out and say he wanted it. He had to pretend to debate the pros and cons with me before putting in an offer."

A clapping noise interrupted Kate's story, and the flame disappeared from the ferns. The dew-like lights still lingered, but they no longer danced, and the hot-from-the-oven cookie smell grew faint.

"Are you all right, Marnie?" Kate's eyes widened. "You act like you just saw a ghost."

Marnie flinched. Kate had no a clue how right she might be. The flame in the ferns resembled the spirit Marnie had seen in her room at The Diana her first night there. Dear God, she was jumpy. But she was pretty sure Kate had not seen the flame or heard the clapping that beckoned it away.

For a moment, Marnie couldn't remember their conversation. Once she did, she tried to cover her tracks.

"You were saying Dutch should've just come out and said he wanted to buy the house."

"Yes." Kate sighed. "Why all the games? I knew he intended to get it all along."

Marnie glanced around. The dew on the ferns once again shone like amber glitter.

"Well," she said, "if that's how you ended up with this beautiful place, I'd say everything worked out all right."

Kate tilted her head, and her eyes brightened. "You know what? You're right."

Good. Now to figure out how to make an escape without seeming too abrupt. After all, she worked for Kate. She didn't want to make things more uncomfortable than necessary.

Kate clasped her hands on her knees and leaned forward. "You know, sometimes pretending not to be a strong woman when you are one—well, it can be exhausting. So we strong women have to stick together, learn to play our hands differently than the boys do, you know?"

Then she shifted gears and moved on. "I'm just so glad you're working this project," she said. "Check out what's on the thumb drive. You'll see a spreadsheet of contacts and some previous research documents and files. Give me a holler if you have questions."

Marnie took that as an opening to leave. As she stood, a neon-blue monster truck thundered up, stopping in front of the house. A red-headed man sporting a long, full beard hopped out of the cab. He lugged a power washer from the truck bed and rolled it up near the porch.

"Zack," Kate greeted. "Thanks. Dutch'll appreciate your bringing this by."

"No problem, Katie," the man replied, giving Marnie an appreciative once-over.

"Oh, forgive me," Kate said. "Marnie Putnam, meet Zack Lightner. You'll want to interview Zack for The Lake Gardner Mill's segment of your book."

Zack's eyes narrowed and took on a glint. "Oh, yeah. The ghost book."

"Yes, sir," Marnie said. "The ghost book."

"Hmmmm." Zack sized her up, making her slightly uncomfortable. "I'm juggling a few more events than usual this week, but I think I could fit you in. Say, today at two?"

The tawny lights in the ferns blinked fiendishly as if to tell her she wasn't ready, which she already knew. She rubbed the back of her neck, knowing she'd agree.

"Today at two sounds great." She hoped she sounded enthusiastic. "At The Mill, right?"

The lights in the ferns dimmed, which didn't deter Kate, who rubbed her hands together like a joy-filled child. Zack rolled his eyes. Then he surprised Marnie, leaning over to kiss Kate, first on one cheek, then the other. Pretty European for such a good ol' boy.

"Mmmm, you smell good," he growled.

Kate smacked him playfully. "Just CK One," she said. "My signature scent."

When he cocked his head Marnie's way, she feared he might move in on her for a similar farewell. Thankfully, he didn't.

"Two o'clock." He waved as he left, his truck chugging at an obnoxious volume.

Kate excused herself to go inside again briefly, returning with a copy of the brochure Willow had already given Marnie. "I'm sure Zack will be good about sharing The Mill's stories. But"—she paused—"you might as well read about them before you two talk."

Marnie rose to leave, again overcome by the smell of chocolate cookies.

She cocked her head at Kate. "Do you smell that?"

"What?"

Spirits, she almost said. Except that would sound absurd. "I thought I smelled something sweet," she said instead. "Like someone had been baking."

"Not me," Kate said.

As the twinkling lights continued to pop among the ferns, goose bumps rose on Marnie's arms. She stopped on the stairs, a question forming strong in her mind.

"What about your place, Kate? It has spirits, too, right?"

"According to ghostlore, yes. Three children." Kate's voice wavered. "Kind of ironic since Dutch and I have only one child." She stared off. "We would've liked more, but that didn't seem to be in the grand scheme of things."

Marnie's throat tightened, but she hoped Kate would continue.

"Neither Dutch nor I have ever seen them," Kate said. "But our son, Garrett, used to claim two 'invisible boys' hid things on him. He'd blame those boys for stealing his money and toys." She stopped here, and her lips turned up, remembering. "That was our unorganized little guy for you. He blamed the spirits for the things he lost." She laughed softly.

"They sound mischievous," Marnie said.

"The boys, yes." Kate's lips bowed down. "But the little girl supposedly stands at the top of the stairs, wearing a yellow pinafore, staring down longingly, waiting for someone."

Marnie's breath caught, picturing the yellow pinafore. Yellow, like the lights in the ferns.

"Do you think she's waiting for her brothers to ask her to play?"

"Who even knows if they were related? This house was an orphanage years ago." She pointed toward Marnie's hand. "You can read more about it in the brochure. Or on the town mural up at the library."

Then she suddenly clapped again, beaming, and changed the subject.

"I hope Willow told you about tonight's soiree? Casual. Here. At seven p.m."

Dammit. Willow had not mentioned tonight's gathering—not in person or via the whiteboard for notes in the kitchen. Could she skip it? Probably not. At least not without coming across as extremely ungracious.

Marnie turned back to Kate. "Thanks for the invite," she said. "See you around seven."

The Lake Gardner Mill

Lake Gardner's 2020 Walking Ghost Tour

*B*uilt as a flour mill in the 1870s, today The Lake Gardner Mill hosts hundreds of guests each year as one of the area's premier event centers, owned by Zack and Bree Lightner. Many believe it is also home to the spirit of Edgar, who allegedly sways from a noose tied to the bar's rafters, and Isabella, whose ghostly cries pierce the night air.

Back in the late 1800s, when machines ran without safety covers and emergency shut-offs, accidental deaths were frequent and heinous. Fingers, hands, and even legs were sometimes lost, later to be found among the exposed gears and mechanisms. But ghostlorists agree Edgar Hodges did not die by accident. He died by hanging in the late 1890s. Some think the man took his own life in the mill's off-hours due to ailing health. But others believe Edgar suffered at the hands of a vigilante who, to avenge his sister's rape, shoved Edgar into the machines, later hanging his body, minus his right leg, from the bar's rafters.

Stories about a second spirit are even more confusing than Edgar's. A ghost hunter from the now defunct Preston Foundation for Paranormal Research visited The Mill in the early 1980s and confirmed the presence *of a woman's spirit, possibly from the facility's 1940s breakfast house years. Cobbling together history and lore, the ghostbuster hypothesized that a woman either fell in an accident or jumped to her death to escape an arranged marriage. His claims have been debunked, but the tale of a woman's ghost lives on. Locals call her Isabella, and some say she perished in more recent years, perhaps when The Mill lay vacant after a fire destroyed the kitchens and badly charred the wood structure, which remained intact.*

While Zack Lightner denies any visits from the ghosts of Isabella or Edgar, co-owner Bree Lightner isn't so sure. "Sometimes when I'm near the bar's rafters, the air gets icy," she says. "And on stormy nights, who knows if it's the wind I hear...or the sobs of one of the ghosts?"

Chapter 7

Marnie guided her Outback over the railroad tracks and into the lot of the Lake Gardner Mill. It towered over the town like a monolith, its energy beckoning in the manner of a great lighthouse. She parked beside a sign that read *Valet Parking Only* and started across the gravel lot toward the patio.

A gruff voice called out to her, "Just gonna ignore the sign, eh?"

She brought a hand to her heart, turning toward the voice.

A boisterous laugh filled the air. "Gotcha, didn't I?"

Zack Lightner grinned at her from The Mill's covered patio, where he sat on a sofa near one of the outdoor fireplaces. He rose from his seat, offering his hand as she approached. Marnie bobbed her head to return his greeting.

"Oooh," Zack said. "A cautious one, eh? You gonna be comfortable touring inside?"

"Absolutely." Marnie would mask up and power on through. "But perhaps first we could visit here outside for a bit?"

"Deal," Zack said. "But only if I can offer you a drink. Cranberry or lemon-lime?"

"Cranberry," Marnie said, making herself comfortable in a chair a safe distance from Zack's sofa. Pre-pandemic—and maybe soon again, she hoped—she could envision large groups enjoying this covered patio area, complete with fans, heaters, and high-definition TV sets.

When Zack returned, he carried a tray that held a pitcher and two glasses. He poured one for her and one for himself.

"Salut." She raised her glass, took a drink, then pulled away from the glass. "Oh!"

He had made them sangria. Cranberry sangria. She wasn't a teetotaler, so no harm. But what if she had an alcohol issue? He should've asked. But she needed his story.

"I'm usually more of a Jack and Coke man." Zack raised his glass and grinned.

She placed him at close to forty, and despite his gruff ways, sort of attractive. As she took another drink, she felt his warm brown eyes staring her down, his grin growing wider.

Her cheeks flushed, but she took charge. "So tell me your story, Zack."

"Ah..." He placed his drink on the table. "What d'ya want to know?"

"You've owned the building here for about three years, right?"

"Yep." Zack rubbed his red beard. "I first fell in love with the place when it was a restaurant, maybe twelve years ago? The owners moved back up north, and it sat empty for a few years. The more I talked to people, I kept hearing all these great memories of the place. From even before its restaurant days. Stories from people whose parents worked in the mill years ago."

Marnie glanced about her, trying to imagine the old brick structure as a flour mill. Or a textile mill. Her sketchy research beyond the ghost tour brochure indicated it had been both at various times.

"So you took the plunge." Marnie sipped her sangria, which tasted quite good. And strong.

"Bree and I did, yes."

"Why didn't the two of you want to reopen as a restaurant?"

"Too much work." Zack laughed. "Plus, this town doesn't need another restaurant." He took another swig. "But I loved the bones of the place, and Bree agreed it had some great investment potential. As an event venue, though, not a restaurant. So she got to work, filing for a liquor license. We opted for a full bar, a couple floors, a wide-open space with some side club rooms." He motioned to the lot opposite of where she had parked. "The side lot provides plenty of room for bringing in food trucks, which gives us more options."

Marnie's phone rang. Glancing at it, she moved to send Lee's call to voicemail but accidentally hung up on him. Crap. She couldn't be lightheaded from the sangria already.

"Want me to show you around now?" Zack suggested.

"Sure." She hoped they'd talk longer out here, but what the heck?

She followed him inside, stepping into a place that housed close to 150 years of history. An expansive dark wood bar took up one entire wall. Tables of the same dark wood dotted the space. Restored brick, high ceilings, and a grand chandelier dominated the room.

"See that area beyond the chandelier?" Zack pointed. "Those are the scars from The Mill's first fire in the early 1900s. It wasn't rebuilt until years later. Pretty wild, eh?" He didn't wait for a response. "And then in the 1940s, the roof caved in. See there?"

He gestured toward the second floor, visible from where they stood. Charred wood peeked from its walls, once nearly burned down, now an artful backdrop for massive sections of piping and a boatload of old oak barrels.

"Those bricked-up doors?" He checked for her attention before continuing. "They led to the machine rooms. Some of the bricks are originals from back in the 1870s."

"It's an amazing place." While Marnie didn't pick up any unusual orbs or scents, she was compelled to ask, "I'm surprised you haven't included any stories of ghosts on our tour."

Zack smirked. "I can tell you the stories. But I want to go on the record that they're just stories." He pointed again to the bricked-up doors. "Up there's the spot Isabella jumped from. To escape an arranged marriage."

He gestured next to the rafters above the bar. "And folks say old Edgar hung himself over there during the early mill years. Supposedly because of his ailing health. But there are also tales that one of his legs was severed." Zack frowned. "Depending on who you talk to."

Marnie got a strange vibe from the way Zack relayed these stories. Like he'd memorized them to recite if ever asked to share. But he definitely lacked any conviction about them.

"You don't believe the stories?"

Zack raised his eyebrows and escorted her back to the entrance. He motioned to an area in the middle of the room. "At one point the roof collapsed, and a tree grew right over there, inside, if you can imagine that!" He grinned, then kept talking as he escorted her back outside. "It's a miracle they ever brought the place back to life. From what I've heard, the seventies, eighties, and nineties were especially rough years financially."

Marnie followed him back onto the patio. "I can't imagine the past year has been easy for you and Bree. With the pandemic and all."

"We've done all right." He refilled both their sangria glasses. "The big outside entertainment area helps. Plus, we've had more leeway than we would have if we'd gone the traditional restaurant route." He took a large gulp, put down his drink, and surveyed her. "So, what else can I tell you?"

Marnie referred to something she'd circled on The Ghost Tour brochure, the words *now defunct* in front of *the Preston Foundation*. She studied him closely.

"Stories dug up from the 1980s ghost hunter were debunked, right? So why do you think the stories of Edgar and Isabella live on?"

Zack made a sour face. "Because people are fucking crackers." He smoothed a hand over his red-brown beard. "Believe me, I did a lot of research before we made an offer. Commissioned a survey through another paranormal research group. No ghosts. Plus, I worked with a woman up at the library. Anita? No. Maybe Renita?" He waved a hand at his lapse in memory. "An Indian woman. She helped me pull historical and field mapping documents. No graves."

Marnie's interest piqued at the obvious reference to Vanita.

"So I'm also curious…" she said. "Why do you think the Remingtons have commissioned me to do this book if they already have a town history of sorts?"

Zack's face pinched into a scowl. "Because they're not interested in accurate, historical information. Sure, a little history's okay. But they don't care so much about accuracy as they do good old-fashioned haunting entertainment."

"Are you saying Kate and Dutch, even Bree, are concocting their own ghost stories?"

"Nah." Zack waved his hand. "The ghost stories already existed, passed down through the years. Do Bree and Dutch love to embellish 'em? Yeah. But they've never had to fabricate 'em. There are enough folks out there already doing that."

Another question occurred to Marnie. "Bree and Dutch?" Her face flushed, but she pushed forward. "Do they have some special connection?"

"They have kind of a love-hate thing going." Zack grinned. "But with Dutch being the mayor, and Bree being the city comptroller, they're in the know about every friggin' thing that goes down in this town."

She leaned in toward Zack. He'd caught her attention.

He continued, unabashed. "All the land deals...the scoop on whose business is failing...the dirt on who's sleeping with who. If it's happening, they know about it."

Okay, Zack hadn't exactly spilled the beans on any specific behind-the-scene activities in this town. But he'd thrown the mayor—and his own wife, for God's sake—under the bus, at least as far as ethical practices went.

She hesitated. "Are you okay with Bree and Dutch's, um, interesting relationship?"

Zack viewed her with an odd expression. Then his eyes lit up. "You think Bree and I are married?" His eyes widened. "Holy shit, lady. No! She's my sister. Ewwww. My sister."

He slapped his leg and let out a rip of guffaws.

Ow. Talk about reaching the wrong conclusion. She joined in his laughter.

"You know what? That makes more sense."

Zack wiped his eyes. "Here's the deal, Marnie." He tapped his fingers on the table. "The Lightners and the Remingtons have had some ups and downs through the years, but we've all learned how to play nice in the sandbox and get along. Bree's got the brains. I've got the brawn. Dutch has the connections."

"What about Kate?"

"Oh, Kate has her place. She has the eye, the class, *and* the smarts. She knows how to tie up everything with a big bright bow."

Okay. This little hamlet had more going on than the alleged activities of a handful of ghosts—none of which were vying for her attention here at The Mill, by the way. No harm. The human stories proved even more provocative, starting with the Dutch-and-Kate-and-Bree-and-Zack partnership. For one thing, Dutch and Bree sounded a little too cozy. But what about Kate and Zack? His affectionate overtures toward her earlier that day seemed off. Something about their cultural European nature didn't jibe with Zack's good-old Southern boy façade.

"So," she mused, "I can access The Mill's property transactions at the public library, right? Along with surveys tied to its alleged ghost stories—the ones nobody believes."

Zack's brown eyes locked in on hers. "Let me be very clear here, Marnie," he said. "I did all that research before we bought The Mill because I *do* believe in ghosts." His brows bunched low. "If the survey had said there *were* ghosts here at the mill, I never would have gone in on an offer with Bree."

She narrowed her eyes, trying to sort through all he'd said. She didn't have to wait long.

"When it comes to the spirit world... No, ma'am, I don't fuck around with that."

He chugged his drink and stood. They were done talking.

Chapter 8

Still feeling a trace of a buzz from the afternoon, Marnie strolled with Willow up the walk toward the Remingtons' place.

"What should I expect tonight?" she asked. "Are people going to be talking business? Politics? What?"

"All of the above. Plus sex and religion." Willow glanced Marnie's way. "In Lake Gardner, those are all major topics of interest."

"And ghosts," Marnie added lightly. "Don't forget the town loves its ghosts."

Willow stopped walking. "Well, this is the time of year when the veil is its thinnest."

"Say what?" Marnie stopped walking, too.

"The veil between the earth and the spirit world. It thins at dusk and dawn and during certain seasons, like Halloween. It supposedly eases the way for souls to cross worlds."

"Do you really believe that?"

"Plenty of cultures do. For example, there's Mexico and its Day of the Dead." Willow dug through her bag and moved the conversation elsewhere. "Now, as far as this little party goes, who knows who will be here and what might go down?" She pulled out a mask. "As for Lake Gardner tales—ghostly or real time—be careful what you believe. And who."

She donned her own protective mask and left Marnie to fend for herself.

"Greetings!" Kate called from the wrap-around porch. She radiated flair and self-assurance in a boho wrap dress of deep coppers and purples. A color-coordinated mask hung around her neck, and cute little peep-toed booties completed her look.

Marnie hoped she could perhaps rebrand herself like Kate when she grew up.

"What's your pleasure, Marnie?" Dutch asked from a makeshift bar in the corner.

She pointed to Kate's martini-shaped glass, filled with frosty clear liquid and a lemon twist. "That's tempting. But could I start with a seltzer water?" She turned to Kate and added, "And a restroom?"

Marnie accepted the drink from Dutch and followed Kate into the house and down a hallway. Kate pointed her past a home office with rich dark cabinetry, an animal hide throw rug, and lots of gold accents. Marnie used the facility, then stopped to take in a picture on the hall table outside the office before going back to find Kate.

"That's Emmett Lightner," a voice behind her boomed with the cadence of Jamaica.

She twirled around to face a large Black man, accompanied by a slender silver-haired white man.

"In the picture," the big man said. "Emmett partnered with Dutch in the early days when he and Kate first started flipping houses. Before he died."

Marnie turned her attention back to the photo, which depicted Dutch and Kate with a red-headed man she felt like she should know.

"Zack's the spitting image of his old man, wouldn't you say?" the slender man said, pointing to the redhead in the picture.

Ah, of course. Zack Lightner was Emmett's son. Scrutinizing the photo again, Marnie had to agree. The two looked more like twins than father and son.

The larger man bowed his head toward her. "I'm Andre," he said, "and this is my partner, Randy. We run Andre's Chop House."

"Oh?" She perked up. "I hear it's amazing." Okay, she'd read that during her online research.

"I trust you'll come visit us soon." Andre spoke with a rich tone and with a wink.

"I will." Marnie nodded. Andre's was, after all, one of the venues of her assignment.

Back outside, she followed the sound of Kate's musical laugh. It came from amidst a small group gathered around a built-in fireplace tucked into a nook farther back on the porch.

"There you are." Kate gestured for Marnie to join them. As Marnie approached, Kate motioned toward a striking brunette standing beside her. "I'd like you to meet Bree Lightner."

Marnie lit up. "I met your brother earlier today. At the mill."

"I'm happy for you," Bree said.

When Bree turned away to talk to someone else, Marnie's eyes widened. Kate laughed silently but ushered Marnie quickly back toward the front of the porch.

"Bree's sense of humor can be biting," she said in a low tone. "I'd hoped you could meet her new fellow, but he couldn't make it tonight." She leaned toward Marnie and spoke in a confidential tone. "I shouldn't say it, but he's an absolute dream." Then she laughed. "Oh, what the hell? I may be married, but I'm not dead. Right?"

Marnie nodded absently, about to mention she'd met Andre and Randy when Kate grasped her arm as if to brace for something unpleasant.

"Oh, no." Kate pointed toward the front end of the porch, where Willow made broad, exaggerated gestures at Dutch. "I hope they're not getting heated over religion again."

Marnie's gaze bounced from Dutch to Willow. From the looks of things, they weren't discussing something warm and cozy, like Dutch's cocktail recipes or Kate's splendid fall décor.

"We're talking about people here." Willow jutted her chin and crossed her arms.

"No, we're not," Dutch said.

Tall as she was, Willow's stature and voice did not measure up to Dutch's bluster.

"You're pushing socialism, Willow. It's a flawed system. It always fails."

Okay. So they *were* taking on an explosive topic. Politics.

Willow uncrossed her arms and pointed an index finger up at Dutch. "It's nice you can take care of yourself, Dutch. But what about those who can't?"

"Oh, dear." Kate stopped mid-step, probably well aware of how Dutch would respond.

"To hell with 'em!" he thundered back.

Willow turned abruptly away from Dutch. As she passed Marnie and Kate, she muttered, "Ass." Kate sighed but then still smiled coyly at Dutch, who waved them over, unshaken, his eyes twinkling. He leaned in and kissed her.

"My beautiful wife." He beamed at Kate, then at Marnie. "And her ghostwriter."

What a tool.

Marnie accepted when he offered to get her another drink, a real cocktail this time. It didn't completely ease the undercurrent of tension, but, sipping on the icy lemon libation, she had to admit it helped. After a moment, there was a little less pressure in her shoulders.

"Mr. Mayor?" A voice cut the air, and a man bounded up the porch steps.

"You gotta be fucking kidding me," Dutch sputtered.

Marnie stepped back, wary of his quick change in temperament. The other man, slight, especially next to Dutch, didn't back down.

He pressed on. "I wanted to follow up on our interview of earlier today. You left a lot of my questions unanswered."

"Because your questions were bullshit!" Dutch clenched his hands into fists. "About something that happened a long time ago."

"Sir, it's my job to report local stories—the current ones, but also past ones that reflect on our town's history."

Okay, the man must be a reporter. So why was Dutch acting like such a pit bull?

"Honey." Kate rubbed his arm in a soothing fashion. "What's this all about?"

Dutch yanked his arm away, and Marnie's stomach clenched at the way Kate retreated.

"Nothing," he snarled at Kate. Then he practically spit in the reporter's face. "The Dalton Creek Bridge Expansion happened ten years ago." He cocked his head. "Oh, I forgot. You weren't here then. I guess you'll need to check your archives if you want details."

"This is a *ten-years-later* story," the reporter countered. "And I have checked the archives. People were divided about refurbishing the bridge back then. You and Lightner pushed hard for it. Some say it ruined your friendship. And then he died. On that very bridge." He paused. "So, what do you have to say about it now?"

Dutch balled his fists, eyes blazing. Marnie feared he might punch the poor reporter in the face.

"Lightner was a drunk," he snarled. "He chose to drive when he was three sheets in. He killed himself."

Bree Lightner came out from the shadows, scowling, pointing a finger toward Dutch.

"Don't act all smug." She glowered at her boss. "You could have stopped him from driving that night. You or Kate. And now you rub salt in the wound with this damned book?"

Whoa. Zack had described the Remington-Lightner ties as a love-hate relationship. The hate side was definitely letting itself be seen here.

Bree brushed abruptly past Dutch. Before descending the porch steps, she turned toward him one more time and muttered, "Talk about bullshit."

For a moment after she stormed off, Dutch just stared, too stupefied to make a retort. But when he regrouped, he turned toward the reporter and cocked his arm back, fist poised.

"Get the fuck off my property, Finster," he snarled.

Finster shielded his face with his hands, but he still didn't back down. "Go ahead," he chided. "Attack me on top of avoiding my questions."

Marnie glanced around the porch, uneasy. Wasn't there someone here who might intervene? Sad to say, it didn't appear that way. The Remingtons' guests were too engrossed in the shitshow Dutch was stirring up. As for Finster, he had to be a nutball, staring down the mayor, whose arm was still poised, fist aimed to land smack on the nose.

Then Willow stepped in between the two, her arms reaching out to each of the men in a way that resembled an eerie take on the crucifixion. Marnie's legs weakened, partly from the unnerving visual, but also because Willow clearly hadn't taken her own safety into account.

"Mr. Finster," she said, "you're on private property. You need to be moving along."

The reporter hedged, frozen in place for what felt like an incredibly long time. Marnie watched, too awestruck to say a word. Finally, shoulders slumped, Finster retreated, loping back down the porch steps into the night.

Willow turned to Dutch. "You and Kate go inside now. We'll all see ourselves out."

Marnie held her breath. When Dutch relaxed his arm and cradled Kate to his chest, she melted into him. Only then did Marnie let out her breath, watching him escort his wife inside. And then, dear God, people started to leave. Indeed, maybe Willow Maddox *was* a witch.

Then again, maybe not. Willow's ringed fingers trembled as she picked up her half-full glass for another drink. And that was when Marnie let her own guard down.

"Why did you step in like that?" she scolded softly but firmly. "You could've been hurt."

"I know." Willow's face took on a flush. "But a voice inside me just told me to do it."

As she spoke, a gentle breeze stirred, and the porch ferns flushed with bright yellow lights, flashing in a flurry. At the same time, the scent of cinnamon and chocolate cookies swirled in the air, and a flame bounced among the lights like a gleeful child.

Oblivious to what Marnie was sensing, Willow finished her drink and set down her empty glass. A clapping noise cut the air, the flame snuffed out, and the amber lights stilled.

"You ready?" Willow asked.

But she was already heading down the stairs before Marnie could muster a response.

Chapter 9

What a night.

Marnie lay in the quiet, staring up at the fan. She couldn't decide which character or what incident made it most memorable. She had plenty to choose from, like the saga of the Dalton Creek Bridge Expansion. Her freaking book. And now, Bree Lightner's sudden show of animosity toward Dutch. All that deserved attention.

But Marnie's mind kept returning to the spicy-sweet air on the Remingtons' porch and the bluish-orange flame that danced with the golden lights in the ferns. She had a pretty good inkling who they all were. The flame was CeCe. From its cinnamon scent and playful bounce, she was almost certain. And the little amber lights were the Cozy-Remington orphans.

Okay, so their timelines didn't mesh. Roxy and CeCe had died in 2012, the orphans, years earlier. But maybe that didn't matter. Perhaps ghosts from different generations hung out, trying to resolve each other's stories in order to finally cross over.

If so, these spirits were trying to get her help.

That, or Marnie was imagining shit, having a mind-blowing midlife crisis before its time.

She fussed with her covers, struggling to better understand the other-worldly sights and smells and sounds she'd experienced since her temporary move to Lake Gardner. Fighting back a lump in her throat, she tried to conjure her mother's spirit. *C'mon, Mom. I need you.*

But Patsy remained mum. So much for the thin veil easing the way for the spirits.

Rolling onto her side, Marnie tried to ignore the pain in her heart. And that was when it came into focus. A faint opal orb glowed near the attic portal.

The pear scent of her mother brought tears to Marnie's eyes. She sat up slowly, afraid abrupt movement would chase her mom's spirit away.

Then her phone pinged.

No! She wanted to scream.

She reached for it, hoping to silence it quickly. But it had already scared Patsy away.

Cussing under her breath, she picked up the phone.

"Hey." Lee's tone sounded light.

She tried to make her greeting sound equally casual while checking out the ceiling, wishing her mother's spirit back. Perhaps he could tell she was pissed, though, because a thick silence hung between them. She waited for him to break it, perhaps to ask about her work. She'd be happy to talk about it with him, but she didn't plan to volunteer it if he didn't ask.

Finally, he broke the quiet. "How does Denver sound?"

She sat up straight. "I'm sorry?"

"For a long weekend." He laughed. "My Charlotte trip got switched to Denver. I know it's spur of the moment, and I have back-to-back meetings Thursday and Friday. But that would give you time to shop and visit the spa."

She struggled with what to say.

"We could drive to Breckenridge or Vail for the weekend."

"I can't, Lee." She tried to keep the defensive tone out of her voice even as she waited for some negative retort from him about her little gig. But he surprised her.

"I know the assignment you're working on is important to you." He paused. "But couldn't you negotiate for a few days away by offering to make them up on the tail end?"

This touched her, his trying to find ways for them to be together. She supposed she could broach Kate about adjusting her schedule.

"You love Denver," Lee added, his tone expectant.

She did love Denver. She enjoyed its clear blue skies and mountain views. She liked its size—big enough for her to experience some Western culture but not be suffocated by constant activity. Lee remembered that about her, which made it even more difficult to decline.

But she stood her ground. "I can't, Lee. I'm sorry."

He sighed. "Can't? Or won't?"

Her stomach tightened. She hated conflict so much.

"Here's the thing, Marnie," he said. "I'm trying to meet you halfway, and you're refusing to budge. That disappoints me."

She bit her lip. He disappointed her more.

"Tell you what." His tone shifted again. "Why not sleep on it? Maybe you'll feel differently about it in the morning?"

"Maybe." Her voice sounded flat, even in her own ears.

"I'll touch base with you then," he said, ending the call. No *I love you*. So like Lee, not one to squander those words during mundane daily exchanges. He preferred to save them for special moments, often spiced with champagne or rose petals or a new piece of jewelry.

Marnie stretched to place her phone back on the night table. Her lower back ached with what she recognized as tension. She lay back down, focusing her attention away from the fan, which showed no signs of phantom visitors.

A bubble of a laugh tried to surface, an ironic snigger at something far from funny. She felt so disconnected, from her mother's spirit, from Lee, from everything.

She rustled, trying to get comfortable, unable to resist checking the fan and the portal door one more time. As she suspected, nothing. Lying on her back, she attempted her *I am here, I am now* chant. Again, nothing. The same happened with her *Lord is my shepherd* chant. No sense of peace. No grounding connection with her faith—tried and true *or* newfangled.

And that made her saddest of all.

Closing her eyes, she pulled up the covers and willed herself to sleep.

She woke with a sliver of a headache. Her phone shined the time: 8:44 a.m. She sat up, surprised to have slept this late, irked for being off her game. She rose and padded toward the bathroom to brush her teeth and splash water on her face. As she approached it, she heard voices.

Her attention darted back to the attic portal. It remained undisturbed. As she listened, she distinguished two very different but familiar voices. A conversation. Coming from an area downstairs beneath her bathroom. Not Willow's office. Perhaps the kitchen?

Marnie's attention shifted into overdrive.

"I'm not connecting with my mama anymore." The voice belonged to Kate Remington. "For a while there," she continued, "I sensed her spirit walking along beside me, helping to ease my burdens. I felt…I don't know, calmed and energized by it at the same time."

"You mentioned your energy ebbing the last month or so," Willow replied.

Marnie's fingers flew to her lips as she recognized a real life-coaching session in progress. An impromptu one, she guessed. And while she knew better, she couldn't help herself. She lowered herself onto the rim of the tub to sit and listen.

"I can blend you some tea and give you an essential oil recipe for energy," Willow said.

"Maybe." Kate sounded uninspired. "What about meditation?" Her voice perked up at that. "Dutch brags he's a master of meditation and mind control. Can you teach me about that?"

"We could do a meditation to stir up your chakra centers." Willow's voice carried an odd tone Marnie couldn't read. "Why don't we go into my office? It'll just take five minutes."

Kate's laugh sounded tinny. "How 'bout a spell to shoot me to the moon instead?"

"Kate...." Willow hesitated. "I'm having a tough time reading you. Do you feel unsafe?"

Marnie jolted at the question. But it made sense, given Dutch's antagonistic behavior, even toward Kate, the night before.

Willow continued. "Do we need to discuss an escape plan for you?"

"No." Kate's laugh turned sardonic now. "Only if I can escape from myself."

"You're safe here. Physically, but also from judgment." The older woman's voice grew more encouraging. "Let's go into my office, unblock you, and open up your energy fields."

Power to Kate and Willow, but Marnie preferred to open her energy fields with coffee, not meditation.

"Actually," Kate blurted, "what I'd like to open up is my ability to make myself heard!"

Marnie's eyes shot wide.

"I need to know how to stand up for myself," Kate continued. "There are things I want to say or do. But I can't help myself. I keep holding back."

Marnie waited. In the silence, she imagined Willow and Kate locking eyes.

"Why do you think that is?" Willow asked. "Do you think you hold back because you're afraid of something? Or someone?"

If Kate gave Willow an answer, it was inaudible.

"Why don't you stay here?" Willow suggested. "At least for tonight? This *is* your house, after all. And we all can use a little breather now and then."

Marnie could relate to that.

"I've got to go." Kate's tone took on urgency even as it faded.

"Wait!" Willow called out. "I want to give you something."

Marnie wanted to cry out *wait*, too. Except that would give away the fact she'd been listening. She crept out of the bathroom, begging the floor not to creak. Edging to the head of the stairs, she hid out of view, hoping to hear more. She got lucky.

"This gemstone is jet." Willow's voice came from the foot of the stairs. Marnie envisioned her standing there, squeezing Kate's fingers around a stone.

"It absorbs negativity and anger," Willow continued. "It can also help you gain influence over difficult people. Let it be a talisman for you. For self-control and power."

"Thank you." Kate's voice was barely audible.

The front door squeaked as Kate left. Marnie held her breath, hoping Willow would return to the kitchen and not trek upstairs to find Marnie eavesdropping. She waited in silence, hesitant to breathe. When the back door smacked shut, she rushed to her window where she saw Willow heading to the garden squares out back. Once certain Willow was not going to call her out for eavesdropping, she exhaled quietly and went downstairs to grab some breakfast.

She had just finished packing up her laptop to take to the library when her phone rang.

"Hey." She didn't jump for a change. Seeing Lee's name on the caller ID, she steeled herself for more Denver conversation.

"I had a feeling I wouldn't be able to convince you to come away with me." At least he didn't sound irritated. "So, may I propose an alternative?"

"Sure." Glancing out the large window, she caught Willow, still working out back.

"I've made dinner reservations at Andre's Chop House tonight. How's nine sound?"

"Like it's past my bedtime." She laughed.

"Think you can stay up a little bit later just for tonight?" He paused. "Please."

Marnie hedged. She had told Lee this assignment was a trial to retest her writing chops, not a much-needed break from her marriage. And Lee. She still needed more time and space. Plus, what about after dinner? What would he expect then?

She had hoped he would compromise, and he had. Her turn now, right?

Making herself smile, she said, "Dinner at nine sounds great."

"Excellent," Lee said. "I'll pick you up around quarter till."

Chapter 10

Willow came back into the house just as Marnie was set to leave for the library.

"Did you get breakfast?" she asked.

"Yes, ma'am." Marnie patted her stomach. "Figure I need to walk it off about now."

Willow chuckled. "I can show you my favorite loop along the lake if you'd like. It goes up to the church before heading back this way again. It's about a forty-minute trek."

Marnie had only planned to walk to the library, but she figured the extra steps wouldn't hurt. Her laptop bag and purse weren't heavy. Not to mention, she had questions for Willow.

"That would be great," she said, waiting for Willow to grab a few things of her own.

They turned left off the porch and walked toward the beach. The scent of dead leaves and apples followed them to where the street ended and the earthy smell of the lake grew stronger. They crossed the lot onto the lake's east shoreline, dotted with picnic pavilions, swings, and a swimming beach, now closed. When Marnie saw a sign for the *Emmett Lightner Day Use Area*, she had to stop walking.

"So, what's the deal?" she asked. "With Bree and Zack's dad. I noticed his picture with Dutch at the Remingtons' place last night. At a ribbon-cutting ceremony, I think. But the next thing I know, all hell's breaking loose on the Remingtons' porch between the reporter and

Dutch. And Kate and Dutch." She frowned, noticing a pattern. "And Bree and Dutch. But always pointing back to Emmett Lightner."

Willow motioned toward a point on the lake where a modern bridge spanned alongside an old covered one. "The picture was probably celebrating the Dalton Creek Bridge Expansion. Emmett and Dutch worked together long and hard to get that project approved."

"Yeah, I got that much." Marnie studied the bridge in the distance. "But it sounds as though something went sour between Dutch and Emmett."

"Remember that was before my time here?"

Marnie shot Willow the sternest stink eye she could muster.

Willow raised her hands in surrender, her silver rings catching the sunlight. And she smirked. Just a little. "Rumor has it the Dutch and Emmett friendship was waning. Emmett was always rough around the edges, but he was getting even more so."

Marnie nodded, thinking about Zack and how the apple didn't fall far.

Willow continued her story. "The night of Emmett's death, he and Dutch had been eating and drinking together at a restaurant north of town. I'm not sure if Kate was with them or not. But apparently they got into a heated argument, partly over how much they'd had to drink and the fact that neither of them should drive home."

"But Emmett did?"

"Yes. In Dutch's car. Without Dutch."

"Youch. Dutch gave him the keys?" If that was the case, no wonder Bree was so angry.

Willow's gray eyes clouded. "It's not exactly clear how Emmett got them. The bartender backed up Dutch's story that Emmet was raging—completely out of control and practically beating Dutch to get his keys." Willow started walking again, albeit slowly. "But Bree's always felt that Dutch could have stopped Emmett if he'd just tried a little harder."

Marnie walked along beside her, and for a stretch, neither woman spoke. After a bit, Marnie broke the silence.

"Do you think that's how Bree got promoted so quickly at such a young age? Because Dutch felt guilty?"

"I decided long ago not to try to figure out Dutch's logic."

Marnie understood Willow's thinking, but she couldn't help herself. She had to ask.

"Given the givens, why would the Remingtons want to remind folks about the questions tied to Emmett's death?" She shivered at the thought. "In a book of local ghost stories, of all things?"

"I don't know. Seems like someone didn't think everything through." Willow glanced back at her. "But Emmett Lightner is not the only ghost to reportedly haunt that bridge. Ask Vanita to steer you toward its history when you visit the library."

Willow led them farther along the shoreline, its brown sugar sand dotted with feathers and shells. Marnie followed her along the water's edge, passing a fisherman and two kayakers gliding on the lake. She looked away from the lake to a place where well-shaded trails and extension paths meandered into the woods. Her mind wandered. She pondered how to frame her next question without outing herself for eavesdropping earlier.

"I noticed Kate leaving your place this morning," she finally said to Willow. "Is everything okay with her?"

They stopped at a history marker denoting a battle of the Civil War.

"Why do you ask?" Willow prodded.

An osprey soared overhead. For a second, Marnie stood frozen in nature's wonder. With some reluctance, she returned her attention back to their conversation.

"Dutch came so unglued last night," Marnie said. "At the reporter, but at Kate, too. Do you..." She didn't want to go where her mind was taking her, let alone say it out loud. But she couldn't help herself. "Do you think Kate's in danger? From Dutch?"

"No." Willow wrinkled her forehead. "And believe me, I don't take your question lightly. I know Dutch can be hotheaded."

"So let me ask you this," Marnie continued. "If you *did* think he presented a threat, who could you go to?" She didn't add, *in this insular town,* but Willow seemed to follow her gist.

"I'm not sure." Willow's forehead relaxed some, and her eyes shimmered. "But I think Kate's fears right now are more tied to herself than to Dutch."

Marnie hoped to hell Willow was right.

They picked up their walk, continuing to where the trail tapered onto a less maintained path. Signs on a nearby dock read *Private Property*. Willow veered right, up a set of steps built of railroad ties. She stopped at the top, where the public trail picked up again. Marnie stopped alongside her, unsure whether—or how—to press further about Kate. Willow made the decision for her, changing the subject altogether.

"Would you like to talk a bit more about your ghosts?"

In a way she hadn't expected, Marnie was tickled by Willow's abrupt diversion. For years, she had steered away from discussing her ghosts. She understood why people might not believe her. Worse, some would figure she verged on some kind of a psychotic break. Willow had presented a golden opportunity. But for Marnie to take the conversation forward, it would have to be on her own terms, starting with gaining a better grasp on the root of Willow's interest.

"I lost my mom," Marnie said, "and she sought me out. Not to sound glib. That's just how it started for me. But you lost a daughter." She stated her words as fact, not a question. "Is that what attracted you to pursue your line of work?"

"Indirectly, yes." Willow's eyes shined. "Everything changed after we lost Olivia."

Marnie mumbled how she was so sorry for Willow's loss. What else could she say?

Willow peered out over the water. "It was an Easter Sunday. Olivia, her husband, Hank, and their daughter, Natalie, attended services at their church, with plans to join us for dinner afterward."

Marnie bit her lip. Willow had a granddaughter. Marnie listened for what came next, despite a growing sense of dread.

"Charlie took the call." Willow started to walk the path again. "I could tell it was bad news from the way his body slumped." Her voice cracked. "A drunk driver hit them. Livvy and Hank died on impact. Natalie had to be airlifted." She faltered. "She died in transit."

Willow stopped walking. "The first year hit us hard. We both struggled to get out of bed each morning. I had to be medicated. Charlie relied on the bottle. It's a miracle we hung onto the business." She added, "He sold insurance. I helped with the books."

She stared ahead, still not walking. "By the second anniversary, the pain had dulled. Just barely. Charlie had gained a lot of weight, stuffing his grief deep inside by overeating and still drinking too much. I got off my prescription pills but still joined Charlie for our evening alcohol escape." She laughed, a bitter sound. "I preferred drinking over eating. So Charlie got fat, and I melted away. Got diagnosed with osteoporosis on top of it all.

"When my doctor prescribed protein supplements and yoga, what did I have to lose?" She sighed. "I followed his orders. And in spite of myself, I began to feel better. My yoga instructor also practiced as a spiritualist and grief counselor so I scheduled a session with her."

"And that's how you got introduced to the work you do?"

"Sort of," Willow said. "My work has changed, or evolved, through the years. But I suppose that's how it started. During that very first session, I was hypnotized, and Livvy and Natalie visited me, floating in white gauze like angels. They glowed."

Her hands fluttered to cover her heart.

"They didn't talk to me in a traditional sense, but through hums and sound waves, I understood Livvy's message. 'We're okay. We're whole again. See?'"

"And I did see," Willow continued. "Their images flashed before me in hazy colors. When they started to fade, I panicked. 'Don't leave!' I cried. But my daughter told me, 'We're always here with you. Get better for us. We love you.'"

Willow started to walk again, toward a gate at the end of the pathway. Marnie tried to push away a nagging feeling about why Willow wanted her to pursue her gift. But she had to ask.

"Are you hoping I can help you see them again? Their ghosts?"

Willow turned to Marnie, her eyes widened. "I can see why you might think that." She opened the iron gate, her sleeve rising to reveal the Celtic cross tattooed on her forearm. "But no. My girls—or their angels or ghosts or whatever—visited me. They're at peace. They don't need to come back. Not to this world."

Marnie tried to blink away a gumminess under her eyelids. How could a person bear to lose a child—*and* a grandchild—and still stay so hope filled? She glanced into the sky, where two white egrets soared above the treetops. Willow followed her gaze, her face lighting up.

"I hope there's a heaven," she said. "And angels, too. But who knows? Maybe those egrets carry the souls of my girls, reincarnated and watching over me as my spirit guides."

Willow finally looked away from the sky. They were on the edge of the Lake Gardner Community Church property, and Marnie followed Willow as she started to walk again.

As they grew closer to the church, Willow said, "You asked me earlier who I'd turn to if I feared for Kate's safety. I think the person I'd seek out would be the pastor here. Stan Meadows."

On hearing that, Marnie did a double take. "You belong to this church?"

"Oh, butterfly. We don't belong to churches. Churches belong to us."

Chapter 11

After Willow convinced her to meet Pastor Stan, Marnie breathed with relief to learn he had stepped away from his desk.

"He should be back any time," his secretary said, "if you want to wait."

Willow told her no thank you and led Marnie through a maze of hallways, trying to coax her to pop in on some volunteers working on props for the upcoming *Boo for Christ*.

Marnie begged off. "I ought to get to the library."

"See you at dinner then." Willow had already headed down a hallway by the time Marnie remembered she had alternate plans for her evening meal.

Marnie wound her way out of the church, this time by way of the front door. In the front lot, several adults and young teens gathered. Scattered about them were sawhorses and tools, poster board and streamers. A couple youth were trying to duct tape together some PVC pipes.

One of the adults turned her way. "Marnie!" he called out.

"Dutch?" She edged closer to get a better look.

Dutch held up one end of a PVC pipe. "Social distancing candy chutes. To keep Halloween safe for everyone."

"Nice."

She tried to hide her surprise that he'd actually acknowledged safety concerns over COVID. In Atlanta, everyone still wore protective masks everywhere. The pandemic was far from over. Yet here in Lake Gardner, it was hit or miss. Did these people not tune into the news?

As she observed the little assembly operation in process, she softened. Perhaps Lake Gardner folks felt safe after an early COVID outbreak. Maybe Dutch's earlier ugly behavior was atypical. Perhaps the real Dutch was here with this mix of middle school boys and girls, who seemed to look to him as the quintessential project manager and role model.

"Like this, Grayson." Dutch guided one of the boys on how to make safe cuts.

"Nice, Maggie," he said to a girl painting a sign that read, Place buckets here. Dutch turned back to Marnie. "That'll go at the end of the chute so trick-or-treaters will know where to hold their bags to receive their candy."

If Dutch was embarrassed about how he'd behaved last night, he didn't let on.

"What brings you this way?" he asked after a bit more work with the kids.

"A loopy walk by way of the lake." She laughed.

"Good for the soul, isn't it?" Dutch grinned at her, and his eyes lit up like a child.

"Willow convinced me to walk by the lake with her instead of straight to the library," Marnie said. "Then she wanted to introduce Pastor Stan, but he was busy. Which led me here to observe your handiwork."

"The kids do a good job." Dutch observed a group of girls shaking cans of orange spray paint, ready to apply their magic to the cut PVC pipes. He turned back to Marnie. "But you *should* pop in and meet Pastor Stan before you leave. He's the best. His office is through the side door." He pointed, then returned his attention back to the construction in progress.

"Thanks, Dutch."

Marnie lingered a bit longer before deciding it *wouldn't* hurt to meet Pastor Stan, who seemed to walk on water—at least according to both Willow and Dutch.

Following Dutch's directions, Marnie re-entered the church. She slowed down to take it in this time. To the right lay the Narthex, which led to a freestanding altar with lecterns on either side. Not ornate like her childhood church, but she found the rich oak handsome, its crisp, straight angles a lovely contrast against the cream-colored walls.

She followed a sign pointing left to the Church Office. It sat empty now, but a male voice, hushed but audible, wafted from an open door off the secretary's office.

"This virus is going to kill me one way or another," he said. "I'm so tired of not being able to pull out all the plugs for a sermon."

"I know." Kate's reply came out rich as caramel.

The male—Pastor Stan, she presumed—spoke again. "Not that I don't appreciate all you've done to get us back to a more normal service." He likely lamented the current hybrid-style of worship most area churches now offered—services still hosted on Zoom while socially distanced in-person gatherings were phased back in.

"Can I run something by you?" Kate asked. "On a different topic?"

"Of course."

Marnie rubbed her clammy palms on the legs of her jeans, debating whether to continue to eavesdrop. But who was she kidding? Until today, it hadn't been a common practice for her. At this point, she might as well anoint herself *The Queen of the Eavesdrop*.

"I want to get your opinion," Kate said.

"My opinion's worth a lot less than my spiritual guidance." The pastor laughed.

"Well, your guidance then. About a silly thing." Kate's voice held a tinge of embarrassment now.

"The things that trouble the soul often start out as trivial," Pastor Stan said.

"It's about Dutch."

Oh. Marnie straightened as her interest piqued.

"He..." Kate seemed to be searching for words.

The pastor didn't push her along.

"I learned we're in arrears on some loans Dutch has consolidated."

Pastor Stan paused before responding. "That isn't a mortal sin, Katie."

"I steamed open some mail addressed to Dutch to find out about it." Her voice wavered. "I had to break the lock on his private safe in the process. It made him furious."

"I can see the frustration on both your sides." The pastor spoke with a steady tone.

Kate's voice escalated. "Why does a husband need a private safe filled with things he doesn't care to share with his wife? Believe me, I've asked that question plenty. Dutch always turns the tables on me, making *me* feel like I'm in the wrong for not trusting him." She stopped to take a breath, but barely. "Why would a married man need to lock his wife out of his life?"

Marnie's mouth went dry. *Did Lee do that to her, at least on an emotional level?*

She forced her mind away from Lee and back to Dutch. She hadn't liked how he treated Kate, even before hearing this, even if Kate seemed to take it all in stride. And she didn't think she was just being too sensitive.

"Katie," the pastor said.

Marnie held incredibly still to focus on Pastor Stan's words.

"Dutch is a good man. But even good men do things that make them hard to understand."

Was he *really* passing along this schlock?

"So I should just get over it?" Kate wasn't buying that. Not based on her tone.

"That's your call to make." Okay, score one for Pastor Stan. "It's surely a good idea to make sure you're financially set. Both of you. Whether you move forward together or not."

Whoa. So true. Especially for a woman who wasn't the major breadwinner. But, geesh, what the pastor just said sounded so un-pastor-like.

"Stan!" Kate apparently agreed. "Don't be so drastic. It's not like we're splitting up, for Pete's sake."

"I know, Kate." He spoke gently. "But let me ask you this. Do *you* not have things you like to keep private from Dutch?"

Marnie stiffened. Some people had reasons for keeping secrets. Haunting ones.

"Why?" Kate's words came out sharp. "What have you heard?"

"I didn't hear anything." The pastor sounded surprised, practically wounded as if from an attack. He recuperated. "You're not being petty, Kate. But just because Dutch digs his heels in on this doesn't mean he's doing something unsavory." He hesitated, then asked, "Do you want to see if he'll come in with you and we can talk?"

"Not right yet."

The conversation seemed to be winding down. Marnie moved away from the pastor's office, primed to make a quick exit.

"Let me think about all this, okay?" Kate's voice grew stronger as she approached the pastor's door to leave his office. "And Stan?" she added. "I'd rather you not say anything about this to Dutch."

Marnie might have heard the pastor say, "Of course." She couldn't be sure, though. She had already started on her way out, not about to stick around and let either Kate or her pastor know she'd been listening in on them.

She slipped out the door Dutch had directed her to, but instead of heading up front toward the lot, she walked out back, away from the church. Stepping through tangled leaves and weeds, she worked her way toward a rustic old fence and an arched iron gate anchored by stone angels on each side. Bare limbs from lofty trees blocked some of the sunlight. Dappled light bounced off chalky rock and cold slabs of stone.

Holy hell. She'd come upon a graveyard.

She froze still, taking in the headstones, old and worn, jutting from the ground higgledy-piggledy. The beauty of the old graveyard drew her in. But something troubled her here. If she could sense phantom energy in places like The Diana and on the Remingtons' porch, why did she get no sense of that here?

A hint of breeze brushed against her as she studied her surroundings to get her bearings. If she continued on the unmarked path down the hill, that should take her to Spring Street and the library. The town didn't sprawl. Even if her directions were off a bit, she should be okay.

She glanced back at the church, still alive with activity. A wad of orange and black crepe paper danced across the ground in skittering movements, just like a tumbleweed. She bent to catch it, but the wind played a trick. The wad of refuse drifted just out of reach. She chased it to where it lodged against the gate to the graveyard.

"Gotcha." She laughed at herself, leaning down to retrieve it.

As she picked it up, she surveyed the ground, where grass and weeds gave way to the patchy dirt that formed a makeshift path through the gate. She stood, her eyes glued to the rustic trail, holding her breath as she tried to make out what she saw.

In crooked print, probably scratched into the dirt with a stick, a message read:

HELP THEM.

Chapter 12

She stumbled backward, pressing a fist to her mouth. A dizzy feeling washed over her, and everything around her intensified. The smell of the earth. The rustle of fallen leaves. The sound of her heart thrashing in her ears.

Sweat beaded at her hairline despite a sudden uptake in the breeze. Clenching her jaw, she stole farther into the graveyard, half expecting one of the *Boo for Christ* teen volunteers to jump out and scare her.

When no one did, she spun around, glancing in the direction of the church again. Everywhere she turned things appeared still. She guessed activity continued down near the lot. Still, she could see or hear no one. Which likely meant no one could see or hear her.

HELP THEM. Who had written that message? And with what?

She crept back toward the gate, scanning the tombstones and the ground around her, in search of a stick. Finding none, she bent to examine the cryptic message, to see how the earth had been broken where the letters appeared. She started to reach down to touch it but couldn't make herself do it.

"Okay, Marn. Calm the hell down." Nothing like talking to oneself out loud.

She grappled with her purse for her phone. Bending over the scrawled note, she tried to click a picture, but her camera wouldn't focus. She jiggled it and tried again but got the same result. *Damn.* She shifted, aiming her lens on a headstone nearby. There, the camera worked fine.

But when she turned back to try shooting the note in the dirt again, no go. It had a mind of its own.

She studied the ominous message again, the script wobbly but clear to her naked eye.

"Damn kids," she muttered, as though that could explain any of this. Ignoring the quiver in her own voice, she walked away from the little graveyard and down the hill toward town.

Who had made the note in the dirt? The lettering appeared childlike, which fit with the explanation she wanted to believe: Kids playing Halloween tricks had written it, finding it funny. But that didn't explain her malfunctioning camera. Plus, it all seemed too coincidental, the discarded crepe paper landing on the note, drawing her attention to that precise spot. In her gut, she didn't buy it.

Reaching the municipal lot, her mind remained on the message. Did *them* refer to Roxy and CeCe? God must be having quite a chuckle, giving her a gift *and* an assignment but no concrete instructions on how to proceed.

Inside the library, the circulation desk sat unattended. Marnie took a cleansing breath and phoned Vanita to let her know she'd arrived. To calm her jitters, she studied a photo display of town history. She read the caption accompanying the exhibit.

Lake Gardner – Yesterday and Today. *The area now known as Lake Gardner was first settled by the Cherokee Nation, forced toward Oklahoma during The Trail of Tears. In the 1840s, a railroad engineer named the town after his birthplace, Gardner, New York. In the 1950s, the town was renamed Lake Gardner after the U.S. Army Corp of Engineers completed work on the body of water that anchors it today.*

Body. More like bodies. Bodies in a graveyard.

Good grief. She was losing her shit.

She glanced down the hall toward the area where she figured Vanita worked. *What was taking her so long?*

Licking her lips, Marnie tried to regain her focus. She stopped in front of a framed illustration of the house she recognized as the Remingtons' old Victorian. Its caption read:

The Cozy-Remington House – Yesterday and Today. *Before the Civil War, Walter Cozy built a multi-room Victorian home with hopes his children and grandchildren would visit for years to come. After Mr. Cozy died in battle, Mrs. Cozy, recognizing the needs of homeless children orphaned by the war, partnered with local ministries to create the Cozy Home for Children in 1872. It remained in the family for years, housing dozens of children until the Great Depression. Lack of funding eventually forced the Cozy Home for Children to close.*

Marnie closed her eyes, remembering the smell of chocolate cookies and the sight of twinkling amber lights on the Remingtons' porch. The children.

"Ready for a tour, Marnie?" Vanita's voice jogged her back to the present.

Her eyes popped open. "That'd be great."

She wanted to bring up the spooky dirt message in the dusty warmth of the library, but she held off. After the tour, Vanita handed her an index card of Internet links and passwords.

"Can I help you with anything else before I go back to my desk?" she asked.

Now or never. Marnie gestured for Vanita to have a seat across from her.

"Something weird happened to me up at the church graveyard just now." Marnie's heart stuttered, but she continued. "A message was written in the dirt. It said, HELP THEM." She couldn't bear it if Vanita tried to explain it away so she preempted her. "I know, I know. Maybe kids working on the *Boo for Christ* event were trying to be funny? Except..."

Vanita's eyes were kind as she reached over and put her hand on Marnie's knee. Marnie sucked in a deep breath and steadied her leg, only now realizing how much she jittered with nerves.

"Except what?" Vanita asked gently.

"I tried to take a picture. But my phone camera wouldn't focus."

"That happens at the worst times, doesn't it?" Vanita's eyes narrowed.

Marnie sensed Vanita's doubt, but she didn't care. "Do you think *them* might be Roxy and CeCe?"

Vanita sat up slowly. "Anything's possible. But if *them* is Roxy and CeCe, who—or what—sent you the message to help them?"

Marnie was thinking maybe the Cozy-Remington orphans. But she picked up the card of database codes and kept her hypothesis to herself. She could tell the librarian didn't buy the ghost thing one hundred percent, but she appreciated being able to talk about it rather than bottle it up.

"I'm a researcher." Vanita lifted her hands up, then let them fall. "I dig up facts to back up theories."

"And are your theories about the Blue Moon killings based on the facts?"

"The facts about that night have never quite added up." Vanita pressed her lips together. "In my mind, at least. From everything I've gleaned, the evidence just wasn't there."

Marnie pushed on. "And what about Willow? Does she think like you do?"

"Willow thinks like Willow." Vanita sighed. "She cares more about truth than facts."

Marnie scowled, wishing Vanita would stop speaking in riddles.

"Just do your job, Marnie. Don't fret about ghosts." But Vanita's dark eyes widened. "Unless you feel threatened, in which case, tell us." She paused. "Otherwise, carry on and research your venues. Especially The Diana. Sift through the facts for the truth."

Marnie cocked her head. "How are they different? Facts and truth?"

"Truth may include facts. But it may also include beliefs. Facts are indisputable."

As Vanita returned to her desk, Marnie tried to understand the distinction.

Don't overthink it, Marn.

She pushed herself on, starting with a search for information on The Diana Homestead. Off the bat, she learned the house originated as a Sears, Roebuck & Co. kit home, one of an estimated 70,000 built between 1908 and 1949.

Her skin tingled. She lived in a haunted house. A ready-to-assemble haunted house, ordered by mail.

Enough. She narrowed her search by date and topic to land on articles about The Diana's murders. Skimming through information, she settled in, taking copious notes. Even using Vanita's links with their powerful filters, she still pulled up some questionable information. But she landed on credible sites as well and kept on working.

Mid-afternoon, her stomach rumbled. She'd been ultra-focused and forgotten lunch. Heading back to The Diana, her mind still raced with all she'd learned. Or, in some cases, confirmed.

On August 31, 2012, members of a group called Andromeda's Coven held a cleansing festival to celebrate the Blue Moon. Three days later, Roxy Tripp, age 73, and her daughter CeCe, age 35, were found dead at The Diana Homestead. Authorities arrested Jackson Mott, Roxy's former foster son, in early 2013 for the murders. At a press conference, they said they had no proof that Mott had any ties to black magic or witchcraft.

Stumbling over a crack in the sidewalk, she scolded herself to pay more attention to her surroundings. Approaching the Remingtons', she scanned the porch. No amber lights twinkled today. There were, however, not one, not two, but three *Trump for President* signs in the yard. Because apparently one didn't cut it in these times of uncertainty and overindulgence.

She continued walking, her mind already back on her research.

Nothing had been stolen from the Tripps' home the night of the murders. That fed the theory that the murders had been a crime of passion. Again, fingers pointed to Mott, who knew the victims better than most and whose prints were all over the house. In his defense, Mott said of course his prints would be there; he visited often. To his detriment, he admitted to what he called other-worldly practices, and two separate articles referenced a room in his house filled with books about the occult and witchcraft.

How closely had the authorities examined Mott's ties to black magic or witchcraft?

Passing the Remingtons' house, Marnie switched her laptop strap to her other arm and chewed on another name that had turned up in her research: Dutch Remington. In the months following the crimes, Dutch, at the time an alderman for the city, frequently spoke on behalf of a group convinced of Jackson Mott's guilt. He posited the murders were part of an initiation requirement into Andromeda's Coven, which, not surprisingly, infuriated the Wiccan community. As Mott's trial neared, a local professor of comparative religions agreed to testify as an expert witness on behalf of the defense, but that never happened because—

A cackle broke the still afternoon, and a witch lunged from the bushes. Marnie's heart caught. *Holy shit.* First ghosts in the graveyard. Now this. Clutching at her chest, she ran from the crone's screeches and croaks.

Only when she realized the hag hadn't followed her did she dare to stop and look back. Heat flushed her cheeks as she made out the wires attached to the witch. In spite of herself—or more likely *because* of herself and her reaction—she bent over in laughter. The folks who lived across from Willow had gone above and beyond to pull off the best Halloween prank ever. Good for them.

Crossing the street into The Diana's front yard, another sight accosted her. Willow's sign, a big-lettered *NOPE* swiped across a swatch of Trump-ish orange hair. Amazing. Who would've ever guessed that wrangling ghosts and witches would become easier than dealing with the uncertainties and divisiveness of real life in 2020?

Marnie neared The Diana's porch, and a small black cat skittered from beneath the bushes. She continued up the steps, and a spark of light popped from a pot of mums by the door.

She stopped. The spark grew into a translucent flame, and she detected the familiar scent of cinnamon. The flame dimmed, then flickered in fits of excitement, springing up and down in the pot like a Roman candle. At one point, it jumped to the pot on the other side of the door, where yellow lights flashed to life alongside it. *Hippity-hop.* The smell of cinnamon *and* chocolate cookies filled the air.

The flame and lights poured more energy into their dance, their childlike joy contagious.

Her skin tingled as she whispered to the tongue of fire, "You're not Roxy. I know."

Three sharp claps cut the air. That, Marnie knew, *was* Roxy. CeCe's flame flickered out, and the yellow lights dimmed but remained aglow.

Marnie touched a finger to her lips as things began to make sense.

CeCe, familiar with the drill, had been called to stop horsing around by the clap of her mother's hands. The ghosts of the Cozy-Remington orphans, less aware, had frozen in place, hoping to avoid Roxy's wrath. Even as ghosts, children hated making adults angry. Apparently.

Her mood grew more pensive as the ghost children's lights dimmed and left.

The more she thought about it, the more she believed CeCe's orphan friends were the ones who'd left her the message in the graveyard. The scrawl had been childlike. So sweet. Were they asking Marnie to help CeCe and Roxy by solving their murders?

I don't think the dead continue to haunt us unless they think we can help them.

Entering The Diana, Marnie pondered the words Willow had said to her after her first night there. What chilled her to the bone was how spot on Willow had called it. Marnie hadn't pursued the spirits; they'd come to her.

Granted, not all of them. Roxy's ghost still seemed tepid at best.

Still, Marnie felt a surge of energy. Perhaps the spirits *were* her reason to be here. Maybe they continued to seek her out because she could help.

Did it make sense? Not exactly. She was compelled to learn more.

Because really, what, if anything, had made sense about 2020 so far?

Andre's Chop House

Lake Gardner's 2020 Walking Ghost Tour

*O*nce upon a time, Andre's Chop House was called Long's Uptown Gin Joint. Step into this beautiful old corner building on Main Street today and take in its 100-year-old beams and brick, first-class food and drinks, and unmatched hospitality. The century-old structure has kept its nostalgic ambiance much like when it first opened as a popular nightclub in the 1920s. Some say it might have even survived Prohibition and the Great Depression if, shortly before the crash, owner Tibbott Long hadn't killed an out-of-towner for cheating in a poker game.

Long went to jail and the nightclub folded. The facility reopened through the years under different owners to little success. In 2011, current owners Andre Ennis and Randy Mason re-opened the place as Andre's Chop House, an upscale eatery credited with helping bring Lake Gardner into the new, more prosperous millennium.

According to Ennis and Mason, the place is not without a ghost or two. Visitors like to venture that Tibbott Long haunts the bar, seeking revenge on the ghost of the man who led to his demise—all over a crooked exchange similar to the "draw poker" game played today.

The owners are not so sure.

"I've never seen or heard from the spirit of Tibbott Long." Ennis gestures toward a spot at the end of the bar, and his voice booms. "But see there? A man named Reggie used to sit there smoking cigarillos." He raises his eyebrows. "He's been dead for years, but even today, we sometimes still smell the stink of those damned cigars."

Chapter 13

Andre himself delivered their meal. "Bon appetit." His voice boomed through his mask. When Lee took a bite of his Randy-Dandy Steak and gave a thumbs-up, the chef broke into a deep-throated laugh before leaving them to enjoy their meal.

Marnie found her Blackened Sea Scallops divine, too. She offered Lee a bite. The intimacy of it—him eating from her fork, something they'd done since their earliest days of dating—made her look away.

Andre's made for a lovely date venue and provided relief after the weird events of the day. Over the meal, she and Lee visited companionably. But they talked of nothing deep.

"How's your work?" From the way he cocked his head at her without blinking, she could tell he was feigning interest.

"It's good." Then, feeling guilty that she, too, was just going through the motions, she pointed toward the bar. "The original owner shot a man over there for cheating in a poker game."

"You don't say." He flagged down the waiter and ordered a slice of cheesecake for them to share.

Their dessert arrived, and the hostess led Bree Lightner by their table. Marnie gave her a prickly half-smile. Then her stomach did a major flip. Alongside Bree stood a very real ghost from Marnie's past.

"Josh Smith?" she stammered.

The man jerked, coming close to spilling his cocktail. "Marnie?"

Bree fixed her gaze on him, then Marnie. "You two know each other?"

Butterflies fluttered into Marnie's heart and tried to climb out of her throat. She more than knew him. He looked older—even better, to be honest. He'd cropped his dark hair shorter and wore a scruff beard. His eyes were still blue as the deepest part of the ocean.

"It's been a while," she said in an even tone.

"Eight or nine years?" He shook his head. "What are you doing in Lake Gardner?"

Bree answered for her. "Marnie's working on the book for Kate."

"The ghost book?" Josh studied Marnie with care before breaking into a big grin. He turned to Bree. "Marnie's an excellent writer." Then, still disconcerted, he turned to Marnie. "Sorry. This is Bree. She's one of the owners of The Lake Gardner Mill."

"We've met." Marnie bobbed her head toward Bree. She motioned to Lee. "And this is my husband," she said. "Lee, this is Josh and Bree."

Lee stood up halfway as a courtesy.

Bree beamed back at him and then asked Josh, "So how do you two know each other?"

"We dated once upon a time," Josh said.

"A lifetime ago," Marnie added.

Truth was, she and Josh hadn't just dated. They had talked about marriage. Marnie tried to fake her way through her awkwardness, though, because like Josh said, that had all been once upon a time.

Bree rubbed Josh's arm possessively as the hostess laid menus on a nearby table, pantomiming they should sit there. But then she held up her finger, gesturing for them to wait, and she waved a bus person over to wipe off the table again. Marnie glanced at Lee, who wore a stony expression.

"Are you still with the fire department?" Marnie asked Josh, not sure how else to fill the awkward silence. "And running your own company on the side?"

"No," he replied. "And no."

Bree beamed. "He's a nurse now."

SECRETS OF THE BLUE MOON

Marnie almost choked out the wine she'd just sipped. "What?" She dabbed her mouth with her napkin. "I'm sorry, I never saw that one coming."

He shot her a sheepish grin. "Neither did I."

Bree again spoke for Josh. "After getting his EMT certification, he felt a calling. Got into an accelerated nursing program, and voilà!"

"Wow." Marnie couldn't shake off her surprise. Or her irritation at the way Bree liked to speak for other people.

Bypassing Bree, she spoke directly to Josh. "I thought you wanted to do something with construction." She added, "You were always so good with your hands."

Oh, my God. How in THE hell had that slipped out?

Her cheeks grew warm. She didn't dare make eye contact with Josh. Or Lee. From the corner of her eye, she noticed Bree fold her arms.

Struggling to make it better, she murmured, "You were good at the hard sciences, too."

"I'm sure." Bree smirked.

At least she spoke. No one else would. Or could.

The hostess gestured—thank God!—and Josh placed his hand on Bree's back to move her along to their table. His face flushed as he turned to Lee. "Nice to meet you."

"Likewise," Lee said.

Marnie felt Lee's stare and silently begged him not to say anything that might make things even worse. Which might not be possible. Dutch Remington saved the moment when he approached with two glasses of port. He sat them on the table, then stood back to apprise Lee.

"I'm Dutch Remington." Surprisingly, he did not offer his hand.

"Lee Johnson." He nodded in Dutch's direction.

"Andre says the port's on the house. I asked if I could deliver it so I could also apologize." Dutch glanced sheepishly at Marnie. "I got a little worked up last night."

85

Marnie hoped her surprise didn't show on her face. "No worries," she murmured. She wanted to say he should apologize to his wife, not her. But she held her tongue.

"It's okay," she finally said, noting his eyes still locked on her.

He left. They drank their port in silence, and Marnie excused herself to use the restroom.

As she exited the stall, Bree entered the restroom. Un-freaking-believable.

"Ah," Bree said, "it's the woman with good taste in men." Her voice poured out like rich cream. "Your Lee is a handsome man. He wears his confidence like a well-tailored jacket."

Was that a bad thing? As Marnie proceeded to the sink, a second thing occurred to her. Who says something like that to someone they'd just met?

Marnie tried to brush all that negativity from her mind. A worried frown creased Bree's forehead.

"Can I offer some friendly advice?" Bree's tone dripped with concern.

Marnie wanted to say, "Oh, hell no, you can't." Instead, she held her tongue and stilled her nerves for what might come next.

"I know you're writing this book," Bree continued. "And for some reason, the Remingtons are excited about it." She pursed her lips.

Speaking of the Remingtons, Marnie wanted to say, *what the hell was the deal between you and Dutch last night?*

No time, though. Bree kept talking. "I worry that, with you living with Willow, you might get a skewed picture of things around here."

Bree's audacity irritated Marnie, but she appreciated that the woman wasn't digging into things more personal. Like Marnie's taste in men.

"I'm not sure what you mean." She tried not to scowl at Bree.

"Willow's spiritual practice, for one thing." Bree made air quotes at spiritual practice. "She plays it up as helping people, but, well, come on."

Marnie took her time drying her hands on the disposable towel. "How is running a life-coaching business a bad thing? Plenty of people find those kinds of services helpful."

"Not the way Willow runs things. She hypnotizes vulnerable people and makes them think they can talk to the dead. Naïve, vulnerable people. Like Kate."

Marnie's muscles tensed. "I don't see Kate as naïve."

Bree leaned in and spoke in a low tone. "Kate turned to Willow to reach out to her dead mother." She blinked hard. "You think an ethical woman would take Kate's money to do that?"

Marnie shifted uncomfortably. She hoped if she said nothing, Bree would move along.

She tilted her head and met Marnie's eyes. "And then there are those wild bonfires."

Bonfires? Marnie perked up. "It's not like we're in a drought."

Bree sighed. Loudly. "The big worry had to do with the one a couple weeks ago. The one scheduled for the night of the waning crescent moon."

"You've lost me." Okay, a white lie. Dutch had been outraged about the same fire.

Bree pulled her phone from her purse and swiped at the screen. When she found what she sought, she thrust the phone at Marnie. "Here. Check it out."

Marnie squinted to read the small print, but Bree couldn't wait that long.

"On nights with a waning crescent moon," she recited, sing-songy, "witches conduct rituals to oust the current U.S. President from office. It's been going on for some time now. Worldwide." When Marnie had no words, Bree added, "Bizarre as F, isn't it?"

Marnie tried to shut out Bree's nattering long enough to read the small text on the phone. She zoomed in on a list of magical spell ingredients: an unflattering picture of POTUS, a feather, a piece of an orange candle, and a Tower tarot card.

Struggling not to laugh, she handed the phone back to Bree. "You think Willow scheduled a bonfire for the purpose of casting spells? Against the President?"

Bree puckered her lips as if she'd just tasted sour milk. "Have you seen the sign in her yard?"

Marnie kept a poker face. Of course she'd seen Willow's sign. Just like she'd seen Dutch's. All three of them.

"Look," she said, "I think you're misinformed. But even if rituals to oust the President *have* been going on, they're not working. Know what I mean?"

"Whatever, Marnie." Bree hoisted her purse strap over her shoulder and moved toward the stall. "Just don't take everything Willow says as fact. You need to get more information."

Marnie's body temperature rose as Bree closed herself in the stall.

"I appreciate your concern," she lied to the stall door.

Gritting her teeth on her way out, she tried not to picture this bitchy, gossipy woman involved with *her* Josh. Except he was no longer her Josh. That Josh would not have been drawn to a woman with such a brash, brassy style.

A sudden thought roiled inside her, making it hurt to swallow. Maybe that was what Josh liked best about Bree—the fact she was so very different from Marnie. After all, that was how Marnie had moved on from Josh, by latching on to his polar opposite. But she was starting to wonder if she'd traded a fun-loving, daring doofus for a disciplined, self-centered brat.

Sucking in her breath, she walked back to her table.

Back to the man with the safe, self-disciplined manner who had wooed her back when.

Back to the husband she no longer knew.

Chapter 14

"Dutch brought us the port, right?" Lee asked once they left Andre's.

"Yes. Why?"

Given the coolness at the end of their meal, he surprised her by offering his hand. Tentative, she accepted it, comforted by its warmth.

"Why the apology?" he asked.

"Dutch is the mayor. He and his wife Kate had a gathering last night. A reporter showed up with some questions, and Dutch got a little hot when responding."

"Well"—Lee squeezed her hand—"I'm not sure I blame him."

Marnie chewed on that for a beat. "The thing is, Dutch didn't just yell at the reporter. He took out his anger on Kate as well."

Lee stopped walking and turned Marnie to face him. "Men do that sometimes when we're feeling helpless. Take out our frustrations on the person who's closest and dearest to us."

His eyes shimmered in the reflection of the streetlight. He smiled a little. She didn't.

"Marnie!" Kate's greeting interrupted the moment. She walked arm in arm with Zack Lightner, and her tone came out light and musical. "And this must be your husband."

"Hey!" Zack's eyes lit up, and he raised a challenging brow. "I didn't know you're married."

A flush crept across Marnie's cheeks as she made introductions. "Lee, this is Dutch's wife, Kate. She's the person who contacted me about this assignment. And this is Zack, who co-owns The Lake Gardner Mill with his sister, Bree. The woman you just met in the restaurant."

Lee appeared to take a cleansing breath, sizing things up. Then his shoulders relaxed. "Good to meet you." He dipped his head to Zack, then to Kate. "Ma'am."

Zack's phone rang, and he pulled it from his pocket. "Hate to be rude, but I've got to take this." He bobbed his head and walked away, phone glued to his ear.

"Good to meet you, Lee." Kate waved and trotted after Zack. "Catch you later, Marnie." She caught up with Zack, clutched his arm again, and the two headed into Andre's.

Marnie tugged Lee's arm to steer him off Main Street back toward The Diana. Now, he placed his hands in his pockets rather than reaching for Marnie again.

"So what's the deal with this Zack fellow?" Lee asked as they walked.

"I only met him once." She couldn't read his tone. "He and his sister Bree co-own The Lake Gardner Mill."

"So you said." Lee stopped walking and turned to her. "But let me ask you something, Marnie. Why did he act surprised you're married?"

"I have no idea." She had also found Zack's comment odd.

Lee studied her closely. "Do you not wear your rings? When you're out and about at all these interviews and parties?"

She drew in her breath, surprised at his overt jealousy. "I do wear my rings, Lee. The interviews are part of my assignment here. And I went to the party at Kate's so she could introduce me to the people I need to interview."

She shouldn't have to explain herself. It wasn't like he never socialized for business.

"Lake Gardner's different than Buckhead." She kept walking. "People are friendlier here."

"A little too friendly if you ask me."

Marnie didn't want to admit Lee might have a point. "The Lightners and the Remingtons have partnered on some real estate deals."

"Hmmm."

They walked in stilted silence past city hall, down the Halloween-festive Amani Way. Scarecrows guarded yards while ghosts floated from porch rafters. At the house across from Willow's, the witch lunged from the shadows again, and again, Marnie startled.

"Gets me every time," she said, turning to Lee, laughing at herself.

Lee's cool glower flattened her mood quickly.

"You know what gets me, Marnie?" He started to cross the street, and she followed. "It sounds like you're not missing our life at all."

Marnie stopped in her tracks, in the middle of the street. When Lee came to a standstill, too, she couldn't read his eyes. She also couldn't trust herself to respond just yet.

Lee had referred to *their* life as though they no longer existed as individuals. And why not? *His* life ticked along splendidly, career booming, home life neat and orderly. Any little problems—say, his wife's lost pregnancies, her job termination—those were just little hiccups in *her* life. *Their* life still purred along, smooth as the engine in the luxury car he drove.

That was unfair on his part. Self-focused. Thoughtless. But she couldn't muster the energy to explain it to him, to deal with his inability to see it.

"I *do* miss our life," she finally said. In her mind she added, *the old version.*

She didn't try to hide her scowl as they continued to walk onto The Diana's property.

"I don't know, Marn." He stopped to examine Willow's *Nope* sign. "You're showing a side of yourself I don't even recognize."

"I'm just being myself." She stomped the ground harder than she intended. "Which you would recognize if you ever pulled your head out of your backside long enough to pay attention."

Lee flinched. "I *am* paying attention, Marnie. And from what I'm picking up, I'm worried I may be losing you."

Something fluttered in Marnie's stomach. "That's ridiculous."

But she had to admit, her feelings ran all over the place.

Lee ogled the *Nope* sign one more time, then turned his attention back to Marnie.

"Nothing knocks a man down a notch or two more than hearing his wife describe a former boyfriend as good with his hands."

Oh, that. She wished she could take back those words a million times for a billion different reasons, including the puppy-like expression in Lee's eyes right now.

She reached out, gently touching his cheek. "Hey, I'm married to you, not him, aren't I?"

In her ears, that sounded ingenuous. She felt like a blinking amber spirit, trying to freeze or back up time, yearning to avoid more trouble than she cared to handle.

But it seemed to be what Lee needed to hear. And she didn't say no when he asked if he could spend the night.

Marnie stirred, half awake. The room loomed darker than usual, and her heart pulsed faster than it normally did. She told herself to calm down. It had just been a dream. But it had been an odd one, the kind that mixes the past with the present until it was hard to tell the two apart.

She steadied her breathing to match the light snores beside her. Nuzzling closer, she still tingled from everywhere he'd touched her.

And then she froze. Lee lay beside her. Not Josh.

Her lungs took in a sharp gulp of air. Of course it was Lee by her side. He was her husband, her present. Josh was now part of her past.

She didn't move. Or rather, she *couldn't* move, overwhelmed by conflicting thoughts and feelings. The afterglow of the sex made her giddy, like when things were fresh and new. But her heart weighed heavy with guilt.

Thinking about Josh while lying in bed beside Lee made her feel dirty.

Gently, she pulled her tangled limbs free from Lee's. For a moment more, she lay still beside him. But she had to get up, to get some space, to think.

The evening had been a comical game of dominos, going from bad to worse. Until the sex. Lee could be extremely accommodating when he chose to be. That had been his MO last night. When she climaxed repeatedly, she felt a powerful connection she worried they'd lost.

But had last night been about love? Or just chemistry?

For sure, it had lacked the emotional urgency she felt when they were trying for babies. Was that okay? Even normal, perhaps? Lee certainly hadn't mentioned their fertility struggles, and neither had she.

Rising carefully, she reached for her robe. Her mind turned toward Josh.

She padded toward the bathroom, trying to shed her shame. After being with Lee, she'd dreamed of Josh. *Dreamed of him*, for God's sake. But it hadn't been *that* kind of dream. And it hadn't just been him in her dream.

Closing the bathroom door, she turned on the light. Her own tired, befuddled face stared back from the mirror. Not quite the scrambled bewilderment she felt inside. But close.

She washed water over her cheeks, then sat on the rim of the tub in the quiet.

Her dream seemed so random now. Her lamb, Ollie, had been in it. And her mom, Patsy—which amplified her confusion. Her mom had died before Marnie ever met Josh.

Dreams could be strange, though.

In this one she heard the horrible bleating. Not like an ewe during birth, that combination of straining noises and harsh maas. These were panic bleats, coming from down by the river.

Marnie's knees wobbled, but she raced toward the sound, through the milkweed and butterflies, to a place where the river churned in her ears and cricket chirps choked the air.

By the time she crested the field, the bleating stopped. Her knees buckled as she stared into the rushing water. She fell to the ground, frozen in disbelief. Straight ahead, Ollie bobbed in the logs dammed up between the river's shores. Her mom lay facedown, very near the lamb, like she'd been struggling to help her before getting swept into an eddy herself.

Marnie fought off the weight of her grief.

"Stop blaming yourself." Josh had cradled her tight, sweet as always, her Josh. Even in a dream.

But her mother's death *had* been her fault. In her heart, she knew it. Despite the contorted timeframe of the dream and the fact her mom had been gone for years, it still haunted her.

Marnie rubbed her eyes with her fingers now, still blaming herself as an image circled the doorframe. It resembled a flame licking the ceiling. It appeared so real, even though it couldn't be. It didn't scorch the door or heat the room, but it glowed bigger than before, in deeper oranges and more mature reds. Gone was the erratic jumping bean of a spark. In its place, a blaze crackled, appearing strong enough to spread warmth or destruction in one billowing gasp.

A spicy familiar scent surrounded her. It smelled stronger tonight, more like Fireball whisky than straight-up cinnamon. It wasn't CeCe. She knew that.

"Roxy?" Marnie whispered.

The flame grew larger and more animated. Not an actual flame, she reminded herself. It didn't char the wood or smell like a fire. But in her heart she felt it, this ball of emotions. It struggled to tell her something, which she interpreted as, *Yes, I'm Roxy.*

"I'd like to help you," Marnie said.

Of course, she wouldn't mind if Roxy's ghost could help her, too—say, to connect with her mother's spirit. But first things first.

"I'd like to see your killer brought to justice." The flame remained steady, and she pushed on. "It might help you rest, having the world know what happened that night. To you. To CeCe."

When she uttered the name CeCe, the flame grew huge, its cinnamon whisky odor burning Marnie's lungs.

She recoiled, but she refused to stop with her questions. "Do you like what I just said?" She balled her fists to calm herself. "Or are you trying to tell me to leave things alone?"

The plume belched out a humongous, hellish flame.

And then it huffed out.

Chapter 15

She slept restlessly after that, waking to the white noise of the shower. The room lay still except for the fan, which rotated slow and steady. She donned her robe and slippers and padded downstairs, hoping to catch Willow alone so she could tell her about her latest ghostly encounter. Not finding Willow, she poured two mugs of coffee and took them upstairs.

Fresh from the shower, Lee smelled of bergamot and citrus. He leaned down to kiss her. "Hey, babe." His eyes shone as he accepted a mug from Marnie. "You want to pack first? Or shower?"

She opened her mouth, but he never gave her the chance to ask her question.

"I got you a last-minute flight." He shot her a sheepish grin.

Her mouth felt dry. "We talked about this, Lee. Why I can't go with you."

He raised his hands, palms out, his grin widening. "I know you're committed to this project. But I got to thinking, the whole world is teleworking these days. So why can't you? From Denver?"

"I—" Could she access the library databases from Denver? "I don't know."

"Oh, c'mon." He cocked his head and wiggled his brows. "There must be some things you can work on during the day there. And then we can have our time together at night."

He put his coffee mug on her writer's desk and moved in closer, pulling her to him. "I've gotten lazy, Marnie. About romancing you, like in the old days." He rubbed against her.

She might have laughed at such a horndog move if he didn't look so sincere.

"Remember Savannah?" He nuzzled her ear.

She closed her eyes. "I remember." She pulled away gently. "We had a wonderful time. We've had *lots* of great times. But marriage is more than just a series of romantic moments."

He avoided her eyes. "I feel like you don't even want to try anymore."

"That's not true." But the words left the sour tang of a white lie in her mouth.

His jaw muscle tensed. "Everything I do to try to bring us closer, you push me away."

"We were pretty close last night." She reached for his arm. "Remember?"

But they were talking about something different here. And she couldn't blame their distance all on Lee. While he hadn't exactly pushed for meaningful conversation during his stay, neither had she. *Why not?* Because they struggled to find things to talk about anymore? Or worse, because *she* felt exhausted from trying to make their marriage work?

"I'm not a quitter." She hated the bitterness in her tone, especially when talking about their wedding vows.

"Did I ask you to quit this project?"

Lee's question frustrated her, even though she read his tone as hurt, not confrontation.

"I'm talking about our marriage." She palmed her thighs. "And this is a perfect example of why I get frustrated. Your ideas to bring us closer are all about you."

Lee broke eye contact. "I thought we were good. After last night." His Adam's apple bobbed. "I figured you'd love me to whisk you away for a surprise romantic weekend."

For an instant, everything around her spun. Then time slowed, and the room stood still and dark as Lee's expression. She hated to see him this way. But dear God, why did she have to explain her feelings to him again and again? She shouldn't have to.

"I told you I didn't want to go to Denver." She tried to match his even-keeled tone.

"You said you *couldn't* go. Not that you *didn't want* to go."

"Lee!" She squeezed her scalp, all too aware of his point. *I can't go* because *I have to work* meant something completely different from *I don't want to go* because we were at a difficult place in our marriage.

She ran her fingers down her forehead, stopping at her brows. She needed space. And time. "You're pushing me past my limits, Lee," she whispered. "Honest to God."

He didn't respond to that. Not at first. Then he sighed and touched her face. "Look at me." When she didn't, he gently pried her fingers away from her eyes. He squeezed her hand. "Come to Denver. It'll be good for us, don't you think?"

She still couldn't sustain direct eye contact. "I'm sorry, Lee, but no. I'm not coming."

He dropped her hand and just stood there. When he finally moved to gather his things, his lips formed a tight line. "You need to decide what you want, Marnie. And I'm not just talking about Denver." His flat tone shook her more than if he'd blown up in a rage. He started to leave the room but turned to face her one more time.

"You can't have it all." Fire blazed in his eyes. "Not all the time."

She jerked back. "But you can?" She hated herself for taking his bait, but when he turned to leave again, she couldn't hold back. "You don't get to just walk away!"

The silence that followed weighed a ton. *Would he come back?* Did she *want* him to?

She ran several feet after him, freezing in the doorway as he descended the stairs. She slammed the door.

To hell with it all anyway.

She opened and slammed the door again. Hard.

After she calmed down, Marnie went to the kitchen and poured herself an ice water. She took a sip, then dipped her fingers into the cool wetness and dabbed some on her eyelids. Through the kitchen's picture window, she caught a glimpse of Willow out back, sitting in one of the Adirondack chairs, leaning over something on the table in front of her.

Marnie stepped out into the day, which hung eerily still, the clouds shrouding the sun. As she neared Willow, the older woman looked up from her work in a coloring book to greet her with cool, all-knowing eyes and a "Good morning."

Marnie peered closer to see what Willow had going. A picture of Jason Momoa stared up at her. Painstakingly colored. Everything in the lines with excellent shading.

"It was a gift." Willow's cheeks pinkened as she bent over her work.

Marnie tried not to smirk as she sat in the Adirondack chair next to Willow's.

"Anyway," Willow said, "I trust you had a nice evening with your husband?"

"I loved Andre's. But Lee and I... We're in one of those odd patches when it's hard to connect."

Why did she always tell Willow more than she intended?

"Seems like you connected fine last night." Willow chuckled.

"Oh." Marnie blushed now. "Well, this morning we disconnected again big time."

"You want to talk about it?"

"Oh, God, no." Marnie's laugh rang thin in her ears.

"Okay." Willow returned her focus to the lei around Jason's neck, where she added red highlights to the tips of yellow flowers.

"You know what?" Marnie said. "I'd rather talk about ghosts. About how you help others connect with them."

Willow traded her red crayon for a turquoise one, engrossed in her art. "That's not exactly how I'd describe my work." She moved on to color Jason's shirt.

"Since I met you, I'm seeing spirits all over the place." Marnie might be oversimplifying, but she spoke her truth. "So I can't help but wonder if it's because of you."

Willow lifted her crayon. "What's happening with you has to do with your gifts, not mine. Plus there's the thinning of the veil." She returned to her work, adding a touch more turquoise to the page. "But I'm curious. Whose spirits are you talking about?"

Marnie stood, feeling as though she might burst out of her skin if she didn't move.

"The Cozy-Remington orphans, for starters. I saw them at the Remingtons' place and then again on your porch, playing with CeCe. But then last night, I think Roxy visited. Up in my bathroom..." Her voice caught. "And she didn't seem happy to see me in her space."

Willow tucked the crayons away and closed her coloring book. "Why do you say that?"

"She appeared as this floating flame that flickered and glowed when I asked her questions." Marnie scraped her hand through her hair. "She looked authentic enough to ignite a fire. But she didn't emit heat. And then when I asked her if she wanted me here, she just cut out."

Rising, Willow gathered her art materials. "She could be trying to determine if she can trust you."

"Maybe."

Marnie gave that some thought. It felt as though the younger spirits wanted her help, but the older wraith did not.

"Can't you help me figure out what these ghosts want from me?"

"And how do you propose I do that?" Willow started walking back toward the house. "As I've pointed out, it's your power at work here, not mine."

Marnie jogged along behind her, thinking back to Willow's meditation session with Kate and to reading about Willow's life-coaching services.

"Could you hypnotize me? I mean, that could help me find subconscious answers, right?"

Willow opened the door to the kitchen. "Depends what you're looking for."

Marnie followed her inside, where Willow placed her coloring materials on the old farmhouse table.

"How about today?" she asked.

"No, butterfly. I've got to prepare for tonight's bonfire."

The bonfires. Marnie had forgotten about them. She chose to push some more.

"You know neither Dutch nor Bree are fans of your fires, right?"

Willow waved her off, unfazed.

"You know why?" Marnie pushed on. "They think you time your fires with the lunar cycles so you can help oust our President from office."

Willow froze in front of the refrigerator door. "I beg your pardon?"

"Bree said that's why you hosted the fire a couple weeks ago."

Willow turned, her face red, her fingers fluttering at her lips. As her eyes widened, they filled with tears, and she bowed her head, shoulders shaking.

"I'm sorry," Marnie murmured.

She couldn't believe Willow was crying. Over something so ridiculous.

But when Willow raised her head, she wasn't crying. She was laughing so hard no sound came out. She had to pluck at her clothes to cool herself down.

"Oh, my," she finally said, all shiny faced.

She retrieved a pitcher of tea from the fridge, raising it toward Marnie in a question.

Marnie shook her head, wanting answers, not sustenance. "So the bonfires aren't—what did Dutch call them—some voodoo-hoodoo events to celebrate the cycles of the moon?"

"Oh, for heaven's sake." Willow filled a glass with ice. "Sometimes the bonfires here *can* be quiet and meditative. But more times they're sort of like a happy hour and campfire combined. They're no big deal."

Okay. But if the bonfires were no big deal, what did Willow have to prepare for the one tonight? *Preparing for it* just sounded like a way of putting off hypnotizing Marnie.

Willow glanced over, her steely gaze intent. "Marnie, the bonfires are just that. Bonfires. There's nothing outlandish at play here. No mystery at all."

That reminded Marnie of something else. "Speaking of mystery, did Vanita tell you about the message I saw at the graveyard?"

"Yes."

"Do you agree with her that it was kids playing a prank?"

"No." Willow poured herself some tea and took a long drink. "Sometimes," she finally continued, "when we first activate our gifts, they go into overdrive. So it's possible random spirits are honing in on your energy, reaching out with no rhyme or reason."

"Reaching out from their graves?" Marnie suddenly understood the meaning behind the phrase of making someone's blood run cold.

"It's a lot, I know. But remember it's also the time of year when the veil is at its thinnest. Eventually the spirits will die down." Willow's lips twisted upward, possibly at the bad pun. "And by the way, I'm not opposed to hypnotizing you, if you want me to. Just not today." Quickly, she added, "But not just because of the bonfire." The worry lines in her forehead creased. "You've been through a lot. Miscarriages. Job loss. A roller coaster ride of emotions surrounding your marriage."

Marnie's chest tightened at what an open book of her life this woman saw.

Willow's eyes lit with empathy. "Not to mention, you've been gifted with a special sight but no instruction manual on how to use it. So how about granting yourself a breather from all this ghostly shit? You could take a nap? Or color." She leaned in and winked. "I have a book with poker-playing dogs if you'd prefer that over Jason."

Marnie laughed.

Willow pressed on. "Why don't you take a walk? Or maybe a nature hike."

She plucked a brochure from under a magnet on the fridge, placing it in front of Marnie. On one side, it listed *Hikes Around Lake Gardner*. On the other side, *Historic Sites on Lake Gardner's Outskirts*.

Goose bumps ran up Marnie's arms as her attention honed in on one particular bulleted item: *The Dalton Creek Bridge*.

Marnie's mind raced. The Remingtons wanted her to feature the bridge in her book. Emmett Lightner had died there. Well, he'd actually died on the Dalton Creek Bridge Expansion.

But still.

Her gaze returned to the bulleted item: *The Dalton Creek Bridge*. Andromeda's Coven had met at the Dalton Creek Bridge the night of The Diana's murders.

Marnie shivered.

But suddenly she knew exactly where she'd be taking her afternoon breather.

The Dalton Creek Bridge

Lake Gardner's 2020 Walking Ghost Tour

*T*he original Dalton Creek Bridge is a step back in time to the days of buggies and "horseless carriages" when bridges were covered to protect them from the elements. Located on the outskirts of Lake Gardner, this one was built in the 1880s with just a single lane, its intent to help travelers cross Dalton Creek. Unfortunately, the narrow, curved road leading up to the bridge, along with the bridge itself, was home to dozens of fatal crashes through the years.

Locals have long fueled lore that the bridge is haunted. One legend tells of a mother whose ghost walks the grounds nearby, screaming for her baby, who was tossed from a carriage to certain death. Ghostly lanterns shine, only to disappear without explanation as the mother's cries die out. In other gruesome tales, ropes groan as though holding bodies swaying from the rafters, the air filled with angry and agonized cries. Some claim these sounds come from the ghosts of souls hung from the beams by angry vigilante mobs in the 1930s and '40s.

As iron became more affordable, truss-structured bridges became passé. Even so, the covered Dalton Creek Bridge remained operational *until the 1980s, when a two-lane bridge—the Dalton Creek Bridge Expansion—replaced it. Historic preservationists succeeded with a campaign to restore the original bridge in the early 2000s. One of only several hundred covered bridges left in the U.S. today, it has become a local treasure.*

A final note: Despite its safer structure, Dalton Creek Bridge Expansion still can prove deadly to those who veer off it and into the larger and deeper Lake Gardner it crosses. A tragic example of this occurred on New Year's Eve 2010, when one of the biggest advocates for restoring the bridge, Emmett Lightner, drove off the extended bridge to his untimely death.

Unfortunate coincidence? Or proof that both *bridges are now haunted?*

The truth may never be known, but the ghostlore will likely live on forever.

Chapter 16

A temporary sign stood beside the concrete stumps installed to keep cars off the old covered bridge: *Today's hike cancelled due to inclement weather.*

Marnie found that odd. A storm was in the forecast, but not until later that night. She parked her Outback near the vacant ranger's station anyway, then followed a stone stairway that descended to the underbelly of the bridge. She walked along the creek's edge toward a grassy picnic area dotted with gigantic spindly pines.

She felt no sense of foreboding, no supernatural energy connected to this site. Perhaps Willow's claim would prove true. The spirits would ease up on her the more she leaned into her gift and learned how to navigate it.

The wind picked up, carrying the pungent scent of moss and decayed leaves. Walking away from the creek bank, Marnie closed in on an old stone well, covered and nestled in the grass. A memory caught her off guard as she neared a chipped green picnic table and rickety charcoal grill. It had been at a place like this. Her eyes tingled. The only things missing? Grilled hamburgers and plastic cups of prosecco.

And Josh.

Fresh out of college, they'd been celebrating new starter jobs and toying with moving in together. She had been ready, but Josh dragged his feet. *Why?* Her stomach fluttered, remembering how much she'd loved him. She thought he'd loved her, too, but not quite enough?

Never mind. The past didn't matter. She had chosen her present life. With Lee.

Returning to task, she retrieved her phone to shoot some stills of the picnic area and the ruins of an old mill off in the distance. Amazing, her phone camera worked just fine today. She plodded under the bridge where the water still trickled, but with the lethargy of late fall. A crow cawed, drawing her attention up to the rafters, angled in geometric perfection. Goose bumps dusted her arms as she recalled a description from the ghost tour brochure.

Angry mobs hung their victims from the beams in the 1930s and '40s.

Her stomach roiled, and a pressure clamped around her throat like a vise—like a rogue spirit, telling her not to forget the atrocities. She touched her neck. As the pressure eased, she remembered to breathe and ascended the steps to get to where the bridge met the road.

Her face was flushed by the time she reached it. Thunder rumbled nearby as she followed the narrow road to under the bridge's roof, where beams and trusses formed pristine angles. She turned in a slow 360 to shoot more pictures—the deck and running boards underfoot, the sharp one-lane road leading up to the bridge. Her stomach fluttered, imagining once-upon-a-time travels along that road on starless nights or when storms were at bay.

Lightning slashed and sent her skittering back under the bridge. A crash of thunder made her skin prickle. The storm had arrived early. She glanced in the direction of her Outback, at least a five-minute run with no umbrella or jacket.

She steeled herself to make her escape. Another bolt of lightning cut the sky. The angry sounds of bird squabbles and beating wings raged from deep in the bowels of the bridge.

Her pulse faltered as she clutched for her phone. Steadying her hand, she aimed the phone's light back toward the commotion. She squeezed her eyes to make out an engraved plaque resting in the midst of the bridge's lines and symmetry.

She read the words to herself in a low voice: "In memory of Emmett Lightner – December 31, 2010."

A whooshing ruckus echoed off the trusses, and a flash of black swooped straight for her. She stumbled backward, her grip tight on the phone. Her scalp tingled.

Had she just dodged a bat? No. Something bigger. Probably a bird. She sucked in her breath, tried not to lose her shit.

The black bird landed near her and let out a hoarse grinding caw. It strutted, nervous. When it stopped, it cocked its head and stared at her. Her breath hitched in a panic. She wasn't sure why it freaked her out so badly, but she had to turn away.

The rain still gushed in torrents as her shaking fingers pawed her phone's flashlight on and aimed it toward the entrance to the bridge. It represented her only hope of escape, but a vivid scene from the movie *The Birds* rushed in her mind, paralyzing her to the point she couldn't move.

The black bird continued to screech, raucous and persistent. Marnie's adrenaline spiked, enabling her to start to run. Grunting, she ignored the fire that pulsed through her leg muscles with each step. She pushed forward despite the uneven surface beneath her.

Until she tripped. *Ooopb.*

She face-planted, her phone skittering across the floor beams. She labored to catch her breath and surveyed the area to get her bearings. At least the freaking bird had flown off.

Struggling to her feet, she rolled her neck and shoulders and checked for sprains. She stepped with care to ensure she hadn't twisted a knee or an ankle. When she reached her phone, she picked it up and shined it toward the bridge's entrance.

Lightning sizzled. It backlit the outline of a man. He walked toward her, painfully slow. Her knees buckled and she tried to scream. Nothing came out.

"Are you all right, ma'am?" He kept coming closer. "I'm Ranger James."

Her lips parted. She wanted to cry, but instead, she covered her mouth.

"I'm okay." Her voice came out with a schmaltzy vibrato.

He cleared his throat. "I'm afraid I have to ask you to leave. A severe weather alert has been issued." He tugged at his hat. "I can follow you in my vehicle if you'd like."

Oh, hell no, she wanted to tell him. But she declined more politely, accepting the spare umbrella he handed her.

As she prepared to leave, he asked again, "You sure you're okay? I heard a bit of a commotion in here just now."

She let out a nervous laugh, motioning to where she'd first spotted the bird. "You ever been dive-bombed by a crow? Because I think that's what just happened to me."

He pulled out his flashlight and aimed where she pointed. "That's highly unusual." Spotting nothing, he turned back to her. "In spring, they might swoop down if you threaten their nests. But this time of year…" Thunder rumbled. "Are you sure you didn't imagine it?"

Her mouth fell open again. "No. I didn't imagine it."

"Hmm." His eyebrows pulled down in concentration. "You know, crows can distinguish and remember human faces. They've been known to wreak havoc when they recognize a human who's a threat to them."

She shuddered. That crow had posed more threat to her than she had to it. In fact, it had terrorized her more than the spirits of drowned souls or Emmett Lightner or whoever-the-hell-else she might have encountered here. Now she could only hope to high heaven she didn't have a memorable face. From a crow's perspective at least.

The ranger swept the flashlight through the bridge's cavity one more time.

"No, ma'am. You definitely don't want to mess with crows. You know why?" He stared her square in the eye. "Because crows remember for life. They never, ever forget."

Chapter 17

"The crow is a good omen, butterfly," Willow said from where she sat with Vanita on the porch. "It represents the death and dying of one thing to make room for the growth and transition of another."

Willow had set up a table on the front porch and topped it with candles in lieu of an actual bonfire. Sitting at the fire table alongside her, Marnie regretted telling her what had happened at the bridge. If she never heard one more bit of crow folklore, it would be too soon.

Yet even with the rain pounding on the roof of the old farmhouse, the porch was strangely cozy. A small fire bowl flickered at the center of a black tulle-covered table. Candles and sconces of multiple colors, shapes, and sizes surrounded it. Words had been etched on one round-bottomed sconce: *White Witch – Goddess of Love and Light – Sister and Healer.*

Marnie pointed with a half-smirk.

"You know it's a joke, right?" Willow poured her some wine.

Marnie couldn't be sure. "And the different colored candles?"

Vanita's eyes warmed in the flames' reflection. "Green signifies love, yellow is wealth."

Willow pointed and picked up where Vanita left off. "Red is for strength, blue for good fortune." Then she chuckled. "And white means Kirkland's had a great sale on candles."

The two older women held their glasses up to toast, and Marnie joined them. The wine warmed her, even after just a few sips.

Pointing to the *White Witch* candle base, Willow mused, "You know, if I had the power some folks think I do, I'd heal the racial divide that's been fanned in our country over this past year."

"You wouldn't eradicate the pandemic?" Vanita egged her on. "Or our current President?"

"Yes." Willow relaxed. "And yes again."

Vanita contemplated the flickering candles. "Well," she said, "if I were a witch, I'd be a hedge witch."

Marnie tilted her head, intrigued.

"One who isn't part of a coven," Willow explained. "A solitary."

"You seem to know an awful lot about witches," Marnie said.

"I try to educate myself a little on all religions," Willow said. "Whether I practice them or not."

"Hear, hear." Vanita lifted her glass.

This whole bonfire business struck Marnie as, well, anticlimactic. Things were definitely not unfolding the way Dutch or Bree had led her to believe they might. On the other hand, Willow and Vanita's low-key discussion and camaraderie struck Marnie as interesting but harmless. She felt a twinge of longing for the special bond the two women shared.

"You know what else?" Vanita set down her glass. "I'd have a familiar."

"That's an animal guide, right?" Marnie asked.

Willow nodded. "Sent to serve as a guardian and protector."

"Sent by whom?" Marnie leaned in.

"The devil!" Vanita widened her eyes before bursting into laughter.

"Vanita..." Willow gave her a side glance. To Marnie, she added, "In early European folklore, familiars provided protection for young witches just coming into their new powers."

Kate ran up the steps to join them then, raindrops hitting the ground around her like pebbles. She handed Willow her BYO glass and sloughed off her rain slicker.

"You all know your discussion would give Dutch a stroke if he heard it, right?" Shaking her slicker, she tucked it out of the way, pulled up a chair, and retrieved her drink from Willow. Raising her glass, Kate giggled. "So here's to Dutch." Then she groaned. "How I wish I could mix up a truth potion to give the man." She returned her attention to her glass, taking a righteous gulp. "Not that he's a bold-faced liar," she slurred. "Not an intentional one, at least."

Marnie rubbed her lips. Kate had already been into the cups.

"Would you like to talk about it?" God love Willow, she came right out and asked.

Kate gave her a pouty simper. "As you've told me before, this, too, shall pass."

Marnie cupped her chin, trying not to overanalyze their conversation. Truth be told, she would also love to get her hands on a similar potion and sneak it to Lee. Then he might give her the honest-to-God answers she needed to help choose her path forward.

She couldn't admit that to Kate, though. She could barely admit it to herself.

She studied the candlelight, its shape shifting and flicking like the spirit she'd seen last night. Goose bumps ran up her back. "If I had a truth serum like that, Kate," she said, "I'd use it to draw out the truth behind The Diana's murders."

Kate cocked her head. "That's sweet, Marnie. But everyone knows Roxy's foster son did it. He never got tried because of circumstantial evidence. But everyone knows the truth."

Vanita crossed her arms. "Everyone?" She looked pointedly at Willow.

"It happened before my time here." Willow stared into the candles' flames.

"That's a copout," Vanita goaded, but in a gentle way.

"No, it's not," Kate corrected. "The killings happened before either of you came to town. They were tied to some Blue Moon initiation ritual of the Andromeda's Coven. The foster son did it to earn his way in." The lines of her throat tightened. "It's too heinous to talk about."

Marnie studied her. "If you feel that way, why include The Diana in the book?"

"I had hoped to leave it out," Kate admitted. "But as Dutch said, how could we?"

A bolt of lightning blistered the inky sky. The women jumped. Something small and dark moved at the base of the massive magnolia tree. Marnie rose, peering to get a better look.

A roar of thunder blasted the air. She grabbed the stair rail to steady herself.

Behind her, Kate murmured, "That was close."

"Should we move inside?" Vanita suggested.

Willow's response got lost in another crackle of lightning. This one appeared to spear through the magnolia, lighting the yard like an old-time horror film.

In that split second, Marnie recognized what lurked beneath the tree. "It's a kitten." Her reflexes kicked in, and she bolted from the porch.

"Marnie!" Willow cried after her, but Marnie ignored her.

Closing in gently on the soaking animal, she murmured, "You're okay, kitty."

The cat cowered, but it didn't fight when Marnie scooped it up.

Above them, tree boughs creaked and moaned in the angry wind. Thunder bellowed as Marnie tried in vain to start back for the porch. She squinted to make her way, barely able to see through the torrents.

As the rain pelted harder, the tree limbs groaned. A sickening crack split the air, and the scent of smoldering wood pushed through the rising wind. At the same time, a force yanked her away from the tree, then shoved her onto the ground in the opposite direction.

"Marnie!" Kate screamed from the porch.

Stunned, Marnie lay where she'd been flung. She tasted metal. As she tried to feel her legs, the cat mewled in her arms. She lightened her grasp, relieved it hadn't been hurt. When her toes tingled, she took a deep, grateful breath for her own safe-being as well.

She didn't try to stand right away, knowing her legs weren't steady enough to carry her yet. Finally, she wobbled to her feet and willed her spongy legs to transport her back to the porch.

Willow met her halfway up the steps. Vanita waited with towels. Where had they come from? Marnie didn't care. She let the two women wrap her like a child.

"You could've been killed." Kate's voice sounded thick, angry even. But then she added, "I'm so glad you're okay."

Marnie recognized relief when she heard it.

"But Dear Lord..." Vanita's sentence broke off. "The magnolia."

Sticks and branches littered the yard. A huge bough had snapped from the magnolia's top, landing on the ground in the precise spot where Marnie had rescued the cat. Shaking her head in denial, she began to laugh. Soon her reaction turned to sobs.

Willow soothed her into a chair. "You've got some excellent reflexes."

"No." Marnie peered up at Willow through tear-tinged lashes. She hugged the cat. "I've got a familiar."

Vanita laughed, a little longer than normal.

"Y'all are bonkers," Kate snapped. "You barely escaped death just now, Marnie."

Marnie didn't admit it out loud, but it *had* been scary, running into the storm. Truth be told—and fondness for cats aside—it had been a pretty stupid risk on her part. She couldn't be sure what had prompted her to do it.

Vanita returned to the table, her eyes wide. "Did you feel it, Marnie? It looked like a magical force pushed you to safety."

"Yes!" Kate agreed. "I saw it, too."

Marnie's cheeks flushed with heat. She had felt the force as well.

Willow sat back at the table now, too. "What I saw was one wild shot of adrenaline." But her voice wavered, as though she might not believe her own words.

"Adrenaline, my ass," Vanita scoffed.

Marnie cradled the cat on her lap, leaning toward Vanita's side in this debate.

"What if Roxy's ghost did it?" Kate ran her hands up her arms as though fighting off a chill. When she added, "I'm scared," Marnie shivered.

Willow reached for Kate's hand. "Please don't be frightened, Kate. Most little quirks like this can be explained by science, you know."

"Nope. That wasn't science." Vanita shot a side glance first at Willow, then at Marnie. Her expression grew pensive in the dim candlelight, and she dipped her head toward the cat, which purred like a well-tuned turbo engine as it nuzzled Marnie's hand.

"If I didn't know better, I might say you *did* get yourself a familiar, Marnie." She nodded toward the cat. "A lifesaving one."

Marnie sat back with a contented sigh. "I could almost embrace that. Except it would make me a young crone just coming into my own new powers." She snorted gently, then bent her cheek to touch the cat's head. "Not to mention, I'm not so sure Onyx saved me."

"You named the cat Onyx?" Vanita's lips twitched.

Willow ran a hand through her silvery hair and grinned. "It fits."

Vanita burst into laughter, and Willow joined her. Marnie held back a chuckle, but she couldn't help feeling tickled as well.

"You all go ahead and laugh." Kate drew her lips tight. "But I'm telling you, Roxy was here." She crossed her arms. "Marnie said she wanted to find out the truth behind The Diana's murders. Well, Roxy heard her." Hugging herself, she added, "And Roxy saved her."

Chapter 18

In the wee hours, Marnie's phone pinged. Rubbing her face to help wake up, she felt the drool on her pillow. Gross. But she hadn't slept so soundly in a long time.

Ping.

Kate had sent a message.

Any more strange activity last night?

Onyx, who had been curled up on the window seat to sleep, padded up on the bed now, cocking her head as if curious as well. Marnie scratched the cat's neck and murmured, "Fair question, I suppose."

Shortly after Onyx's rescue, Kate had insisted on leaving. She threatened to march home in the torrents, so Vanita drove her. And Marnie's first bonfire pretty much ended on that note.

Staring up at the ceiling now, Marnie recalled Kate's comment before all the commotion. *How I wish I could mix up a truth potion to give to the man.* Would Kate ask Dutch about his financial secrets?

Or did she have more ominous fears she wanted to explore with him?

As for Marnie, she had initially fantasized about dosing Lee with the serum to discover whether or not he would ever want children. But in the morning light, another question came into focus:

Do you see me as your equal?

She lay completely still now, unsettled by her wakefulness *and* the question. Lee would say, yes, of course, he considered her his equal. But

Marnie had to wonder if he might not, no matter what he told himself or what she wanted to believe.

Coffee. She needed coffee to help her make sense of things. But first she needed to reply to Kate's text. She found a thumbs-up emoji. And a smiley face blowing a kiss. The two icons said pretty much nothing and everything at the same time.

Whooosh.

Message transmitted, she donned her robe and made her way to the kitchen, Onyx rubbing up against her legs as she walked.

Willow filled a mug with coffee for her. "The storm felled some trees in town. A few homes and businesses have lost power." She returned the carafe to its cradle. "Anyway, emergency-response teams are out, and I'm going to pick up some biscuits and coffee to deliver to them."

Marnie took a sip from her mug. How ironic one of the most ostracized women in town also happened to be one of the most thoughtful.

"Are you doing okay?" Willow asked. "You gave us all a scare last night."

"I'm fine." Marnie nodded toward an assembly line of candy on the old farm table. It consisted of piles of miniature chocolates, Airheads, Reese's Pieces, and gummy skeletons. A basket at the end of the line held individually wrapped bags of the goodies.

"Do you expect many trick-or-treaters?" she asked.

"These are for Trunk-or-Treat at the church." Willow bobbed her head toward the bags. "It's part of the *Boo for Christ* celebration. I still need to fill more bags." She frowned. "But when Kate called and asked if I could deliver coffee and biscuits, how could I say no?"

"I can help you with the goody bags if you'd like." Marnie took a sip of coffee.

Willow's face lit up. "Thank you, butterfly. That would be great."

A bit later, Marnie pulled up in front of the Lake Gardner Community Church. She parked as close as she could to the tables that lined the lot area nearest the church. A couple volunteers waved to her, happy to take whatever she'd brought for distribution. She carried the box of treats over to them, aware they were discussing the storm and what a miracle it had cleared just in time for the Halloween festivities.

"These are from Willow Maddox." Marnie set the first of two boxes of goody bags on the table.

"Thank you," said the plumper of the two women working the table, a fortysomething with a gorgeous brunette shag haircut.

The taller woman, a blonde, sifted through the box. She wiggled her eyebrows and grinned. "What? No candy witches' hats?"

Marnie's mouth slackened.

"I'm kidding." Blondie raised her hands palms out and sighed.

Marnie ignored her and returned to retrieve the second box from the Outback. In the process, she overheard another set of women working another table.

"It's not gossip if it's a prayer request," one said.

The other one snickered. Marnie fought the urge to roll her eyes.

When she reached the original set of women, Blondie and Brownie, she tucked the second box nearer the one who'd been searching for witches' hats.

"No broomsticks in this box either." Marnie narrowed her eyes at the blonde. She hadn't intended that to come out with such bite, but, oh well.

"We don't really think Willow's a witch." The brunette's eyes shone sincerely.

"Of course not," Blondie said. "She's just...well, different." Her eyes widened. "I hear she worships the moon and the seasons. Is that true?"

Marnie scrutinized the blonde, trying to determine whether this woman deserved a sincere answer. She didn't, but Marnie chose to take the high road anyway.

"It's not my business." But then she couldn't hold back. "She may seem a bit different to you, but I'd say she behaves more Christian-like than many folks who attend regular services."

Blondie's eyes flashed. Had Marnie rattled her cage? Good.

Brownie dipped her head, toying with her wedding bands. She hadn't been the confrontational one in the first place, but when she looked back up, she pointed to her friend.

"Joni didn't mean any offense," she said, as if she'd signed on to run interference.

"Well, I don't mean any offense either." Marnie crossed her arms. "But I hate to hear people put down what they don't understand."

The two women gaped as she spoke, which only egged her on.

"You know," Marnie said, "your church may not be the end-all and be-all when it comes to Christian doctrine." She jutted out her chin, on a roll. "Where I come from, Jesus is a Jew, and he loves the woo-woo folks as much as he does the traditional Christians."

Where had all that come from? From her heart, she supposed, but she sure as hell hoped the women didn't ask her to expound upon it. They didn't. They just continued to gawp.

"That's a fascinating idea for a Bible study." A male voice cut the air.

Marnie reeled around to see who had spoken. Her breath caught as she recognized the man from pictures she'd seen online.

"Jesus the Jew and the Woo-Woos: A Conversation." The man made air quotes as he spoke. "Do you mind if I borrow that?" He wore a warm grin and didn't appear to be poking fun. "I'm Stan Meadows, by the way. The pastor here. And you are?"

Marnie swallowed hard. "Marnie Putnam. I'm living at The Diana while I work on a project for the Remingtons."

"Ah, yes." The pastor held his finger to his lips. "The book."

Unbelievable. At least the pastor didn't refer to her project as the *ghost* book. Still, Marnie wished she could melt into the pavement. She suspected her expression gave her discomfort away, but she stood firm, refusing to shrink back despite her embarrassment.

"Listen," the pastor said. "I hope you'll give my warmest regards to Willow. She has a deeply generous heart, and for that I'm grateful."

He nodded one more time at Marnie, then to Blondie and Brownie as well. And when he made his way back toward the church, Marnie made her own exit, too.

She steered her Outback into downtown, which had blossomed with scarecrows guarding storefronts as far as she could see. Scary ones reminiscent of crones and ghouls, sweet ones more akin to the Wizard of Oz, and personalized ones, like the one dressed in a Lake Gardner High School football uniform.

A sign above Calvin's Pub advertised "Witch's Brew" specials. Another pointing back toward the church promoted *Boo for Christ*. Nowhere carried much hint that yesterday's storm had threatened to wipe out Halloween altogether. Lake Gardner appeared ready to celebrate with zeal, pandemic be damned.

Tucking her concerns away, she turned her Outback onto Spring Street. As she neared City Hall, she spotted a county sheriff's cruiser idling in the lot. She was almost on top of it when she noticed the sheriff and a young brunette standing in front of the cruiser, sputtering back and forth in a heated confrontation.

Rolling down her window to better see what was happening, Marnie jerked her head.

Oh, my.

The sheriff wasn't the one sputtering and gesticulating; the young brunette was.

And the young brunette wasn't just some rando Marnie had never seen before. It was Bree Lightner, spitting mad. And very much inebriated.

Chapter 19

Bree glared through Marnie's open window, and Marnie tried not to shrink back under her surveillance.

"What are you staring at?" Bree chided.

Marnie didn't have to answer as Kate panted up, seemingly from nowhere, her eyes rimmed with panic. Marnie couldn't tell if she'd come from City Hall, the lot, or somewhere else along the street.

"Bree!"

"Go away!" Bree tried to lunge around to face Kate, but the sheriff held her arm tight.

"What's going on here?" Kate clenched her fingers, tight then loose.

Marnie couldn't help herself. She watched like a rubbernecker, ice-cold hands tight on the wheel.

"Oh, please, bitch." Bree didn't even try to break away from the sheriff anymore. "You're no better than anyone else in this goddamned town. Y'all just want to watch me come unglued and fall on my face."

"That's not true," Kate cried.

The sheriff continued to guide Bree toward his cruiser, but she resisted, stopping short of the vehicle door.

"You have no jurisdiction here," she snarled at him. "You can't arrest me within city limits."

Marnie blinked slowly, taking it all in.

"You're not under arrest, ma'am," the sheriff said. "But you cannot drive yourself home either. You're in no condition to do so."

"Let me go get my car," Kate interjected. "Let me give you a ride home."

"Fuck that," Bree said. "I'd rather accept a ride home from the sheriff."

As the sheriff tucked her into his cruiser, she called after Kate, loud and clear.

"I am so damned sick of you and Dutch gaslighting my family."

"What?" Kate sputtered.

The sheriff slammed the back door of his vehicle, cutting off any response Bree might have given. He nodded curtly toward Kate and got behind the wheel. He drove off in the cruiser, Bree in tow, leaving Kate and Marnie gape-mouthed as they watched.

Marnie exhaled as she let the Outback idle. "Kate?"

Kate flashed a quick and frantic glance at Marnie but then lowered her gaze.

"What was that all about?" Marnie asked. When Kate didn't answer, Marnie changed gears. "Can I give you a ride home?"

Kate paled. "No." Her chin quivered, and she added a feeble, "My place is just around the corner.

"I know, but—"

"I'm fine, Marnie." Kate sucked in her cheeks and jerked her head back.

"Okay." Marnie could feel her own face tighten. "I can see that. You're fine."

Kate turned and marched into the lot, finally disappearing behind the City Hall complex.

The base of Marnie's neck tingled. What in the world was going on?

For sure, she wouldn't learn anything more just sitting here and staring. Shaking her head, she shifted the Outback into gear and wove her way back to Amani Drive and The Diana.

Marnie and Willow discussed Bree's quasi-arrest over dinner, a hearty wild rice soup with kale and andouille.

"Word on the street is Bree had too much to drink at Andre's." Willow scooped up a spoonful of soup. "Unfortunately for her, a county sheriff was also there, making dinner reservations. When she headed out, well, he followed her. Because she was in no shape to drive."

Poor Bree. Not that Marnie was a fan of hers. Or of drunk driving. But talk about an unlucky break.

"Bree was pretty angry with Kate," Marnie said. "She said something about how the Remingtons just want to see her struggle, how they just keep on gaslighting her family. I thought the families were tight?"

"Me, too." Willow wrinkled her forehead. "But who knows? From what I've heard, Dutch and Emmett always had a love-hate relationship. Some of their business deals went great. Some soured. And then Emmett tunneled into alcohol abuse toward the end of his life."

"Until it killed him," Marnie murmured.

Willow's worry lines deepened. "And now it seems his daughter is following in his footsteps. With the alcohol *and* the anger."

Marnie stirred her soup, which still steamed in the bowl. She tried not to think about Bree and Josh and what he possibly saw in her. Marnie felt like she didn't know him anymore.

Worse, she was starting to wonder if she ever really had.

She tried to muster up some empathy for Bree. They had something poignant in common, after all—the loss of a father. Yet the compassion she sought was stubborn in coming. It got overridden by earlier speculations, and she would run her newest by Willow.

"Do you think Dutch promoted Bree through the city ranks because he felt guilty? Maybe she even threatened him with a wrongful death lawsuit if she thinks Dutch let her dad drive drunk."

Willow shook her head. "That's a pretty long stretch."

Her phone pinged, and she excused herself. Marnie sipped at her soup, part of her cursing the call for interrupting, another part of her trying to listen in to learn what was happening. But Willow stepped into her office and closed the door.

When she returned to the table after a brief absence, she said, "I'm sorry to desert you. But a client family has requested me."

"Wow." Marnie couldn't hide her surprise. "It never occurred to me life coaches might work on call."

"Sometimes we do," Willow said. She paused, then softly added, "Sometimes the dying—or even more so, their families—just want someone to talk to. Besides other relatives or clergy." She dipped her head. "I hope you'll forgive me for leaving you with a mess."

Grabbing her purse and keys, Willow added, "Don't wait up. It may be a late one."

Marnie nodded and started cleanup. What a day. Definitely *not* the calm after the storm.

As she finished rinsing the dishes, she caught a whiff of cinnamon whisky. Just a trace. Nothing more. And then it was gone.

Probably good. She was not in the mood for puzzles tonight.

Suddenly aware of a coolness in the air, she walked from the kitchen into the front room to see if the front door was open. It was shut tight. On her way back to the kitchen, she picked up the leather-like scent of sandalwood wafting from Willow's office. She stopped to make sure Willow hadn't left a candle burning. She hadn't, but the picture of Roxy and CeCe outside Willow's office hung askew. She moved to straighten it, but a force pushed her hand away.

She startled. "Hey!"

Again, she tried to even the frame, but again, the force stopped her.

"That's you, isn't it, Roxy?" she asked boldly.

A trace of Fireball edged out the woody scent coming from Willow's office.

"Thank you for saving me," Marnie said, her voice warm and low. "The other night."

A flicker of fire appeared near the picture. Marnie barely breathed, hoping Roxy finally intended to connect. When Roxy didn't respond, Marnie clenched her jaw. She had no time for games, dammit. Too many questions needed answers.

"What do you want from me, Roxy?" She kept her tone even.

The light flickered, casting an amber halo around CeCe's head in the picture on the wall.

"What can I do to make you trust me?"

The flame brightened.

"Can you help me know what you need?"

The flame shone steady. At the same time, a pinging noise broke the air, causing Marnie to jump. Her heart pounded as she pulled her phone from her pocket. It contained a text from Lee: *Sorry things have been tense with us. Let's talk tomorrow. L*

Dammit, Lee. He had scared the crud out of her. Not to mention, his timing sucked. Yet again. The commotion sent Roxy's spirit back into hiding.

"Roxy?" Marnie tried to bring her back.

But the moment had passed.

Later that evening, Marnie rocked on the porch in the cool darkness, Onyx snuggled on her lap. Along came voices and a group walked toward The Diana. The hair on her arms prickled.

A woman's voice broke the night air. "On your left is The Diana Homestead."

Holy hell. Marnie could only guess she was a witness to the Lake Gardner Walking Ghost Tour, the guided outing for a limited number of participants.

"The Diana was built in the early 1920s, ordered from a Sears Roebuck catalog. It served as a personal residence to a family who farmed acres of land behind it. When the land got parceled off, the place became a boarding house. Today it's owned by the mayor and his wife, who operate it as a communal farmhouse managed by a woman some believe may be a witch."

Marnie scowled, somewhat relieved when the group didn't take the guide's bait. She continued to rock Onyx, who purred loudly, oblivious to all but Marnie's attention.

"A resident witch is nothing, though," the guide continued. "Not when you consider the home's history back in the early 2000s, when a woman named Roxy Tripp purchased The Diana and moved in with her invalid daughter, CeCe."

Marnie cringed at the word *invalid*. Down syndrome meant CeCe had likely experienced developmental delays. Why the harsh label?

The guide kept going. "Roxy and CeCe shared a quiet life here until August 31, 2012. On that night, they were brutally murdered in a crime that's never been solved. It wasn't until three days later that deputies discovered the bodies of Roxy and her daughter, dead."

A high-pitched yip sounded in the distance. Probably a coyote. One of the tour participants wheezed out, "Shit!" Quiet followed. Then soft, embarrassed laughter, followed by, "Sorry."

"The community was stunned," the guide continued. "Authorities evaded questions. Townspeople spread hearsay as a way of filling in the blanks. Some said the Tripps had been beaten to death with a claw-tooth hammer, their throats slit ear to ear, positioned in a way that brought to mind a ritualistic sacrifice."

Marnie scowled. She'd read nothing of the sort in her research.

Wind chimes near The Diana's front door twinkled. The hair on Marnie's neck prickled because there was no wind.

"A Blue Moon shone that night," the guide said. "A coven of witches held a cleansing festival out by Dalton Creek Bridge in a special lunar celebration. Many townsfolk speculated the coven committed the murders."

The wind chimes ceased abruptly. Onyx stopped purring.

The guide continued, "The event has since become known as The Blue Moon Killings. From 2012 until the current day, visitors and residents of The Diana have reported seeing a distressed woman searching the house. Dressed in a pink bathrobe and blue slippers, she wanders up and down the stairs, into the bedrooms, the living room, and the parlor. One theory is that it's Roxy revisiting that night in an effort to save CeCe from the hands of the evil witches."

Onyx jumped from Marnie's lap and hissed. Marnie's breath came out in clumps. She tried to focus her attention on Onyx, now grooming herself near the front door.

The guide had the dramatic pause down to a science. Finally, she spoke again.

"But there's another theory. It's gaining ground, especially this year, as Halloween falls on a night with a Blue Moon."

Again, a lone coyote howl broke the silence. "Jesus!" The reaction came from a man this time, followed by murmurs from the others in the group.

The guide carried on, paying them little heed. "Some believe what happened that night is much more heinous than a coven of crones committing a ritualistic murder." Another over-the-top pause. "Some say the ghost is CeCe, trying to hunt Roxy down, burdened with a burning question: '"Why did you kill me, Mother?"'"

Murmurs stirred through the tour group.

A loud crashing noise came from inside The Diana. Onyx yowled. A few of the women in the tour group let out sharp gasps.

"You see"—the guide sounded rather pleased about the mysterious but dramatic distractions—"The Diana doesn't give up her ghosts. They're still here."

JAN HEIDRICH-RICE

Marnie could hear her own heart pulse, feel it in her throat. The guide didn't lose a beat. "Shall we move on?"

Chapter 20

Halloween Day started with a phone call from Lee. Marnie reached for the phone with cold hands and dread at starting the day with an argument.

"Happy Halloween." She forced herself to sound cheery. "How's Denver?"

"Nice," he replied warmly. "You'd be enjoying it."

Okay, if he didn't bring up their fight from two days ago, she wouldn't either. "I'm glad it's been a good trip." She opened the blinds onto the back gardens, which were patched with sunshine peeking through partly cloudy skies. "When are you flying back?"

"Sunday." His tone cooled when he added, "Anyway, I just wanted to check in."

"I appreciate it."

Searching for what else to say, she contemplated the garden squares. Near the lettuce and greens patch, Willow and Kate stood face-to-face, talking fast, gesticulating furiously. Willow shook her head as Kate squeezed something into her hands. They hugged fiercely. Then Kate departed, and Willow returned to the house.

"Marnie?"

Lee's voice, tinged with impatience, made her aware of the awkward silence between them. She really had nothing more to say. Not to mention she wanted to catch Willow and learn what her exchange with Kate had been all about.

"I've got another call," she lied. "Sorry. Can we talk again tomorrow?"

"Deal." He sounded just as relieved to get off the phone as she felt.

Wow. If that stilted conversation wasn't the sign of a marriage on the rocks, what was?

Enough, Marnie. She hurried downstairs to find Willow in the kitchen.

"Everything okay?" she asked.

Willow lifted her chin. "Yes. Why?"

"Kate was out back with you. The two of you looked...intense. She seemed unsettled."

Willow wagged her head back and forth. "She'll be okay." But the older woman didn't sound exactly sure. She switched the coffeemaker on. "She came by for a special meditation."

"Oh?" The two women hadn't appeared in a meditative state.

"Tonight's a Blue Moon, which makes today a good one for focusing on love, protection, and wisdom. That's what brought Kate here."

Marnie opened and closed her mouth. *Protection?*

Willow moved on to another subject. "Are you heading downtown today?"

"I'm not sure." She hadn't planned to. "I could use the time to write."

"I think seeing Lake Gardner's Halloween in action might enhance your project." Willow reached for a coffee mug. "Even if that's not the case, you might find it fun."

Marnie got herself a coffee mug and gave a noncommittal blink.

"Check out my office for a few old costumes I have on hand," Willow said. "Lake Gardner does Halloween big. You'll want to be dressed for the occasion."

Marnie worked until mid-afternoon, pleased with what she'd written so far. She included the ghost stories the Remingtons requested, but now she was tired. Laying her head on her writer's desk, she tried to conjure the muse. But the muse was tired, too. Fair enough. Apparently, they'd both earned a breather.

She popped into Willow's office to peruse her costumes. The older woman had collected a bountiful stash over the years, but Marnie spotted the perfect one almost immediately. A short time later, dressed in a little black dress and a witch's hat with purple boa feathers, she headed for town.

Willow hadn't been kidding. Lake Gardner did Halloween big. Yard décor blew way past pumpkins and skeletons, with added embellishments like giant fake spiders and pop-ups—some creepy, à la The Walking Dead, others more cheerful, like Disney princesses or Candyland.

The historic downtown area crackled with life. People browsed the shops and cast votes for their favorite entry in the Scarecrow Challenge. Political satire abounded. A scarecrow with a Joe Biden mask carried a sign: "If I only had a brain." A costumed space alien towed an inflatable contraption which turned out to be Donald Trump giving a thumbs-up.

In front of Missy's Sandwich Shop, a family enjoyed ice cream. They wore an Alice-in-Wonderland themed group costume with Dad as the Mad Hatter, Mom the March Hare, and the kids as Alice, the Queen of Hearts, and the Cheshire Cat. The dad had the perfect swagger to pull off the role of the Hatter, and the kids looked adorable.

Marnie pasted on her best I'm-having-fun expression and kept moving. A dull sadness washed over her. Not from the political skews or the over-the-top themes of the day but rather from spirits. And not the kind that visited from the beyond. Sometimes ghosts snuck up like a case of the blues, the kind she experienced in spring, when Mother's Day approached and Patsy's absence stung at her heart. The wraiths of Halloween resembled those of spring. Seeing families with children celebrating the fall brought her pleasure. But it was bittersweet.

She turned onto Spring Street. Seeing the Mayor's office made her wonder if Bree had gotten home safely the day before.

"Hey!" Vanita interrupted that thought, calling to her from near a display for *Free Books* in front of the library. Vanita was dressed in a patterned shawl of deep oranges and black, and when she spread her arms, her shawl morphed into an expansive spread of Monarch-like wings.

"Want to walk to the church for an early dinner?" she asked when Marnie reached her.

Marnie couldn't help grin. "Sure, butterfly."

A carnival operated in full swing when they reached the church. Children squealed. Moms and dads struggled to corral them in. The air smelled of fresh-cut grass and funnel cakes. They got in line for food, chicken barbeque for Marnie, a black bean burger for Vanita.

They ate at a picnic table where they could eyeball vehicles decorated for the Trunk-or-Treat celebration. One truck opened as Frankenstein's mouth, gaping and full of candy. White tulle and big fake lollipops garnished another. Its sign read: "'Tis so sweet to trust in Jesus."

"Too bad there's no beer or wine tent," Vanita murmured under her breath.

Marnie snickered just as Pastor Stan stopped by.

"How goes it, ladies?" He wore his amiable grin the way others had donned masks today.

"Impressive festival you've got here," Marnie said.

"Indeed." He nodded. "God bless the parishioners for all they do."

He strolled away and continued to work the crowd.

Marnie and Vanita finished eating and followed a gaggle of trick-or-treating families back to Main Street. There they found Willow, making the rounds dressed as Glinda the Good Witch from the Wizard of Oz. Wide-eyed children gathered around her to get little bottles of bubbles she distributed.

"She's so good with kids," Vanita said, pretty much to herself.

But Marnie picked up on the irony. Some of the parents tried to edge their kids away from Willow, the witch. But from where Marnie stood, none of the youngest children feared Willow at all.

Willow greeted Marnie and Vanita with glee. "My two butterflies."

Marnie got another good kick from that.

The three looped arms and continued toward Amani Way, as if following a yellow brick road that led to The Diana. As darkness fell, the full moon glowed through the pines.

"Look down there." Willow pointed toward the lake, where a small group gathered.

"They're stealing our MO," Vanita joked to Willow.

Marnie scrutinized the spot more closely to find a group congregated around a picnic table covered with candles. Her curiosity piqued. "Are they doing a Blue Moon ceremony?"

"Only the Divine knows." Willow made her way up the porch steps.

Vanita followed, but Marnie held back, curious about the event by the lake.

"I'll be in in a second," she said, bending to pet Onyx, now at her feet.

Vanita turned back toward Marnie, her furrowed forehead highlighted by the porch light.

"It's okay," Marnie told her. "I'll be right in."

Vanita nodded and let the screen door creak shut behind her.

With Onyx on her heels, Marnie slipped down nearer to the lake. Even under the glow of the moon, she couldn't make out everything going on. Lucky for her, a woman dressed in a billowy black gown explained each step of her demonstration as she went.

"Crystal represents the earth, and the seashell is for water. The feather represents air, and lava rock signifies fire." She hung back momentarily and lit a candle. "The blue candle I've just lit represents tonight's lunar event." She raised her arms again. "Ground and center yourself, drawing down on this rarest of moons."

An owl hooted, but the group gathered around the table remained enrapt.

The woman in black continued. "The white candle—and the white rose to its side—signifies the goddess, Selene. Focus on that and then tip your face up to the light in the skies and silently make your request for wisdom and protection."

The individuals at the table angled their faces upward. Their leader held a hand in the air.

"Bless us, Selene," she said, "with intuition and wisdom. Work your blessings and magic in every aspect of our lives." The group remained quiet until the next prompt. "Now close your eyes and make specific requests for wisdom and protection. In your heart. Or out loud."

Marnie couldn't tell what made her more uncomfortable, the otherness of the ceremony or how much it actually resembled Christian services she had attended through the years.

Walking away, she remembered back to when, as a child, a lay leader at a friend's church told her she'd never reach heaven if she didn't ask to be saved. The leader had spoken her own truth, Marnie never doubted it. But it wasn't the same truth Marnie had been taught, which was we don't get into heaven by asking, but rather by God's grace and grace alone.

Both Christian denominations. Both with different beliefs.

So which one was right?

She let herself stew some more as she made her way back to The Diana. Inside, the light scent of sandalwood tickled her nostrils. She'd become accustomed to its presence. It comforted her now as she decompressed from uncomfortable questions she carried with her from the lake.

And then a blood-curdling scream ripped from out back.

Chapter 21

Black noise filled Marnie's head. She stumbled toward the back door and into the yard where the scream had broken the night.

The backyard glimmered with moon-cast shadows. Near the empty fire pit, Willow was hunched, the back of her Glinda costume puffed around her. Marnie stumbled closer.

"Help me." Willow's voice sounded thin.

Marnie's stomach dropped as Willow turned toward her, blood spattered across the front of her costume. She stared at her with blank eyes. She mumbled something, but all Marnie could pick up was "gunshot."

Marnie scanned the area. Her jaw went slack at the sight of a handgun tucked among some strewn dead leaves. She clutched for her purse and her phone—but shit!—she'd left them back in the house.

She jerked toward Vanita, behind her. "Call 9-1-1! Someone's been shot!"

Vanita froze. "Willow?"

"Dammit, Vanita! Just call."

Marnie faltered toward Willow, to put pressure on her wound and keep her warm until the ambulance arrived. But when Marnie reached her, her legs buckled. Willow hadn't been shot. She was tending another woman who had been.

Marnie fell to her knees, trying to make sense of the horror. The injured woman lay dead still, her head to the side, her face blood-caked around the brow line. One of her eyes caved into her cheekbone. Her jaw line was crumpled.

Clutching her gut, Marnie bowed her head and retched. She breathed in deeply to regain composure. Her temples throbbed and her throat was raw.

When a siren droned from afar, Onyx yowled, a deep-throated, echoing wail.

Marnie lifted her head and wiped her mouth with her hand. She had to get it together. Vanita was nearby now, pulling Willow into her arms, whispering comforts when her lips weren't drawn tight in a scarecrow's grimace.

Marnie's mind raced. She hugged her shoulders and rocked in place, trying to process what she thought she had seen, then trying to unsee it. She'd lost all sense of time. How long ago had Vanita called for help? It felt like only a minute. But it could have been twenty.

The growing scream of a siren stabbed Marnie's eardrums like an ice pick. It let out one final belch and then went silent. In The Diana's lot, paramedics slammed down a stretcher and raced toward the fire pit. At the same time, Dutch sprinted up the side yard, gasping for breath. His eyes were so wide the white around his irises popped in the glimmer of the moon.

"I heard the siren," he panted.

Marnie jutted out her hand like a stop sign, warning him, "Don't go any closer."

Ignoring her, he shoved his way toward the firepit and the body, now laid out on the stretcher. His shoulders slumped, likely horrified to be watching the paramedics continue their ministrations.

Marnie let out a long, slow breath. No way had she wanted Dutch to see this. No man deserved to see his wife in this state, damaged and bleeding and fighting for her life.

She inhaled again, sending a telepathic message to any deity who might be out there:

Be with Kate, please. Don't let her die.

A police officer got her some water. Outside the kitchen window, flashlights darted in and out of the moon's shadows as responders wrapped the scene with yellow tape, blocking the area off from onlookers.

Marnie's hand shook less than she expected when she placed her water back on the table.

"Okay." The officer sat across from her. "I want to hear the whole story. Everything you can remember, even if you don't think it's important."

She replayed the scene in her mind, starting with the scream and trying to sludge through what felt like mud to get out back. Willow's blood-spattered clothes and plea for help. Vanita calling 9-1-1. Onyx wailing along with the sirens, then pinning her ears back and running off. Dutch huffing up the side yard, ignoring her pleas to not come closer.

Marnie made herself re-see it all, from the gun in the strewn leaves, to Vanita offering comfort to Willow, to Kate's unforgettable face, half beautiful and intact, half completely ravaged.

The officer took notes as Marnie talked. "We can take a break if you need it."

"I'm okay." But her voice sounded shaky and odd in her own ears. She took another drink of water, just wanting to get all this over.

"Did you hear a gunshot?" he asked.

"No. I never heard a shot."

He leaned in closer, his eye contact steady. "I know it's hard. But is there anything else you can tell me?"

Marnie stared ahead, fighting off tears.

The officer touched her hand lightly and then handed her his card. "If you think of anything else..."

She let the tears well up when he exited the house to join the others out back. Onyx rubbed up against her leg. She reached down to scratch the cat's neck, still staring off into nothingness.

The front screen door squeaked, followed by footsteps and a heavy sigh. Vanita stood in the kitchen doorway, her eyes dull, her butterfly shawl crinkled.

"You doing okay, Marnie?"

She wiped tears from her cheeks. "Where were you?" A muscle beneath her right eye jumped under her skin. "Where's Willow?"

"I was talking to an officer out front." Vanita filled a kettle with water to boil for tea. "Willow's in her office."

Marnie suddenly felt too drained to speak.

"I don't know what to say." Vanita put Marnie's thoughts into words. "As much as Dutch gets under my skin, Kate was...well, my friend."

Marnie's heart caught. She mustered the strength to say, "You used the past tense. Does that mean—"

Vanita's lips grew tight. "Kate *is* my friend. That's what I should've said."

Marnie felt like she'd been punched in the gut. She had watched Dutch climb into the ambulance as it prepared to leave. Something about that had given her hope, dared her to think Kate might just survive. It seemed silly now. Still, she tried to cling to that hope, even when the scent of cinnamon whisky shocked her nostrils.

She prickled, so not in the mood for Roxy's shit tonight.

But when she turned her attention back toward Vanita, she realized she was smelling *actual* Fireball whisky. Vanita poured it into three mugs, then added an orange spice tea bag to each mug along with hot water.

As the tea steeped, Willow emerged from her office, her eyes glassy.

"Kate stroked out on the way to the hospital," she said softly. "She's gone."

The room hung silent, except for the sound of Marnie's blood coursing through her veins, flushing behind her ears.

"How do you know that?" she finally managed.

"I know a couple nurses in the ER." Willow spoke without inflection in her voice.

A touch of nausea stabbed Marnie's gut. Kate was dead.

"I don't understand." She no longer felt much of anything, including the urge to cry. "What happened?"

"I called to ask about Kate, and one of them told me."

Willow didn't blink. It was almost as though she was high.

"No," Marnie said. "What happened *here*? Before the ambulance came."

"I went out back." Willow shuddered. "Kate was there. She stood near the fire pit, wobbly. And mumbling. With half of her face caved in and bloodied."

"She was already shot?" Marnie asked. "Where was the gun?"

"I don't know. I think she dropped it. When she fell."

Willow absently rubbed the mug Vanita handed her.

Marnie tried to reconcile what she was hearing, seeing, remembering. Kate had shot herself. Marnie never heard a gunshot, which she would have if Kate had shot herself here on the property. For sure, she had heard Willow's scream.

"I tried to save her." Willow's gaze bore into Marnie, her expression childlike.

Was she high?

"I didn't think she was gone," she said, "so I just kept trying."

No, Willow wasn't high. She was in shock. Marnie understood. Her own shock, anger, and denial—they all mingled together like an abstract painting run amok.

"You said Kate was mumbling," she reminded Willow. "Could you understand her?"

"She might have said, 'didn't mean to.' I'm not sure."

Vanita wrinkled her forehead. "Maybe she was saying she didn't mean to shoot herself?"

"Maybe." Willow closed her eyes, and a lone tear streamed down her left cheek.

Marnie rubbed her forehead, struggling to piece things together. "I just can't grasp how Kate could have done this. Especially with a gun... Is it possible somebody else shot her?"

"I don't think the police are leaning that way," Vanita said.

"Let's hope they're not." Willow reached over for the Fireball bottle and poured a large glug of whisky into her mug.

A chill prickled Marnie's neck. "Are you saying you hope Kate shot herself?" she snapped.

"That's not what I meant, Marnie," Willow said. "I don't understand it or want to think it. But I also don't want the police thinking *I* shot her."

Marnie jerked. "Why would they think that?" She studied Willow closely, trying to make sense of what she'd said. "Didn't you tell them she was already shot when you found her?"

"I didn't talk to the police."

Marnie tightened her hands into fists and then loosened them. At the same time, Onyx let out a guttural mewl. Willow set her mug on the table and stooped to pat the cat's head.

"Why wouldn't you talk to the police?" Marnie's tone sounded much calmer than she felt. "That doesn't send a good sign."

"I'm not refusing to talk to them." Willow rose. "But I know my rights. And I'll only answer their questions with my attorney present."

Chapter 22

The Diana's ghosts slept soundly that night under the light of the Blue Moon. Marnie only wished she could say the same. She couldn't shake the image of Kate's beautiful face, now half caved in and disfigured. And Willow's refusal to talk to the police made her appear guilty.

But guilty of what?

Sunday morning, Marnie awakened groggy, with the trace of a headache. On her way downstairs for coffee, she lingered in the stairwell, aware of the familiar woody leather scent coming from Willow's office. Marnie approached the door, planning to knock until she heard Willow was chanting something. It was a prayer. The Lord's Prayer.

Marnie pursed her lips. How was Willow still able to cling to her faith? Marnie was pretty much over her own. The God she'd once believed in would never be so cruel to keep piling on all this loss. Her forehead tightened, listening to Willow's steady chant of trust and hope.

She wanted to scream, *God, if you're real, prove it.*

Her phone twinkled. She jerked at the sound of its chimes, their light cheer a stark contrast to the dark mood hovering in the air. But no, the chimes weren't a message from God. She'd apparently changed her ringtone without realizing it.

"Hey, Lee." She tried to make her voice sound light, walking through the kitchen to the Adirondack chairs out back.

How could the man's timing always be so un-freaking-believable?

"You didn't call last night," he said.

"I meant to." She had. "But there was so much commotion. The police didn't leave till way past midnight."

"What?" His voice turned cold. "What are you talking about, Marnie?"

Shit. Of course he hadn't heard what happened. He was in Denver. She winced, pretty sure he wasn't going to like what she had to tell him.

"A woman died here last night. At The Diana. From a gunshot wound."

"What the hell, Marnie?" His tone was rough. "Who?"

"Kate Remington. The mayor's wife."

"What the fuck?" His voice cracked. "A woman died on the property where you're staying. And you didn't bother to call me."

Marnie had to remind herself to breathe. "I should have called," she finally managed. And it sounded weak, even in her own ears.

His intake of breath was audible. "What's going on with you, Marnie? With us?"

She fought back a pain in her throat. "For starters, I'm okay." She couldn't keep her voice from sounding pinched. "But thanks for asking."

"Good." He sounded gruff. But then he spoke more gently. "That's good."

"And as for us, I'm on an assignment. It's taken me away from home. Just for a little while." She inhaled. "People—couples—do this kind of thing all the time."

Her heart pounded in her neck. Silly as it seemed, she repositioned the phone to ensure Lee didn't hear it. Silence hung in the air.

Finally, he laughed. But it sounded forced. "Honey, people take on work assignments, yes. But if they're part of a couple, they decide together if the assignment is good for both of them. And this one isn't."

"It's been good for *me*." She rubbed the back of the Adirondack chair. A sliver of old wood lodged in her finger. *Damn.* "I'm sorry if it's been rough on you. But it's not much longer. And I'm safe. It's not like there's some unsolved active shooter situation playing out."

"How do you know? Was the gunshot wound self-inflicted?"

"The police think so, yes."

"You don't sound so sure." His tone made her feel like this was a business call. "Who discovered the body? Was it that weird lady you live with? What's her name?"

"Willow." Marnie's stomach tightened. "And she's not weird."

"You don't know that, Marnie." Lee was all business now. "Listen, I get back into Atlanta tomorrow. I think you should plan to be at the house when I get home."

She couldn't hold back a small puff of irritation.

"You're giving me no choice, babe," he added.

Her jaw muscles ached. "No. *You're* giving *me* no choice."

His breathing was uneven over the line. "I'm not trying to be difficult. But don't you see? If something *did* happen to you, I'd never forgive myself."

"Nothing's going to happen to me." She fiddled with the sliver in her finger.

"Marnie, I can't make you come home. But..."

When he didn't finish the sentence, she asked, "But what?"

Lee waited to respond. Finally, he said, "I think we could use a go-between to help us solve some of our conflicts." He cleared his throat. "I've heard this guy at the Sunset Law Firm is pretty good at helping couples stay together."

Her breath caught. "A guy? Like a law firm mediator?"

"He's highly recommended." Lee sighed. "But if you'd prefer a woman, I can do some more checking."

"No," she said quickly. "I mean, no, you don't need to check for a woman."

"So I can set an appointment? For some time this upcoming week?"

Her heartbeat quickened.

"This week will be hectic," she said. "There'll be a service for Kate, I'm guessing." She hesitated. "Do you think we could wait 'til the following week?"

"I'll schedule it around the service, Marn." His tone was flat. "But I think the rest of your to-do list can take a back seat to our appointment."

Marnie stared at the phone after he disconnected, trying to sort through a mishmash of emotions. Lee had suggested the high road of a mature adult, wanting to work through their differences. She admired that. But he was asking her to move at breakneck speed, on his own timeline as always. Not to mention, the concept of mediation confused her. Was it just a fancy word for counseling? Or was it a step closer toward divorce?

Impulsively, she pounded out a text to him: *Call me when you get home, k?*

Back in the kitchen, she found some glue and administered it to her sliver. She covered it with a Band-Aid that she'd leave in place for several hours. It was a bizarrely effective old farm trick that would eventually ease the sliver out.

Beneath the robust coffee aroma, the faint woodsy scent of sandalwood lingered. Willow's office door was closed, and Marnie considered knocking to ask if they could talk about everything happening. But then she decided against it. Her emotions were just too raw right now.

Lee's words echoed in her mind. *You don't know.* They were truer than she liked to admit. She *didn't* know with certainty whether the gunshot was self-inflicted. Whether she was safe. Whether Willow...

She couldn't go there. Willow's friendship was one of the only things keeping her grounded.

She took her coffee out on the front porch. Onyx greeted her, and she sat down on the steps to pet her. Instinctively, she glanced up the street toward the Remingtons' house, still decked out with Trump signs and cloth Halloween ghosts hanging on rope from the trees.

Remembering Lake Gardner had an online neighborhood forum, Marnie sought it out on her phone. Sure enough, news about Kate's death was making the rounds. Sipping her coffee, she scanned some of the posts. Many were tributes, like Kate was "kind and always smiling" and "a premier interior designer as well as a partner in a real estate investment business."

Flimsy details from the police assured the community it was not in danger. A few cryptic posts referenced suicide covertly. "May she now find the peace that eluded her in life," one post read. And then there was this lurid headline: "Is Andromeda's Coven behind yet another death at The Diana Homestead?"

Marnie's jaw tightened. She shut off her phone and finished her coffee to the rhythm of Onyx's purr. It soothed her, as did the sunshine, which had grown warmer.

She rose, casting an eye up and down the street before going in. Up at the Remingtons', a woman in a pink kerchief walked down the front porch steps and beckoned her with a wave. Curious, Marnie rambled down Willow's porch steps and crossed the street to meet the woman halfway between houses. Marnie flinched once she realized the woman was Joni, aka Blondie, whom she'd met while delivering *Boo for Christ* treats to the church pre-Halloween.

What else could Marnie do? She'd look like an even bigger bitch than Joni if she retreated now.

"How's Dutch doing?" she asked.

"He and Garrett aren't home right now." Joni made a side glance back toward the Remingtons'. "It's so sad seeing Garrett's car in the drive. It's hard to imagine how horrible it must be, coming home to a house without Mom."

Marnie swallowed back a lump in her throat. "Is there anything I can do to help?"

Joni feathered her fingers through the light tresses escaping her kerchief. "Sylvia and I have it covered. Pastor Stan reached out to us to clean the downstairs and make sure Dutch and Garrett are comfortable."

"Oh?" Marnie imagined the two women reveling in such an important assignment. Then something else occurred to her. "Are the police thinking the shooting occurred inside the Remingtons' house?" Surely they'd investigated there as thoroughly as they had The Diana.

"Oh, it did." Joni frowned. "Kate shot herself in the bedroom."

Marnie tasted a bitter tang in her mouth.

"Pastor Stan contacted Zack Lightner," Joni continued. "To clean the upstairs." Her face flushed. "There was blood all over the place. On the bed. On the carpet. On the dress."

Marnie's scalp prickled. "The dress?"

"Kate's wedding dress."

Feeling dizzy, Marnie closed her eyes. But the image of the bloody wedding gown was too much. When she opened her eyes again, Joni was standing extra close, her own green eyes watering.

"Sylvia and I think Kate must have laid her dress out on the bed." Joni leaned in and spoke in a breathy voice. "Then she lay down beside it and shot herself in the head."

Chapter 23

Marnie's legs felt heavy, but she had to get away from Joni. Her mind raced, thoughts swirling through her brain so rapidly she couldn't follow them. Only one.

Why would Kate have done this horrible thing? *Why?*

Rubbing the back of her neck, Marnie wandered down to the lake. She sat at a picnic table between the children's playground and the water.

In some ways, the day seemed so bizarrely normal. The sun kissed the lake's surface, shining on gentle, hypnotic ripples. It was warm enough for people to fish and kayak but not to dunk one another in the water. From where she sat, she heard drifts of adult conversations and children's laughter. Near the shoreline, a turtle plopped off driftwood into the water.

But Marnie's mind wouldn't stop.

What in the hell was going on here?

For starters, the town was chock full of ghosts, several of whom she'd already met through bizarre encounters. Then someone she knew and cared about up and died in front of her. Meanwhile, she was at a seriously rocky point in her marriage, and—it just occurred to her—she probably was about to lose her job. The project, after all, had been Kate's pet, not Dutch's.

Not to mention something she hated to ask herself but had to. Was she safe?

A familiar country tune blasted from the nearby gazebo. Laughing, a young man rushed to adjust the volume and wave an apology Marnie's way. She nodded absently, her mind on other things.

Something about the church's involvement in helping the Remingtons deal with Kate's death seemed over-the-top. She could understand why Pastor Stan might send church ladies to ensure Dutch and Garrett were comfortable. But why had he sent Zack Lightner to clean the scene of the shooting? Surely there were companies to call for that.

But back to what Joni had told her, that Kate lay down on her bed and shot herself. How could Joni know such a thing just by looking? Yes! She'd looked. Joni had even hinted that Marnie might like to see the scene, too. Obviously, she'd passed, mortified by such a blatant invasion of privacy. She kicked herself now, though. Now that a zillion questions plagued her.

The newest possibility that chilled Marnie to the bone: what if Dutch was the shooter? Or, if he was the master of mind control Kate claimed he was, maybe he convinced Kate to shoot herself. Regardless of who did it, it made zero sense that Kate could have ambled down to The Diana with a gunshot wound in her head. And the wedding gown on the bed.

What was *that* all about?

Marnie laid her head on the table, breathing in the peaty smell of the lake, of hot dogs cooking on the grill nearby. The sun's comfort and warmth must have lulled her to sleep because when she sat up again, the playground was empty. Music still drifted from the gazebo, but instead of hot dogs, she now smelled the sweet char of roasted marshmallows.

Dusk neared, and Marnie continued to stare out across the water, still numb. Less than twenty-four hours ago, Kate Remington had died. Most likely from a self-inflicted shotgun wound.

She'd sent out hints that she was troubled, sure. But who wasn't these days? And why had Kate chosen to die at The Diana, of all places?

Marnie couldn't help herself. She needed answers—to find out not only how, but why. What were the circumstances behind the suicide of Kate Remington?

Onyx greeted Marnie back at The Diana, rubbing up against her leg. She took the hint and filled the cat's empty food and water bowls. The creamy sweetness of sandalwood no longer drifted from Willow's office. Neither was there a sign of her car out back or a note on the whiteboard.

When Marnie was younger, being alone in her family's old farmhouse sometimes frightened her. She wasn't scared now, though. At least that was what she told herself.

She foraged through the kitchen and settled on making an omelet, moving mechanically. After dinner, the evening sun seeped through the bedroom windows, showcasing the dust mites that hung in the air. She felt alone. Worse. She was lonely.

Drawing the shades, she climbed into bed, wondering where Willow had gone. The woman had shelled herself like a turtle and then left without a word. Much like the spirits, come to think of it. Ironic, but part of Marnie longed to breathe in the familiar cinnamon scents of Roxy and CeCe. For better or worse, their presence would at least have filled up this vacuum.

She didn't try to conjure them. Instead she called Lee.

Marnie had asked him to call her to let her know he'd arrived home from Denver safely. He hadn't called. Fine. She supposed it was his turn to be the passive-aggressive one. She punched in his number and pursed her lips as his phone went straight to voicemail.

She didn't leave a message.

Lying in the dark, she tossed on the bed for a bit. Then she found a short story podcast on her phone and set her timer to end it in fifteen minutes. She turned off the light, got comfortable in the quiet, and let the voice of the reader lull her to sleep.

Marnie awakened late Monday morning. She hadn't bothered to set an alarm. An eerie silence still hung in the air. No dishes clanked from the kitchen. No mewlings came from Onyx. That second thing disturbed her more than the first, and she whipped on some sweats to go downstairs to check on things. She was relieved to find Onyx sunning herself near the back kitchen window. The cat purred as Marnie refilled her bowls with food and water.

After coffee and breakfast, Marnie phoned Lee. Again, she got no response. *Dammit.*

She went upstairs to brush her teeth and grab her purse and laptop. As she descended the stairs, an envelope caught her attention, jutting from the front door mail slot. Instinctively, Marnie reached for it. It was addressed to her, her name handwritten in cursive on a Post-it note. *FYI*, the note said. It was signed, but the writing was hard to make out, looking a bit like *Little F*, which meant nothing to her.

Frowning, she sat at the foot of the stairs and opened the envelope.

She pulled out a photocopied newspaper article. The headline read:

Devoted Wife Gets Conditional Discharge for Helping Husband Die

[Pineville Gazette – Week of August 31, 2015]: *Wilma Madison of Pineville, Florida, was spared jail time after admitting to aiding and abetting the suicide of her husband, Charlie, who suffered from debilitating health issues.*

Marnie stared at the clipping, trying to make sense of it all. Next to the article was a photo of Wilma Madison, whom she recognized immediately as Willow Maddox. She read on.

Judge Lance Barnaby granted Madison a one-year conditional discharge, after being accused of aiding and abetting her husband's death by drowning in the family's master bathroom.

Marnie ignored the knot in her stomach—and the fact she wasn't exactly sure what a conditional discharge was. She continued reading.

According to trial notes, Ms. Madison admitted to police she knew her husband's plans to die and was in the home at the time it happened. Her attorneys argued Ms. Madison did not assist in her husband's death but merely allowed him his wish to die with dignity.

She touched her hand to her lips, trying to make sense of what she was reading. Her fingers were ice cold.

The court heard that Mr. Madison had suffered years of depression following the death of his daughter and granddaughter in a drunk-driving crash. In a note he wrote to his wife, he said, "Fifteen years is enough. This has already been a life sentence."

Marnie whimpered. It matched the heartbreaking story Willow had shared with her earlier. Curious, Marnie checked the envelope to see if it had a return address. It did not. It had not been mailed.

She finished the article:

Reaction to the verdict was mixed. Several people who knew the couple expressed their disagreement with the judge's decision but refused to comment further.

The advocacy group, Planning One's End (POE), welcomed the sentence but said the case should not have been dealt with under the criminal law. "Mrs. Madison should have been treated with compassion instead of being arrested and charged with murder."

But the head of the Florida Council for Behavioral Health said, "What kind of message is this sending out to the public? That it's easier to kill a depressed person than support them so they can live, knowing the value of their self-worth?

Marnie folded the article neatly and placed it back in the envelope. Who had sent it?

Beside her Onyx purred, but her own stomach roiled. People who'd never witnessed a loved one die a slow death had no right to judge. Still, she squeezed her eyes to shut out a new set of questions whirring in her head. About Willow. About Willow and Kate. About what happened at The Diana on Halloween night, especially in light of what she'd just read.

Had Willow pretended to help Kate while, in reality, she pretty much stood by and let her die? Or worse, helped even more directly.

Marnie rubbed her forehead. Tough questions didn't bring easy answers.

Resigned, she opened her eyes. At the same time, she picked up a cinnamon whisky scent, sudden and harsh, practically choking her. Roxy's flame flickered nearby.

"Are you freaking kidding me?" Marnie hissed. "You show up now? *Now?*"

Swallowing back bile, she rose and snatched up her laptop and purse.

"Leave me alone, Roxy," she commanded, reaching for the door.

The door wouldn't budge. As she strained to open it, the flame raged scarlet, emitting a smell like burned cinnamon.

An uncontrollable shudder swept through Marnie. "Please!" she cried.

She continued to struggle with the front door as the house closed in on her. No longer silent, it was now filled with the din of cabinets slamming open and closed. A high-pitched hum filled the air, like a blasting teapot. Her hands sweat, slipping as she tried to open the door.

Up to now, fear had fed her adrenaline. But the constant noise in her head exhausted her. She slumped near the door, queasy from the sickly sweet stench of burning spice.

Roxy was out of control.

Marnie clung to the door, trying in vain to open it. Near her, Onyx emitted a bristly drone-like purr. Marnie could feel it, even if she couldn't hear it. When the vibration stopped, Marnie held her breath. *I'm going to die.* Onyx, too. Never mind that Roxy's flame wasn't real.

Onyx's body pulsed now, more of a choking vibration than a drone or a purr. The energy emitting from the cat pushed Marnie to the floor.

Panting, Marnie searched around her, fearing the cat was hurt. Or worse.

But Onyx wasn't hurt. Rather, she was in battle form. Her hair stood on end, her back hunched. She screeched. Even when the cabinets stopped clanging, she yowled. She didn't stop until the door pushed open, Marnie still clinging to it, crying.

That was when Onyx stopped. The house stood dead quiet, except for the sound of Marnie's sobs. The cat rubbed up to her and began to purr again. Its nose nudged Marnie on, as though coaxing her out of the house.

Shaking, Marnie grabbed her laptop and purse and stumbled onto the porch. Then she left The Diana, uncertain if she'd ever return.

Chapter 24

Marnie squeezed the steering wheel to still her trembling fingers. Her breathing hitched as she merged onto the highway.

Onyx! How could she have left Onyx behind?

She rubbed her lips. Onyx would be okay. She had saved Marnie, after all. Just now, and maybe even the night of the storm. She was a familiar, for God's sake. Marnie could go back and get her after the wildness passed. Right now, she needed to get away.

Drive, Marn. Just drive.

To where? It didn't matter, just so long as it was far away from The Diana.

Her strategy seemed to work. Her breathing steadied. But when she approached the interstate, her adrenaline spiked. She had to choose. She could go north to her brother's place, to the Orchards and the past she'd been avoiding. Or south to Buckhead and the future she also feared confronting.

Choosing north, she merged into the sparse traffic and a sense of lightness returned. She placed a quick call to RJ to let him know to expect her. If he had questions, he didn't ask.

"The family and I may be out," he said, "but just make yourself at home."

If she had doubts—and to be honest, she did, about everything—she tamped them down.

On the interstate, she cranked up the radio, rolled the windows down, and let the wind whip her hair wild. The distraction helped. But only so much. She turned down the music, which was muddling her thoughts, not blocking them completely.

As she drove, an unsettling notion lifted the hair on her arms. Roxy and CeCe had died at The Diana, and now, so had Kate. So exactly *who* was haunting her back at the homestead?

She was inclined to think it was Roxy. Then again, Roxy's ghost still perplexed her. On the one hand, Marnie had believed Roxy's ghost saved her from death in the storm. Unless that had been Onyx? After all, Roxy had not completely warmed to having Marnie around.

So perhaps it was Kate's ghost who'd shuttered her in, not meaning harm but simply wanting to get her attention.

Possible? But mostly moot. Marnie had been too spooked to stay and figure things out.

Back on two-lane highway, she followed the hilly road for several miles. She veered right, and the Outback crunched on gravel as the crisp pine-scented air kissed her cheek. Finally, she caught sight of the old wagon wheel and the sign for Putnam Orchards. Seeing it caught her breath.

And it reminded her ghosts resided here, too.

Despite this, there was an old sense of longing. She parked and approached the farmhouse, quiet, yet inviting. A note on the unlocked door said, "Welcome home! See you soon." Seeing it brought to light just how lonesome she had been.

In the great room, the scent of apples and freshly baked bread stabbed her with sweet nostalgia. So did seeing the big black walnut table, weathered from years of enjoying many a Sunday supper. But much was new, too. RJ and Amanda shared a love of mid-century modern décor and abstract expressionist art, which now filled the main room. They had redone it in the years following Putt's illness, when RJ had closed his law practice to oversee their father's healthcare needs along with the orchards.

Wistful, Marnie drank in the black-and-white photo collage lining the stairway wall. A picture of RJ and their dad, whom everyone called Putt, brought a lump to her throat. In it her father's face hung gaunt, savaged by the end stages of liver failure. She remembered how shocked and angry she'd been at his rapid downturn.

All too soon, Putt had been placed under hospice care, and Marnie prayed his transition would be peaceful and without pain. But he lingered, and his pain was unfathomable. His last days cast a pallor on the past that haunted her still.

Suddenly exhausted, she slogged up the stairs to her old room, now the guest room. Soon enough, she'd have to face her present-day demons head-on. First, though, she needed to sleep.

When a little rap sounded on her door, she roused herself awake, reaching for her phone. It was after four p.m. Unbelievable. She'd slept for close to twenty hours.

"Yes?" she said, somehow still groggy.

That was all it took. Her three-year-old niece, Uma, came pattering into the room and popped onto the bed with her arms opened wide. Marnie scooped her in for a hug.

"Sorry, Marn." Amanda hovered at the doorway, hands on hips. "Uma Marie, you do *not* get to barge in and wake people up without permission. You know better."

Uma wriggled farther into Marnie's arms, making her chuckle. This made Uma giggle, too. "See, Mom," she said. "Her's not mad."

Amanda held up her hands in surrender. "Welcome to my life." She surveyed Marnie and the room, perhaps noting her rumpled clothes and lack of luggage. "Why don't you grab a shower? And help yourself to whatever you need." One eyebrow crept toward her hairline. "Like some of my extra clothes, which I keep in this room."

Marnie's cheeks reddened. She *was* a little bit ripe.

Amanda winked. Turning to her daughter, she said, "Uma, come help with dinner."

The little girl ran off with her mother, still chortling. And Marnie took a glorious shower, letting the steam clear her mind and the hot water wash away some of her stress.

"Only two rules," Amanda said. "First, make yourself comfortable, meaning help yourself to anything you'd like from the kitchen or elsewhere." She passed a plate of roast beef and vegetables. "And second, no political discussion allowed at the dinner table. Even if it is Election Day."

Marnie blinked. She'd voted early; certain nothing was quite as important as this year's election outcome. Yet somehow, hauntings and death had changed her perspective.

RJ rubbed his lips and said nothing. He and Amanda had held different political views from the start. Somehow they made it work, without belittling each other or getting ugly.

"Fair enough." Marnie agreed. While she had her suspicions, she still didn't know which of the two leaned red and which blue. Either way, she'd step on toes if she broke their rule. Her brows furrowed as she pictured Willow and Vanita devouring the election results. She definitely knew which way the two of them leaned. But where the hell were they?

After dinner and cleanup, she excused herself to the porch to grab a breath and scan her phone. In the national news, the election was too close to call. At the local level, accounts of Kate's shooting were sparce but firm in that foul play was not suspected. Services were scheduled for Thursday.

She checked her missed calls, one from Lee, who left a message, saying he'd made a face-to-face appointment for mediation that Saturday, the other two from Willow. Marnie pressed in the keys to return Willow's call.

"Marnie!" Willow answered on the first ring. "Where *are* you?"

She wanted to snap back, *Where the hell are you, Willow?* But she held off.

"I'm at my brother's," she said. "I needed a little space." She paused for a moment, then added, "I wasn't sure what to make of a lot of things." She took a deep breath. "Especially the Wilma Madison thing."

The silence grew thick.

Finally, Willow broke it. "I saw the article on the floor by the entrance." She quickly added, "It's not what you're thinking, though."

Marnie bolted upright. "You have no idea what I'm thinking!"

Willow sighed. "I understand. I also understand why Ian probably felt compelled to drop the article off for you to see. Like he said, *FYI*."

"Ian?"

"Ian Finster," Willow elaborated. "The reporter who interrupted the Remingtons' party a few nights ago."

Goose bumps tickled Marnie's neck. "Ian Finster is Little F." It came out as more of a statement than a question because it suddenly made sense.

Willow exhaled audibly. "I'm sure he's digging through old news archives, trying to piece things together given recent events at The Diana. Still, I'm sorry you had to learn about my past that way. I'm sure it unsettled you. Especially after Kate's death."

Marnie jumped up from the swing. She began to pace. "What's unsettling is why you deserted me without a word the day after Kate was shot. And why you refused to answer police questions."

"I would think that last part would be obvious." She sounded genuinely surprised that Marnie might not get that. "The truth is, I panicked. And—it may have been wrong of me—but I felt in my bones you'd be okay at The Diana alone. Given your powers."

My powers?

Marnie pursed her lips, waiting for more. Then she softened a little. Isn't that the same rationale she'd used for leaving Onyx behind when she fled?

"I'm sorry," Willow said. "I had to get away so I stayed at Vanita's. It was thoughtless of me not to let you know."

Of course Willow had panicked about talking to authorities and sticking around, given her history. Marnie might have done the same. She stopped pacing.

"Kate's service is Thursday at one," Willow said. "At the Community Church. And I've moved back to The Diana. We can talk more here after the service."

"No!"

Silence followed.

Willow finally spoke, her tone halted. "Are you not coming back for the service?"

Marnie took a calming breath. "Of course I am. I'm just not sure I'm ready to come back to The Diana yet."

"You're welcome here, Marnie. You know that, right?"

"Yes."

The door to the porch squeaked open, and RJ appeared with a tray of decaf. Marnie had mixed feelings about his interruption. On the one hand, it gave her an excuse not to talk with Willow about what had happened at The Diana yesterday. She was still trying to figure that out herself. On the other hand, she hated to leave Willow blind-sided if the older woman was, in fact, in danger. Intuition told Marnie that wasn't the case. Not to mention, Willow had failed to pay her the same courtesy.

RJ's forehead creased, but Marnie waved him onto the porch, indicating none of this was a big deal.

"Listen, Willow." She turned her back to RJ. "Stay on your toes and go back to Vanita's if things get squirrelly, okay?"

"Okay." It lingered in the air, like a question.

"I'll fill you in more on Thursday," Marnie said. "See you then."

During naptime on Wednesday—Uma still napped, thankfully—Marnie hiked the orchard with her nine-year-old nephew, Quinten. She had worried her visit would make her sad for the babies she lost, but instead it made her grateful for the family she still had. Quinten was serious and not as present as Uma—was anyone? But, like Marnie, he loved the orchards. And unlike Marnie, he was an ace at chess, which he won three times after they returned from their hike.

Before dinner, Amanda knocked on the door to the guest room, carrying a black dress and pumps. "For tomorrow." She opened her lips like she wanted to say more, but she didn't.

"Thank you," Marnie called after her.

After dinner and the kids' bedtime, Marnie opened up to RJ and Amanda about her life these days. She shared a sanitized version, but she was honest. Things were not good with Lee, and her time in Lake Gardner might soon be ending.

"You know you're welcome to stay here," Amanda said.

"I know." Marnie waved off RJ's offer of more sweet tea.

"So you think your writing project will get nixed?" RJ asked.

"Probably." Marnie rubbed the rim of her glass. "It's ironic, you know? Just when I've come to peace writing about the town's ghosts, I'm pretty sure I'll be canned."

RJ's eyes clouded. Marnie didn't mention the stories that touched her most also scared the bejesus out of her, the ones involving The Diana Homestead.

Amanda rose and began to clear the table. Marnie started to help, but Amanda stopped her. "Visit with your brother," she said. "God knows, he's been giddy to have you back home."

RJ held up his hands in a gesture that said his wife spoke the truth.

"It's been good for me, too," Marnie said.

Once Amanda left the room, she added, "I've stayed away far too long." Her voice cracked. "I should've gotten married here. I should've visited more when your kids were young."

"My kids are still young." RJ grinned, impish. "We all are, no?"

Grateful for his grace and humor, Marnie still carried a shameful sadness. "It's just hard to come back, you know?" Her throat ached. "Knowing it's my fault. Mom's death."

RJ's mouth fell open. "You think that?"

"I *know* it." She didn't cry. In her mind's eye she saw the butterflies, flitting between the milkweed and sunflowers. She smiled a little, remembering the gleam of her mom's skin as they gathered chicory, the sweetness of their harmony, rising above the chorus of crickets.

"Oh, sister, come on down...."

But when she remembered the mournful wails, a sob caught in her throat.

"I didn't latch the lambs' gate right," she cried. The memory of the river water rushed through her head. "It's my fault that Ollie escaped, and Mom—"

"Marnie, stop." RJ cut her off sharply, at the same time reaching out and clasping her wrists. "The latch was broken. Dad and I discovered it afterward." His eyes shimmered and he squeezed her hand. "I thought you knew."

Oh, my God. What was he saying?

"It was a tragic accident." RJ shook his head. "All these years..." He no longer held her hand, but he studied her closely, his eyes pooled in sadness. "If that's why you've stayed away, I'm so sorry."

Her muffled whimpers faded, but a small tear worked its way down one cheek.

"There's something else." She gulped. "As long as I'm coming clean."

He sat back, folding his arms.

"Remember when Dad was sick?" Her voice was strong, but it had an odd tremor. "And we couldn't agree on whether to support his wish to withhold food and water?" She drew in a breath, preparing to confess another shame she'd shouldered for far too long.

"Marnie," he said. "I know what you did."

For just an instant, she forgot to breathe.

"You worked with the doctors to respect Dad's wishes." He cleared his throat. "Thank you for doing what I didn't have the balls to do."

She let his words sink in. It was beyond good to hear them.

"But let me ask you..." RJ broke the quiet. "Do you ever get visits from Mom anymore?"

Her heart tugged at his reference, not to *Mom's ghost*, just Mom.

"Not like I used to." She didn't mention recent visits from the orb, smelling of sweet pears, floating around with those little sparkles of pink and blue. "I miss her." Then she clarified. "Her advice."

"Well, I think I know what she would tell you right about now."

Marnie glanced at him sideways. "You do?"

He tapped his index finger onto the table. "First, she'd remind you to keep yourself safe, whatever it takes." He paused for effect, then repeated the tap, only now he did it with two fingers. "She'd also say if you're not comfortable going home, go to a hotel. Charge a room to Lee's card. He can afford it." He glanced away. "After all you've given him through the years, you shouldn't feel bad if you need a little time and space to get your shit back together."

Marnie's lips twitched. "Mom wouldn't say it like that."

"I think she might." RJ reached into his pocket and slapped down an index card he'd been carrying. "And as long as I'm morphing between me and Mom, here's one more thing."

Marnie reached for the card. She recognized RJ's scrawled words. *FAMILY LAW ATTORNEY – ATLANTA.*

Her eyes widened. "What are you saying?"

"I'm saying, Lee doesn't treat you right."

"What—"

He cut her off. "You didn't ask my opinion when you married him. I didn't offer it then, but I'd like to weigh in now." He ran his hand over his cheek and then rubbed his chin.

"For God's sake, RJ." Her laugh felt awkward. "Just say it. Whatever it is."

He pointed toward the card. "I'm saying, if you decide you're ready to explore separation or divorce, this attorney's a pit bull." He rose from the table, bent and kissed the top of her head. "You don't have to get ugly, but you can't play all nicey-nice, Marn. It doesn't work that way."

He started to leave the room but stopped, scrutinizing her once again, more serious than she'd seen him in years.

"If and when you go up against balls of steel—and let's be honest, Lee's got 'em—you've gotta come back just as fierce. Love you," he added, bobbing his head goodnight and leaving her alone in the quiet.

She sat there for quite some time. If asked, she couldn't articulate what was going through her mind. But it no longer raced. A sense of peace and clarity filled her in a way she hadn't experienced in a long time.

Three days ago, she had headed north, not sure what awaited. She had found redemption here, and it felt almost better than Onyx's fur in the sunlight. Yet tomorrow she'd head south, because, as much as she loved the Orchard, it didn't represent home for her anymore.

Home. She had always considered it the place that was safe enough to live with an open and honest heart. The definition still struck her as apt.

There was just one problem. She wasn't quite sure where that place was for her anymore.

Reader Note

Thank you for reading *Secrets of the Blue Moon*. Please consider leaving a review on Amazon or Goodreads and/or tell a friend about it. Sharing a line or two about something you enjoyed in a particular book feeds a writer's soul. (And it helps with the algorithms, too.)

Please sign up for my newsletter to learn more about what's coming next:

www.janheidrichrice.com/contact

(Pssst, speaking of what's coming next: *ONE WRONG TURN AT A TIME* is coming your way in 2025. In this humorous creative nonfiction book, I share some of my favorite personal adventures experienced over the course of fifty states, forty-five years, and one marriage. It's definitely not a how-to book! But it's filled with fun and love and—I hope!—a good hearty laugh or two along the way.)

Chapter 25

The dining room smelled of breakfast sausage and fresh-from-the-oven biscuits. Amanda insisted on feeding Marnie before she left the orchard. Uma hopped onto her lap as soon as she'd scooped up one last bite of eggs and wiped a smudge of apple butter from the corner of her mouth.

"I miss you," the little girl said.

Quentin was less sentimental. "You better brush up on your chess." He reminded her of RJ so much. "So I don't whip your butt even worse on your next visit."

Amanda pantomimed cuffing her son playfully on the side of his head. "Don't be a stranger," she told Marnie.

RJ walked her out to her vehicle. "You've got this." He winked and gave her a hug.

She hit the road, hoping to hell he was right.

※

Marnie arrived at the church fifteen minutes early. She had planned to slip in, sign the guest book, and choose an inconspicuous spot to sit in back of the church. Upon her arrival, she quickly determined she needed a Plan B. The parking lot was jam-packed, and people congregated on the church steps outside the entrance, waiting to get inside.

She donned her protective mask and exited the Outback. Her shoes clacked against the pavement as she crossed the lot and joined the throngs. Her breathing quickened at the feel of being closed in, at the smells permeating her mask—fresh-cut grass, cologne, the stench of tobacco wafting off someone's clothes.

Marnie recognized faces but didn't know anyone well enough to engage in chitchat. Fine by her. She only wished she could close out the natter she overheard. Or fine-tune it to ensure she was hearing correctly.

A woman's whisper whipped the air behind her. "Willow was involved, I'm guessing."

Another low voice nearby piggybacked on that comment, but Marnie only heard the last part: "...mind control."

Marnie closed out the rumors and inched her way along to the narthex, where she stopped to sign the guest book. Inside the nave, she squeezed into a spot in a polished wooden pew near the back. She studied the pulpit, or, more specifically, the table in front of it draped in white cloth. It was adorned with an urn, a picture of Kate, and a bouquet of bright-colored flowers. Marnie shifted her gaze to catch a glimpse of where Dutch and his son, Garrett, sat. Her heart was heavy. For them and certainly for Kate. But also for herself. She felt Kate's loss more deeply than she fully understood.

Pastor Stan took to the pulpit and asked the congregation to rise and join in singing "Abide With Me." Marnie's voice caught on the words as she sang along, recalling the same music at her father's funeral.

Kate's service progressed much like her parents' had, with plenty of scripture readings and mumbled prayers. Marnie's grief was different today—less intense perhaps, but still deep, Kate being so young and all. The Remingtons' church was less formal than what she was used to. But aside from small differences, like Pastor Stan dressed in a suit instead of the traditional vestments and stole the pastors of her youth wore, Kate's memorial carried few surprises. Babies cried. There was coughing and shuffling feet. Occasionally a pew creaked.

Before the closing hymn, Pastor Stan spoke directly to Dutch and Garrett. "Your sweet wife and mom is no longer in pain. She has been made complete and finally free."

After a beat of silence, he continued. "Does God approve of suicide?" Marnie squirmed at the pastor's directness. "No, he does not. But his grace is sufficient even for those who have taken their lives. Our God is that good."

He studied Marnie intently, or so it seemed. She had to turn away.

"Please rise," he said, "and let us celebrate Kate's joyful meeting with Jesus by singing "Amazing Grace."

Marnie snuck out before the hymn ended. In the restroom, she rinsed cool water on her face. It eased the prickling in her eyes and nose, but a tightness gripped her chest and refused to loosen. The service had left her feeling profoundly lonely.

Once composed, she exited the restroom and was immediately overwhelmed by the after-din of the service. Her mind swarmed with the hum of conversations, the sounds of dishes rattling from the kitchen, the clink of ice hitting glasses. She edged toward the smell of fresh-brewed coffee but decided to pass as her stomach was already sour. From the kitchen, women delivered casseroles, macaroni salads, cheese trays, and desserts to tables already assembled in the congregational meeting room. The sight and smell of these foods didn't help her acrid stomach either. As she debated her next steps, someone said her name.

Turning toward the voice, she came face-to-face with Zack Lightner.

"Zack." She froze, started to offer her hand, then settled for a head bob instead. "I'm sorry about Kate." Her ears grew hot. She hadn't seen him since Bree's arrest. "About Bree's run-in, too."

Her face burned as she said this and felt even hotter when Josh joined them. If he'd heard her comment about Bree, he didn't let on.

Zack greeted Josh with a curt nod, then turned back to Marnie. "Bree's fine. She got caught in the wrong place at the wrong time." He smirked. "It happens."

Marnie flushed some more, suddenly aware that whatever had happened to Bree, it was one hundred percent not her business.

"She's pretty devastated about Kate," Zack said. "We all are. But Bree just didn't think she could handle being here today."

Marnie remembered the last encounter she'd observed between Bree and Kate all too well. Bree had behaved badly. No wonder she didn't feel good about making an appearance.

Zack frowned. "The Remingtons and the Lightners go way back. Dutch will understand her absence." He shot a cool glance at Josh. "We get each other. It's all good."

The room was closing in on her. Maybe Zack perceived that all was good between the Remingtons and the Lightners, but Marnie wasn't so sure.

Her cheeks went red as she tried to read the undercurrent between Zack and Josh, which felt stilted. Or maybe it was just all these people, crowding their way into the multi-purpose room from the service, making it hard to breathe. Desperate to escape this awkward encounter, she murmured, "Listen, I probably should go offer my help."

Frantically, she scanned the area around them. Remembering the door marked kitchen, she strode toward it. A woman's voice floated from around the corner, not even trying to be discreet. "I heard Kate might be sleeping with Zack Lightner. But I also heard that Kate and Dutch were playing the partner-swap game with Bree and her new boyfriend."

Oh, hell to the no.

Marnie spun on her heels, not giving a rat's behind to hear more. As she turned, she ran smack into Dutch.

"Oh!" A tiny gasp escaped her. She took a second to balance herself, struggling to find the right words. Finally, she reached for his hand, pandemic be damned. "I am so, so sorry for your loss."

"Thank you, Marnie." His eyes clouded when he spoke.

Tears prickled her eyes. She felt as though time had stopped. When she spoke again, she pulled her hand gently from his. "Please let me know if there's anything I can do for you."

Dutch gazed at her vacantly. He started to walk away but stopped himself. "Oh, Marnie?"

She glanced back his way, expectantly.

"You don't need to work on the ghost book anymore. That was Kate's deal."

Her mouth went dry. She'd half expected this, but not today. She should have let it stand, but something inside pushed her not to. "I'd like to finish it."

Dutch's eyes darkened under his furrowed brow.

"I won't expect the stipend, of course," she added quickly. "But I'd like to complete it as a way of honoring Kate's memory."

Out of the corner of her eye, Marnie caught Willow and Vanita approaching.

Dutch scowled. "I suppose I can't stop you from completing the damned book. But don't pretend you're doing it to honor Kate. If anything, it will diminish her memory. She'll become just another woman who died during a Blue Moon death spree at The Diana Homestead."

Marnie's mouth fell open.

A quick spark returned to Dutch's eyes, and then he narrowed them. "But that's what you want, isn't it? A juicy story. Perhaps even a *real* book deal and a big whopping payday."

Marnie had no words. That wasn't what this was about.

Willow interrupted. "May I offer my condolences, Dutch?"

She tugged him gently away from Marnie and toward a vacant corner to continue their conversation.

A pain gnawed at the back of Marnie's throat. Dutch had accused her of wanting to write Kate's story for money. Blinking slowly, she turned and sought the nearest exit. Once outside, she stopped to catch her breath near one of the church's winding pathways.

"Marnie!" Vanita panted up behind her, startling her.

Somewhat in a daze, Marnie asked, "I don't suppose Lake Gardner has a Hampton Inn?"

Vanita furrowed her brow. "There's Carly's Motor Lodge out near the Dalton Creek Bridge Expansion. But—"

Bustling up the pathway, Willow cut her off. "You don't need to leave The Diana." Apparently, she had overheard Marnie's conversation with Vanita. The one with Dutch, too, because she added, "It's not like you've been evicted."

"True," Marnie said. "But Dutch pretty much called me a mercenary, wanting to write Kate's story for profit. He might as well have kicked me in the gut."

Vanita snorted. "Dutch is talking out of his ass."

Willow stared at her sternly. "He's grieving," she said. Then she turned to Marnie. "But people grieve in different ways. And in Dutch's case..." She left her statement unfinished, which Marnie interpreted as *yes, he is indeed talking out of his ass.*

Marnie let out a silent, sardonic laugh, appreciative of the older women's levity. But she grew more somber, trying to think of how to articulate her torn feelings about returning to The Diana.

"It's not just Dutch," she said. "Honestly, when I left The Diana on Monday, I vowed I'd never return."

Vanita leaned in. "What happened?"

An iciness ran up Marnie's spine, remembering. "You know those horror movies where the house starts to moan and doors slam open and shut on their own? That's what happened."

Willow nodded. "Xander warned me the spirits might be restless."

Marnie's chill turned into a prickle. "Xander?"

"My attorney." Willow stared fixedly at Marnie. "He recommended I leave The Diana. Just until the bulk of negative energy cleared."

Marnie narrowed her eyes and let out a long breath. "What you're saying sounds more like some magical realism bullshit than legal advice to me."

"Well..." Willow shrugged off the black shawl she'd worn to the service. "Xander *is* an attorney. But he also happens to be a spiritualist."

Marnie let out a puff of exasperation. She glanced at Vanita, trying to read her expression, as she had the fleeting notion the two older women were messing with her. Even the name sounded hokey. Xander.

Vanita opened her mouth to speak, but then, shaking her head, she closed it.

Marnie stared at Willow. "So Xander recommended you leave The Diana until its negative energy cleared?" She threw her hands in the air. "Did it cross your mind you should have passed that information on to me, too?"

"I wasn't thinking clearly." Willow ran a hand through her silver bob, now disheveled. "I really thought because of your gift, you wouldn't be in danger."

Hearing that again, Marnie was lightheaded.

"It was wrong of me." Willow gestured back toward the church, where a few people had begun streaming out. "And I understand you have questions. But can we talk somewhere more private? Back at The Diana, outside on the porch?"

"Or there's my place," Vanita interjected, pointing in the direction of Spring Street. "It's pretty close. Between here and the library."

Marnie glanced back toward the church, where more mourners had started to leave.

"Let's go to Vanita's," she said. She didn't try to hide her irritation when she added, "But for the record, I can't take much more of this magical mystery tour shit."

Chapter 26

The three women walked down the church pathway toward Spring Street.

"So..." Marnie addressed Willow. "The day after Kate died, you went to Vanita's and just holed up there? Because Xander told you to?"

"Yes." Willow let out a long sigh but kept walking. "Xander and I go way back. He helped me process my daughter's and granddaughter's deaths all those years ago. I didn't know he was a practicing attorney, too, until... Well, until I got arrested for my husband's death."

Marnie shot a glance from the corner of her eye. "You mean for assisting in his suicide?"

They had reached a crook near the end of the path, and Willow stopped there.

"What are you trying to say, Marnie? Because I was acquitted, you know."

"An acquittal doesn't mean you didn't do it." Marnie studied Willow with care.

The older woman's steely eyes went cold. Vanita looped her arm through Willow's to get her moving again, and Marnie backed off.

As they reached Spring Street, Willow spoke again. "The living get so worked into a frenzy, you know?" Her voice trembled. "When it comes to the afterlife, they debate about the rapture and judgment day. And they say suicide is the ultimate mortal sin." She jutted her chin upward.

"Well, the dying don't give two shits about those things. They just want their pain to end so they can find peace again."

Marnie swallowed back her emotions. She knew all that.

They walked in silence again until Vanita said, "We're here."

She pointed to the neat gray shotgun-style house to their left. Leading them up to the gabled front porch, she asked, "Shall we go inside?"

"Let's visit out here," Marnie said. She pointed toward the two chairs on the porch, encouraging Willow and Vanita to sit while she perched on the steps.

Willow sat. "Passing over should be peaceful." Her voice no longer carried a tremor. It was as clear and focused as her eyes. "So, yes, I *do* believe assisted suicide should be legal."

Marnie studied her. "Is that what happened with Kate? Did you help *her* pass over?"

"No." Willow's lips turned downward. "Kate's situation was different. I could tell things weren't right with her. I tried to help her through the darkness. Because she still had so much to live for. And I hoped I could help her see that."

Vanita reached for Willow's hand. "Do you think Dutch was...I don't know...somehow behind her taking her life? Kate always said he was a master of mind control."

Marnie had heard Kate tell Willow the same thing. Of course, she'd also heard the church ladies voice something similar about Willow.

"Dutch loved Kate." Willow's tone sounded defensive. Interesting, considering what a thorn in her side he had been at times.

"I believe that," Marnie said quickly. She didn't add that the yin to love's yang was hate because, frankly, that hit too close for her own comfort. Instead, she said, "But so many things here just don't add up. For starters, why did Kate choose a gun?"

"Firearms are the most effective method." Willow's response was mechanical, like she was reciting from a statistics chart she'd studied for an exam.

A vision of Kate's half-crushed face flashed in Marnie's mind, making her gut twinge. She pushed the picture from her mind and moved on.

"I also keep seeing Kate's wedding dress on the bed," she said. "What was *that* about?"

Willow stared off into space. "We'll probably never know."

"I don't think I can accept that." Marnie recoiled, thinking back to one of the last things Kate had said to Willow. *I need to know how to stand up for myself. It's getting harder and harder.*

Those words weighed particularly heavy on Marnie. Being a strong woman and standing up for oneself shouldn't be hard. She understood and agreed with Kate's statement. But the part about it getting harder and harder. Had Kate meant it in more than just the figurative sense?

Marnie had heard her say it while eavesdropping. The question on her lips might give that away, but still, she had to ask.

"What was Kate afraid of?"

Willow flinched visibly. "I don't know."

"Did you ask her?"

"Of course." Willow's eyes flashed. "At least, I tried to. When she wasn't forthcoming, I invited her to stay at The Diana if she didn't feel safe."

A couple walked in front of Vanita's house. Marnie waved in an exchanged greeting, and silence enveloped them all on the porch until the couple passed.

Willow said, "Xander thinks Kate was afraid of something tied to The Diana's deaths."

The hair on Marnie's arms stood on end.

"Where is Xander that he can weigh in on what's what at The Diana?" She thought back to the article about the trial of Wilma Madison. It had taken place in Florida, which might be where Xander resided. "Does he conduct readings with you by phone from Florida or something?"

Willow raised her chin. "As a matter of fact, he does."

"Of course he does," Marnie muttered.

"He *does*!" Willow shuffled through the bag at her side. Finding her phone, she punched a speed dial number and waited. "He's reading energy. It can be from a distance or over the phone. I'm calling him now. You'll see."

Marnie waited, but she was disappointed on hearing Willow leave a message, asking Xander to get back to her.

When Willow disconnected, she shot Marnie a defensive expression. "The spirits have settled. That's what Xander said the last time we spoke. It's why I returned." Then her expression lost its edge and a flush crept over her cheeks. "Again, I'm sorry I up and deserted you. It was wrong of me. But I wouldn't ask you to return now if I didn't think it was safe."

Marnie gazed downward. "I'm not sure I'm ready. Which sounds ridiculous, I know."

"No, it doesn't," Vanita said, her voice kind. "A lot has been going on in your life, Marnie. Even before..." She didn't have to say it. Kate's death weighed on them all.

"I agree." Willow rose. "In fact, a more appropriate question might be, do you *want* to stay? I don't just mean at The Diana but anywhere in Lake Gardner?" Her silver eyes seemed to be probing into Marnie's soul. "You know I want you to. But no one would blame you for wanting to leave. Least of all me."

"But I can't leave!" Marnie pounded her fists on her thighs. "Can't you see, I don't *want* to write these stories; I *need* to?"

For starters, she needed to come to terms with her gift. Not to mention, she also had to learn to stop jumping on cue every time someone—Lee...Dutch...almost always a man—told her what they thought she should do. And then there was this. She needed to get to the truth.

She rubbed her thighs, smoothing out her black dress.

"I feel called to write these stories for my own sense of purpose and well-being...but also to speak for the Kates and Roxys and CeCes who no longer have a voice."

After a brief silence, Vanita said, "I get it."

"And I want to come back to The Diana, but..." Marnie didn't want to say the next part aloud. *I'm afraid.*

Willow said, "If you feel like you need a night or two more away, trust your gut. Whatever you need to get back your mojo."

Marnie fought rolling her eyes. "I'm not sure I had any mojo to start with."

"Don't sell yourself short." Vanita rose now, too. "If you're hell-bent on staying in town, I have a small guest room. You can stay here if you'd like."

"Thanks, Vanita," Marnie said. "But I think I'll check into that motor lodge."

Willow maneuvered the steps with more energy now. "Then I'll go gather your things. And we'll schedule some time with Xander." She spoke warmly. "You'll be ready to come back soon. It'll all be good, you'll see."

Vanita walked Willow to the street and hugged her goodbye. When she returned to the porch, Marnie was careful to check her tone, but she had to ask.

"With all respect, Vanita, how do you put up with her?" She bobbed her head toward Willow, now easily out of earshot. "I mean, she's a handful."

Vanita's dark eyes gleamed. "She is. But I love her." She patted her chest. "I trust what's in here."

Marnie fought the urge to wince. Trust was something she'd all but forgotten how to feel.

A lingering melancholy weighed her down on her walk back to get her car. Pastor Stan stood outside the church, visiting with folks beside the sign announcing this Sunday's sermon: *Death with Dignity or Life with Hope?* Wow. She had to hand it to him. He definitely wasn't one to shy away from controversy. When she reached her car and pulled out of the lot, the pastor seemed to be staring right through her. But he didn't wave or gesture. She didn't dawdle at Willow's either. She picked up her things and moved on.

The crisp fall weather had attracted a slew of bikers to the back roads around Lake Gardner, and Marnie followed them along her route. The lake gleamed like a diamond as she crossed the Dalton Creek Bridge Expansion. Vanita had told her to watch for the lodge shortly after the bridge, and she glimpsed a sign for it exactly where promised.

Traffic slowed almost to a stop. In front of her, some of the bikers and plenty more cars turned into a drive opposite the lodge. A mass of people congregated in a field. A large banner stretched across a makeshift stage. It read "Stop the Steal." A woman with a megaphone, wearing a MAGA cap, addressed a group in front of the stage. Marnie couldn't make out her message, what with the rumble of the motorcycles and the shouts from onlookers. But not everyone here was on the same side. The undercurrent was anger. Dissenters carried signs that read "You Lost – Go Home" or large MAGA logos X'ed out in bold black spray paint.

She bypassed the gathering and turned right into the parking lot. As she did, a flash of black hit her windshield. *Thwack.* On reflex, she squeezed her eyes shut and slammed on the breaks.

When she opened her eyes, her heart thundered. The windshield was intact, and she touched her fingers to her lips and inhaled with gratitude. But as she regrouped, a flutter of black flapped close to her window.

Crows never forget.

She touched a trembling hand to her heart. The black bird had likely hit her windshield, been stunned, but then recovered. Weird, but possible.

Fighting off a sense of foreboding, she took her foot off the break, parked her Outback, and went inside to register.

Chapter 27

Carly's Motor Lodge was clean, just as it had appeared online. The mild weather allowed her to enjoy her takeout salad from the nearby Piggly-Wiggly with a Diet Coke at a picnic table in the courtyard. Some added upsides: the crow had apparently survived and flown off, and only once or twice did noise from the rally distract her, when chanted protests got extra loud.

She tended to emails and phone calls while she ate. Her first and most important call was to Lee. She had kept him apprised when she went home to see RJ, but she hadn't touched base since. Until now.

When he didn't answer, she cleared her throat and left a message, confirming tomorrow's meeting. She already knew the time and place from an earlier text he'd sent. Frankly, she would have preferred meeting by Zoom rather than face-to-face. But Lee was trying his best to make things work. She could at least pay him the courtesy of recognizing that.

After the call ended, she stared into the dusk. Her stomach roiled at something she'd been trying to ignore. She wasn't leaning toward a reconciliation. As much as she hated contemplating divorce, enough with the stigma. She could no longer picture herself married to Lee five or ten years from now. Or even one, if she was honest with herself.

Where had they gone wrong?

Or had they been wrong from the start and just too stubborn to give up trying?

She opened some work files, but she was distracted, to the point that drafting anything now wasn't going to happen. The thought of ending her fragmented marriage felt like creating an invitation to death, and it made The Diana Homestead's history weigh extra heavy. Three women had died there, two by probable murder, one by suicide.

Goose bumps brushed up Marnie's arms.

Something about The Diana's Blue Moon murders may have prompted Kate's suicide. Willow had suggested as much to Marnie. Correction: Willow had quoted her attorney as saying that. The attorney who was also a medium. Xander.

Damn. She wished she had asked for his full name so she could research him now.

Rubbing cool fingers over her lips, she had another thought. How many attorneys in Florida were likely to have an unusual name like Xander?

Spurred on by a small surge of energy, Marnie tapped the words *Xander – Attorney – Florida* into her Google search bar. She hit pay dirt immediately. His website popped up right away: *Xander Rhodes, Attorney-at-Law.*

Marnie scrutinized the headshot on his home page, wondering what she had expected. If she was truthful, part of her imagined him sporting a long gray ponytail and a Grateful Dead T-shirt. But based on his picture, he wasn't like that at all. She pegged him at fortyish, a big man, well-groomed, in a gray dress shirt. His face was clean shaven, his hair cropped close.

His site was crisp and professional, spotlighting his experience in and out of court. Marnie clicked on a testimonial.

"*If you've been charged with a crime, you need an attorney like Xander. His knowledge of the law and justice system is second to none. His experience and record of success cannot be beat.*"

Marnie clicked on a few more of his site links, which connected to the Florida Bar Association, several professional associations, and a couple *pro bono* projects, including the Innocence Project. Her chest tingled when she spotted a link to *The Psychic Attorney*. She followed it to a Q&A with Xander, talking about the work he did when he wasn't practicing law.

Q: *What is the biggest misconception about your work?*

A: *That I'm a psychic lawyer. That's how people have labeled me through the years, and I've grown tired of fighting it. But a psychic foresees the future. A medium connects with the past, with those who are no longer with us in body. People confuse the two all the time. But I'm the latter.*

Marnie rubbed her fingers over her lips and skimmed some more.

Q: *"So you see ghosts? What do they look like?"*

A: *"I connect with their energy...if they think I can help them and if they choose to connect. Some mediums hear from the spirits in dreams. For me, they appear when I'm conscious, through sound waves and patterns. Or they manifest as a vision of the person they once were. (Pauses) I can only speak for myself. The work of a medium isn't a one-size-fits-all science. A lot of it's up to the spirits—whether and how they choose to interact, whether they feel trust has been established. But I suppose you could say, the same rings true for the medium."*

Q: *"Is Xander your real name?"*

A: *(Laughs) It is. My parents were quite nontraditional. In fact, my mom and her mom were mediums, too. It's a hereditary trait.*

Q: *How do you reconcile your legal work with your efforts as a medium?*

A: *I don't. I consider them two completely separate vocations. My spiritual work is conducted through The Spiritual Guidance Center of Pineville.*

Marnie spotted a link to go to that website but passed on it to read further here.

Q: *How do you feel about your gifts as a medium?*

A: *We don't get to choose our gifts. But I've accepted mine without too much struggle. As a medium, you hold more power if you just own it.*

Pursing her lips, she scanned down the rest of the article, stopping only when she landed on the last question.

Q: Do you ever get frightened, working with—what should I call it—the other side?

A: For the most part, my spiritual work is very uplifting and positive. Most so-called evil spirits are just trapped, forced to repeat the same unfulfilling behaviors over and over. I've found a simple yet effective way to deal with them is to tell them they're not welcome, they have no power here. And then I ignore them. They're a lot like misbehaving children, best dealt with by not giving them the attention they seek.

Wow. Marnie exited the computer window and took a deep breath.

Xander didn't come across as wonky as she'd expected. Not that she suddenly had faith he was all great and powerful. She still had concerns. As much as he talked about calling ghosts out and declaring them powerless, she didn't know if she had the strength and focus to do that. Not yet. Not with her faith in a wringer and her mind all over the place.

She stared through her window into the lot, surprisingly full. From across the road, she heard the chant, "Not my president."

For some random reason that tugged at her heart, her mind turned to Kate. Borrowing Willow's logic, Kate probably wouldn't give two shits about who had just been elected. Her inner pain had outweighed external world events.

What had prompted Kate to take her own life? Maybe the dead could tell her, but she wasn't ready to go back to The Diana to find out. Instead she made a list of everyone she knew who was living and might be able to fill in gaps in her stories.

Willow, The Diana's operations manager – check. Marnie had plenty of contact with Willow. (Same for Vanita.)

The Remingtons – co-owners of The Diana – no check. Kate was out of the Q&A running forever, and Dutch deserved to mourn in peace. At least for awhile.

The Lightners – ugh. Marnie sensed there were gaps they could fill. But would they? Bree seemed too angry to see things objectively, while Zack... Well, Marnie wasn't sure what to make of Zack.

As she found herself short on contact options, she racked her brain to expand her list. She came up with Little F—aka Ian Finster. Ah, yes. Maybe he'd have information to share.

She googled his name and found a couple listed numbers. The first one, linked with *The Lake Gardner Weekly,* went directly to voicemail. She hung up, leaving no message, and tried the second number. This one also went to voicemail, but this time she left her name and number, thanked him for sharing the Wilma Maddox article, and asked if she could schedule some time to ask him some questions.

Who else? Her stomach fluttered, thinking of one more source who might or might not be helpful. Turning to Google once again, she typed in a name and then punched in the number it showed before she lost her nerve.

"Hey," Josh answered on the second ring.

"Hey, it's Marnie." *It's not like he doesn't have caller ID, idiot!* "I'm continuing my project in Kate's memory, and, well... I'm reaching out to folks she knew who might be able to shed some light on the direction to take this book."

"Oh?"

Was he going to make this hard?

"I could do lunch tomorrow." He redeemed himself. "How about Andre's? Say 11:30?"

She felt a sudden relief of tension. "That would work. Thanks."

Immediately after they disconnected, Ian Finster returned her call.

"I could meet late tomorrow morning," he said.

Two morning meetings? Yes, please.

"Any chance we could make it mid-morning?" she asked, not wanting to butt up too closely to the time she'd set to meet Josh.

"I could do 10:30," Ian agreed. "The paper's located next to Missy's Sandwich Shop."

"Deal," Marnie replied. "See you then."

Flushed by a double dose of success, Marnie gathered her things to return to her room. She could still hear the occasional hum of nearby protestors, but she couldn't see them. The sun had set. Carly's neon sign glowed and, coupled with the moonlight, cast a warm kaleidoscope of light onto the door to her room.

Inside, the room suddenly seemed to close in on her. Dust mites floated in the dim hotel lighting. She reached for a bottle of water she'd been given at check-in. Once hydrated, she felt better. Despite occasional noise from the parking lot—car doors slamming, murmured conversations—she got ready for bed and settled in. She slept well.

At first.

In the early hours of Friday morning, her phone rang. She grasped for it in the dark, but the ringing stopped before she could get to it. She searched caller ID to see whose call she had missed, but there was no indication the phone had ever rung.

Shuddering, she put it back on the night table. Something was wrong. Her arms were coated in goose bumps, and she could see her breath in the ice-cold air. Yet sweat matted her hair, and her nightshirt clung to her.

From the bathroom, pipes creaked and water ran. Cabinet doors rattled. Her heart raced, but she lay still as a stone, trying to figure out what else she was hearing.

Angry whispers. And then nothing.

Marnie rubbed her forehead, hot beneath her icy fingertips. Her head throbbed. She swallowed the lump in her throat and listened. Once she was sure all was still, she edged out from under the covers.

A strong scent assaulted her. Sulfur. She wilted at its stench, clamping her fingers over her nose. She tiptoed toward the bathroom, where a light flickered off and on in a staccato rhythm. Her heart thumped, watching a shadow flap over the tub. Its wing-like appendages put up a furious fight, as though it was stuck, although, on what, she had no idea.

She squeezed her fists. It was the fucking crow. In shadowy, ghostlike form.

When she tried to scream, nothing came out. She clasped at her throat, desperate to catch her breath, to regain her voice. In the back of her mind, she remembered Xander's online advice for dealing with angry spirits.

She sent a telepathic message. *You don't belong here.*

For an excruciating moment, she and the shadow stood at an impasse. She swallowed hard, waiting to be attacked. When she tried to speak again, her voice came out scratchy.

"You have no power here," she said, her words weak but clear.

The black thing flustered and flapped. It batted against the tub wall. Finally, it swooped by her head and flew out of the bathroom. A violent smash followed.

"Damn!" A woman's voice, almost a whisper, broke the air. Marnie froze, aware of a new shadow billowing above the tub—a floating puff of red, angry smoke.

"Oh!" The same woman's voice came from the puff. "You startled me."

Marnie's heart pulsed in her throat. "*I* startled *you*?"

The puff of red emitted a bigger cloud, and the woman's voice stammered. "You could help, you know."

Then the puff vanished.

Marnie tried to ignore the prickling sensation along the back of her neck and a sudden difficulty to catch her breath. She inched her way back to the main room, still again, with only a faint scent of rotten egg lingering.

Grasping for the desk chair, she sat, wrapping her arms tight around herself. Her breathing improved. She grew calmer, feeling less tense as the putrid hot spring odor faded. A sudden sharp pang stabbed at her chest as the smell of pear cologne replaced the earlier stench. An opal-and-gray bubble, almost transparent, danced near the ceiling.

"Mom?"

The bubble grew more opaque and glimmered. Marnie's skin warmed in its presence. But the warmth didn't reach her heart. The orb was void of the pink and blue lights it once carried.

Where were the babies?

She felt a horrendous sense of grief and whispered, "What are you trying to tell me?"

The light source now throbbed, a ball of aqua gray. Then it started to fade, and the smell of pear diminished.

"Please, don't go!" Marnie cried out.

But she pleaded in vain. The glow of her mother's spirit disappeared, leaving no message.

Chapter 28

She was sluggish on her drive into town the next morning, foggy-headed as she passed a now familiar roadside farmer's market. A new hand-painted sign promised "the most amazing" fresh cider and donuts, plus seventy-five percent off seasonal crafts and signage, much of it woodcrafted and harvest related.

A lone lake-themed directional sign stood among them, its neon-painted arrows pointing out choice destinations. Lake Superior = 902 miles. Lake Ozark = 728 miles. Lake Gardner = U R HERE! As Marnie drove by, the destination and mileage marks became a blur. The sign spun out of control in her mind, its bright arrows pointing out the dismal conditions of her life. Lost pregnancies = unbearable. Kate's death = unfathomable. Crumbling marriage—

She jammed on her brakes, barely missing a tractor-trailer that crept out from a side road. Her heart beat like a snare drum gone rogue. She'd come close to hitting the vehicle head-on. Less serious but still irritating, she'd missed her turn into Lake Gardner.

What was going on with her? Finding a safe place to turn around, she backtracked, vowing to pay more attention.

Near the bridge into town, a young couple walked hand in hand along the shoreline. Back in the day, she and Josh held hands like that. Her stomach tightened. Everything seemed to make her think of him these days. It was probably normal to have unresolved feelings for him—he had been her first love, after all. But this was a business lunch. It didn't matter that he was her ex. Lee was still her husband. For now.

Plus, she had a meeting with Ian Finster to get through first.

She found a parking spot on Main Street halfway between Missy's Sandwich Shop and Andre's. When she arrived at the newsroom, Finster was busy, leaning into the phone secured between his ear and his shoulder, typing frenzied notes onto his laptop. He motioned her in, and she stood in awkward silence, waiting for him to finish the call.

Marnie sized the place up quickly. It was a one-man shop. No printing presses. No staff abuzz, except for Finster, and his side of the current conversation consisted mostly of grunts and affirmatives. He probably relied on outside contractors to print and distribute and do whatever else needed doing.

To one side of Finster, file cabinets flanked a wall, their drawers ajar in a jagged pattern reminiscent of a Jack-o-lantern's grin. On the other side of the room, stacks of newspapers lay strewn on tables in front of a whiteboard, which listed what looked like story ideas.

A Small Town Through the Lens of ... [the Pandemic?... the 2020 Election?]

Ten Years After the D.C. Bridge Restructure

And in a different color marker, probably more recently added:

When Ghosts Walk Among Us [The Blue Moon Killings]

Toward the back of the room, the surface of a work cubicle overflowed with a printer, a police scanner, and some fancy camera equipment. Sharing the space, an old coffeepot teetered precariously, reeking of scorched brew.

"Sorry to keep you waiting," Finster said, disconnecting his call. He rose to retrieve an extra chair from the back of the room. "Please, sit."

Marnie sat as instructed. "Listen, I wanted to thank you for the article you left for me about Willow. Although I confess, I didn't initially know it was from you."

He laugh-coughed at that and pointed toward the whiteboard of story ideas. "I was digging through archives, trying to bring myself to speed on some Lake Gardner history I missed."

"Aren't you from here?" she asked.

"Born and raised. But after college, I worked an accounting position in downtown Atlanta and vowed I'd never return. Then the Big F got sick." He smiled sadly. "That's what some folks called my dad."

Marnie fought back a smile. "Which makes you the Little F."

"I prefer Finn. But some traditions die hard." He shook his head. "Even some we wish we could shake free of."

He got up to turn off the coffeepot, maybe just now aware of its stench. While standing, he stretched his small frame and let out a sigh.

Marnie herself knew all too well how sitting at a computer screen for hours could take its toll.

"You want to take a walk?" she suggested.

His eyes lit with gratitude. "You know what? That'd be great."

She snatched up her purse and followed him outside. Finster locked up shop, paused for a moment, then pointed in the opposite direction from Andre's, his eyebrows raised.

"Your town, your call," she told him.

They started to walk. "Okay, remind me. Where were we?"

"You were saying that sometimes traditions die hard."

"Ah, indeed." He sighed but kept on walking. "I wish I could say the same about small town weekly newspapers. They seem to die easy. And fast."

She had no response to that. The newspaper business must be super tough these days, given ever-changing technology and the many new ways people access their news. She read somewhere that the U.S. sees newspapers die at a rate of two per week.

They strolled in silence, passing a storefront for a secondhand shop. Halloween costumes, ranging in size and marked seventy-five percent off, flanked its entrance. Her gaze lingered on the tiny wing of a firefly costume that caught the sun's light.

"What year did you come back?" she asked.

"In 2016 when my dad got sick. He passed in 2017, and I took over the paper." He looked her way, his expression neutral. "His last wish."

Finn's story paralleled her brother's. Both sons had left chosen careers behind to honor their father's legacies. She hoped RJ was more at peace with his plight than Finn was.

"I take it you weren't here when Emmett Lightner died?" she said. "Based on your questions for Dutch the other night."

"Correct. That was in 2010." Finn stared ahead and strode onward. "Dad said he used to get pretty good stories from Dutch, often at his weekly soirees." He stopped abruptly, jolting Marnie to do the same. "Apparently, the old man had a better touch than I do."

"Maybe." Finster *had* come onto the Remingtons' porch uninvited. He started to slog forward again. "But Bree became pretty unglued, too. I hate that I reignited bad memories. Or old resentments."

Oh, man. This poor guy did *not* belong in the newspaper business.

"You were doing your job," she said, grateful when he picked up his pace, turning left again. "And speaking of your job, you were here when Jackson Mott got tried for the Blue Moon killings, right?"

"Yes, ma'am." He slowed his pace. Again. "That was the start of my own trial by fire, so to speak. I wanted to present myself as a solid newsman, reporting all sides of the story...and let's just say, it bit me on the backside."

"What do you mean?"

"Dutch wanted to get the trial over and done. He had a point, in that an unsolved local murder doesn't enhance a town's economic development plan. It's a small town, and lots of folks picked up with Dutch's crusade, pushing for a slam dunk guilty verdict against Mott."

"Tying it to his initiation into the Andromeda Coven, right?"

"Yes, ma'am."

A shrill whistle cut the air. They'd wandered a block away from the tracks, but it was fruitless to try to talk over the din of a cargo train chugging through town. Marnie took a moment to process what Finster had said. People don't like unfinished business. That was for sure.

Once the train passed, Marnie said, "It sounds like you wanted to report an even-sided story from the standpoint of innocent until proven guilty. That's fair. So what can you tell me about Andromeda's Coven?"

"Well... the head priest had a big ego, you know?"

Marnie couldn't help it. She laughed. "Kind of like a certain town leader we've just been talking about?"

"Your words, not mine." Finster's lips puckered a bit at the corners. "But I think you get my gist. The trial became about personalities, not facts. Most of the coven members came across like everyday folks. But the head priest flaunted an air of self-importance. He showed an arrogant impatience toward people who didn't grasp his views, which only fueled the flame of Dutch's fan club. They dug in their heels, pointing back to the coven. The story spread that the members brainwashed Jackson Mott to commit the murders."

"As part of a Blue Moon ritual." Marnie nodded, and this time it was she who slowed the pace. "I know the trial got tossed due to insufficient evidence, but ... Do you think Mott did it?"

"No."

Partly this surprised her, partly not. "Did you know him?"

"I interviewed him."

Marnie stopped walking, her eyes wide. "What was he like?"

"He was a strange, jumpy dude. Socially awkward, which made Andromeda's members uncomfortable. They never intended to welcome him in, and he knew that."

She couldn't help but feel bad for Mott, an outsider, just wanting to fit in. Somewhere. Anywhere. But that didn't mean he hadn't committed the crimes. She scoured her mind for other motives.

"Did Mott think he was going to inherit money—or maybe the house—after Roxy died?"

"If he did, that angle got buried." He sighed. "For what it's worth, Mott seemed genuinely sad about Roxy's and CeCe's deaths. He was awkward, so maybe people didn't read his reaction as grief. But I did."

They had stopped walking at a spot across the street from the City Hall complex. Dutch strode out the front door, paused by the foundation, and waved. Apparently, that greeting was only meant for Marnie because when Dutch looked toward Finster, he scowled.

Finster picked up their walk again, acting as though he hadn't noticed Dutch's snub. "I interviewed some of the Wiccan folks back then, too. I learned a lot. Pagans, Wiccans, even magic—those terms mean different things to different people."

"That makes sense."

They passed a small music shop on the corner, one Marnie had passed several times on her walks around downtown Lake Gardner.

Finster leaned in close to Marnie and spoke in a low tone. "The owner of Carly's Motor Lodge is a practicing Wiccan."

She swatted at him playfully, thinking he was pulling her leg. Then she realized he was serious. "Sorry," she murmured. "Go on."

"Not much more to tell," he replied. "People are people are people. Sure, some of the Andromeda Coven folks used Tarot cards and owned wands. But my gut tells me they're more about love and positive energy than anything Satanic."

They walked some more, finally turning the corner onto Main. Andre's was steps away, and Marnie's heart raced a little at the thought of her upcoming lunch meeting.

As they approached the restaurant, Finn slowed his pace one last time. "You know that phrase, 'Thou doth protest too much?'"

"Why, yes, Mr. Shakespeare." She smiled. "I do."

"Well, the Blue Moon case reminds me a little of that. People kept pointing their fingers at Mott and the coven, insisting on guilt. Did they really think Mott did the deed? Or were they trying to deflect from themselves...or whoever else they thought might be guilty?"

Marnie shivered. "You make it sound like you think a cover-up took place." She studied him. "Do you?"

Finster shot her a noncommittal smile. "As a rule, I believe people are good. But small-town folks like their justice. And fairness sometimes looks different to folks in small towns."

Her heart lodged in her ribs. "You're freaking me out a little bit here." She paused. "If you really think that, surely you have the tools and connections to help make things right?"

His smile faded. "I'm an outsider here, Marnie."

"You were born and raised here!" she countered.

"But I left and came back with a new way of looking at things." His eyes dulled. "Not everyone likes that."

Slowly, a flush crawled over her face. "You're right, Finn," she said. "I mean, I get why you feel that way."

He opened the door to Andre's for her, and she thanked him.

As she entered the restaurant, she reminded herself of something. She, too, was an outsider here. That was something she'd best not forget as she moved forward.

Chapter 29

With a sense of unease, she entered the restaurant and immediately caught a whiff of cigarillo smoke. She glanced toward the bar to see who was smoking. No one was. Then she remembered the tale of Reggie, the sexagenarian whose ghost still visited his old stomping ground.

Josh waited in a corner booth, already enjoying some chips and salsa. Marnie took a deep breath, greeted him with a nod, then took a minute to study the menu before a waiter appeared to take their order.

After the waiter left, she took a drink of her water with lemon.

"So..." she said. "You're a nurse."

It wasn't a question. She'd learned as much the other night.

"Yeah." He grabbed a chip and dunked it in salsa. "Like you, I thought I'd be managing construction projects." He grinned. "But I loved the EMT work. So now this."

Marnie softened, remembering how at ease Josh had been visiting with her dad when Putt had grown gaunt with illness, never letting it show if he was troubled by his decline.

"I'll bet you're an excellent nurse," she said.

His cheeks reddened a little. "Enough about me. You're married now. Congratulations." He cocked his head to the side. "Any kids?"

She tried to sound casual. "No children. Just a niece, Uma, and my nephew, Quinten."

"I remember Quinten." The blue in his eyes deepened. "Sounds like RJ and Amanda are doing well."

She twinged at the comfortable familiarity and wondered if he also remembered she always wanted three children. Trying to keep things professional, she changed the subject.

"I've decided to complete this project in Kate's honor. And I'm trying to piece together some things by talking to different folks around town. Timelines...relationships." She tapped an index finger to her lips. "For starters, how in the world did you end up with connections in Lake Gardner?"

He laughed. "Small world, right? That we'd run into each other here, after so many years. And we'd have Zack Lightner to thank."

"Zack?"

"He and I met through the Roswell Fire Department. It sometimes pulls in firefighters from other area departments to work part-time."

"Interesting."

"Roswell's deployment model is pretty progressive." He shrugged. "Anyway, when Zack learned I worked construction, he invited me up here for drinks and introduced me to Dutch. That was back in 2012."

There was a dullness in her chest. That was the year her dad died. The year she and Josh broke up.

He continued. "I did a couple small jobs for Dutch that year. And then a few years later, when he was looking for help to renovate The Diana, he called me."

A chill ran up Marnie's spine. "You worked on The Diana?"

"I did."

Josh made room on the table as the waiter brought their food. They took a minute to doctor the crispy fish tacos with spicy coleslaw, avocados, and lime juice.

"Mmm," Marnie said, dabbing a napkin to her lips. "Tell me about The Diana renovation. Before I eat my way into a coma."

He laughed. "Let's see." He wiped his mouth as well. "The renovation had plenty of challenges, like shipping problems and unplanned upcharges in materials. The contract wasn't clearly written, which caused snags with the bank and some of the larger accounts."

"You're making it sound like Dutch was a horrible contractor."

He picked up his taco and shrugged. "The house itself is just incredible. The bones...the design. The craftsmanship. Did you know it's a Sears, Roebuck & Co. catalog house?"

"Yes." She got a kick out of the passion he still showed for his onetime craft. But she was here to talk business. "Y'all were renovating during the Blue Moon murder trial. Do you remember much about that?"

Josh nodded. Then he stopped eating. "It was surreal. There was like this Salem, Massachusetts vibe. Everybody got caught up in the modern-day witch hunt. Literally. Even Dutch said it was bizarre at first. Everyone in town was pointing a finger at Roxy Tripp's foster son, blaming him for the murders and linking him to Andromeda's Coven."

"What did *you* think?"

"I'm *still* not sure." He picked up his taco again. "There was all this talk about rituals and spells and black magic. As The Diana's renovation problems worsened, Dutch joked that supernatural voodoo-hoodoo must be at the root of all the project's glitches. At least, I thought he was joking." He took another bite.

Marnie shivered, given her moments-old discussion with Finn Finster. "Do you think Dutch was just trying to deflect from his own poor project management skills? Or did it run deeper than that?"

"I don't know." He frowned. "It was like a forest fire, lit by a spark, out of control in a flash. People talked about these coven folks like they were monsters. I didn't ever meet any of them personally, but in the news accounts, they just looked like regular people."

So far, Josh's memories jelled with Finster's.

"When the trial got thrown out," he continued, "plenty of folks were pissed. But I was exploring nursing school about then and cutting way back on my work with Dutch. So I didn't spend a lot of time in Lake Gardner after that." He took a big chug of water. "In fact, I didn't see Zack again until a few months ago, when he introduced me to Bree."

Okay, so Josh and Bree were *not* a long-time couple. Her cheeks warmed.

Refocusing, she asked, "Do you think he treated her well? I mean Dutch. Do you think he treated Kate okay?"

He frowned. "Who knows what goes on behind closed doors?"

She cringed. Who knew, indeed? Kate seemed to have it all. Looks, smarts, a prominent position in the community.

"I just don't get why a woman like Kate would shoot herself." Marnie tapped her lip.

Josh's eyes clouded. "When someone takes their own life, they've usually been battling their own internal demons for a long time."

"I get it." Intellectually, she did. But she flinched because something else still troubled her—something Josh, as a medical professional, might be able to explain.

"But why shoot herself in the head? And how did she manage to walk all the way to The Diana afterward?"

"Head wounds are unpredictable. And with a GSW, a lot depends on the kind of bullet and its trajectory. And where it lodged." He hesitated then. "Sorry. Not very nice lunch talk."

"I asked." Marnie pushed her plate away. "But *why* would she walk to Willow's?"

"Willow's the woman they call the witch, right?"

"She's not a witch." Marnie prickled, feeling protective of Willow despite how much she'd irritated her yesterday.

He held up his hands. "Sorry, I'm just trying to distinguish all the players here. If it makes you feel better, I've heard good things about Willow around the hospital. About her work as a death doula."

"A *death* doula?"

Josh motioned to the waiter for more water. "They're like birth doulas. Except they're working at the other end of the life cycle."

Marnie chewed on that for a moment. "So you think Kate had it planned all along, to walk down to Willow's after she shot herself? For what? Comfort?"

The blue in Josh's eyes paled some here. "She might have just been disoriented." He paused. "Or maybe she *did* go to Willow for comfort. They had a close relationship, I hear."

"Really?"

How did Josh know so much about Kate?

"It's a small town." He grimaced, almost as though he was reading her mind. "Kate was a sweetheart. What happened with her is tragic."

He shifted in his chair. "But what about you, Marnie?" His voice lightened when he changed the subject. "What are you hoping to find out by staying at The Diana?"

"Honestly? I started the project to pick myself up after losing my teaching job due to COVID. But now I'm haunted by wanting to know why all these women were silenced before their time." She fiddled with her wedding rings. "I'm starting to think it might be easier to solve their murders than to tackle the pressing questions facing the world today. How sad is that?"

He let out a low whistle.

"Yes, I'm still too earnest, I know." She smiled to cover a bit of embarrassment. "But I'm not at The Diana anymore. I checked into Carly's Motor Lodge. Because…"

She stopped. Josh was aware of her history, of how her mother's spirit used to visit. Marnie had always been able to talk to him about anything. But now it seemed too intimate to discuss something with Josh that she hadn't already broached with Lee.

"Marnie?" He pushed gently. "Because why?"

She threw her hands in the air. "Since I've come to Lake Gardner, I've become a freaking magnet for spirits. The Cozy-Remington orphans. Roxy and CeCe. Ghosts in the graveyard."

"Whoa." He narrowed his eyes.

The waiter interrupted to see if they wanted anything more. When Josh asked for the check, Marnie tried to take it, but he wouldn't let her.

She waited until the server left to say, "It sounds like I'm losing my shit, doesn't it?" But the truth was, she felt an unexpected release of tension being able to share what she had. She laughed a little again, knowing well it didn't hide her self-consciousness. "I have no one else to talk to about this."

"Not even your husband?"

Her face went slack, and, fearing she might tear up, she turned away.

"I talk to Willow sometimes. I *think* I can trust her." She glanced back at Josh now. "And RJ listens, God love him." She didn't mention that RJ listened to *all* her woes these days.

Josh's eyes gleamed with sympathy. "Death and the afterlife are tough topics. Especially sharing them with those we love."

He studied the bill, which saved her from having to run from the table. She mourned all they'd once shared. She even missed their intellectual sparring, which had sometimes driven her wild. Hearing him talk about life and death and love again today left a dullness in her chest, making it hard not to long for a life they might have built.

Josh reached for his wallet and placed cash in the bill holder, giving Marnie a chance to collect her emotions and bring her thoughts back to the pertinent parts of today's conversation.

"The more I hear," she said, "the more it sounds like Kate liked The Diana a whole lot more than Dutch did."

"Definitely." For a moment, Josh stared off. "I'm sure part of her attachment to the place is the fact Roxy left it specifically to her."

"Oh?" That was curious. "I figured the Remingtons bought The Diana at auction."

"No. Roxy left the house to Kate. Not the Remingtons. Just Kate."

Actually, that was more than curious. It surely could have caused some marital friction.

"Well," Marnie tried to reason, "Roxy was single. She probably didn't think in couple terms."

"You could be right." Josh waved the bill holder toward the waiter. "But I remember Dutch being beyond pissed when Kate decided to keep it that way. In her name only."

"Knowing Dutch, I'm sure he wasn't pleased."

Yet from what Marnie heard Kate tell Pastor Stan, she probably felt more of a need to protect her finances than to placate her husband.

"Do you plan to go back?" Josh rose. "To The Diana?"

As he pulled out her chair, she laughed lightly.

"Tell you what?" she said. "If you hear I'm doing something that wild, will you give me a holler and try to talk me out of it?"

He cocked his head. "Who are you? And what have you done with my Marnie?"

Her face flushed. She wasn't *his* Marnie. Not anymore.

Pointing toward the ladies' room, she attempted a grin. "Nature calls," she said, needing an escape. "Thanks for lunch."

She started to walk away, but he touched her arm, sending jolts of electricity through every inch of her body.

"I could come with you," he said.

When she startled, he broke eye contact and his face reddened.

He cleared his throat. "What I meant was, if you're uneasy about going back to The Diana, I could come with you." He laughed lightly and added, "If you'd like."

Her face flashed hot. If she'd been nervous to respond before, she absolutely knew she couldn't trust her voice now.

He seemed to recover more quickly. That or he knew how to fake it better.

"Give me a call if you'd like that, okay?" he said.

Then he shot her that grin she thought he had always reserved just for her. And he left.

Chapter 30

I could come with you....

Marnie replayed Josh's words in her mind in Andre's ladies' room. They weren't a poem, for heaven's sake. He'd said them in his good-old kind style. All the same, they made her feel warm inside.

Stop it, Marn. She chided herself to get a grip, then washed her hands and reapplied her rosy lip gloss.

Coming out of the bathroom, she turned toward someone calling her name. Her gaze landed on the place at the bar Reggie purportedly used to sit, smoking his cigarillos. There, instead of the ghost of Reggie, sat the in-person Zack Lightner.

But it wasn't Zack who had called her name. It was Andre. He stood behind Zack and motioned her over. Unfortunately, she wouldn't be able to avoid Zack if she went to talk to Andre. So went life.

"How'd you like the fish tacos?" Andre asked as she sidled up to the bar beside Zack.

"They were excellent. Can I get the recipe?"

Andre shook a finger at her, a grin forming at the corners of his mouth.

"I take it that's a no?" she said.

He laughed outright and then went about his business.

A waft of smoke from Reggie's cigarillo tickled her nose, but she ignored it.

"Don't you have any big events keeping you busy at The Mill this weekend?" she asked Zack, sensing it would be awkward if she just ignored him.

"I do." He took a long draw off his beer. "Just confirming the catering and bar orders for tonight and tomorrow night." He pointed to Andre, who was now engrossed behind a computer at the bar. Then he turned to Marnie. "And I see you were enjoying a little special time with your old sweetheart, eh?"

Her jaw tightened, and she hoped he didn't see it. She eyed him directly.

"Perhaps I could have a little time with you, too?" she said.

He played with his glass. "Depends on what you have in mind."

She chose to ignore any hidden innuendo he might have intended.

"I still have a few questions," she said. "For the project I'm working on."

"The one Dutch asked you not to finish?"

She tried to ignore the prickling in her scalp. "He didn't flat out make that request."

Zack rested back on his stool, studying her closely. Then he leaned in and slammed a palm on the bar. "Hot damn, you're a piece of work." He laughed. "So...what more do you want to know from me? I already told you all I know about The Mill's ghosts."

"Yes, you did. But I'm focusing on The Diana Homestead now, which got me wondering... Were you all working with the Remingtons at the time they renovated The Diana?"

"By you all, you mean me and Bree?"

"Yes."

Scratching his jaw, he grunted.

"Hey!" Andre's booming voice cut the air. "You wanna come review your order here?"

Zack rose and ambled over behind the bar. This gave Marnie a few precious extra moments to strategize on how to take this conversation forward. When she'd met Zack the first time at The Mill, he stole the advantage, serving her cranberry sangria to catch her off guard and loosen her lips. She remembered it clearly, including his comment that usually he was a Jack man.

She helped herself to the seat next to Zack's, wrestling with the old adage about catching more bees with honey than with vinegar. Or, in this case, gleaning more information with alcohol than with charm.

Zack ambled back to his seat as Andre approached Marnie, asking, "What can I get you, ghost lady?"

"A bottle of Jack Black, please," she said. "And two glasses."

Andre's eyes gleamed, and he placed two tumblers on the bar promptly.

Marnie's cheeks burned under Zack's scrutiny. But she had his attention.

"So..." she said while they waited for the liquor. "You were telling me about the partnership you and Bree have with the Remingtons."

He finished his beer as Andre delivered the bottle and poured them each a hearty serving.

"Since you asked so nicely..." He touched the tumbler but didn't move to drink yet. "The first place we renovated together was the house on Blakely. When we were able to turn a profit there, we did a couple houses on Ashford."

"What about The Diana Homestead?" Marnie asked again.

"Nah," Zack replied. "Dutch and Kate worked that one on their own. Bree and I were knee-deep in negotiations and plans for The Mill."

She reached for her own tumbler, lifting it into the light to study the rich amber liquid it held. "That's also the time Jackson Mott was on trial for the Blue Moon killings," she said. "Did you follow that very closely?"

"It was hard not to because it *was* a shitshow. Definitely too wild to ignore."

"So...do you think Mott did it?"

"Probably." He held up his own tumbler now. "Even if he didn't, karma got him for something." He tapped his glass against Marnie's. "So, here's to karma." He paused before adding, "And projects—including this book of yours—that refuse to go away."

His words left a bitter taste for Marnie. First, he'd made light of a man's death. Then, he mocked her work, the project she refused to let die. Ignoring all that, she took the shot. It went down smoother than expected.

Andre brought them both waters, and Marnie mouthed *thank you* to him. She wondered how long Zack had already been drinking. If it had been a while, she hoped another old adage would hold true as well. *Loose lips sink ships.*

With that in mind, she said, "You know what I find interesting?"

"No." Zack cocked his head. "Tell me."

"Well, the talk around town—"

He interrupted. "You mean up at the church? Or between Willow's lips and your ears?"

Heat flushed her cheeks. She looked around, but no one was within hearing distance. "Talk is that Kate and Dutch were swapping partners with Bree and Josh." She bit back a bitter taste as she said it, then glanced sideways at Zack.

He reached for the bottle and refilled their glasses.

"You gotta pay to play," he said, placing the bottle back on the bar.

Marnie reached for her glass. "Tell me about the swapping first."

Zack countered. "Drink and I'll tell you about the swapping."

She put down her whisky glass and took a big gulp of water, partly to slow this game down, but also to delay answers she might not like hearing. Raising her tumbler again, she tapped it with Zack's.

"To finding answers," she said.

He drank down his whisky and snorted. "I don't see Kate and Dutch as swingers. Now Josh and Bree…who knows?"

Oh? Her neck warmed, and she hoped her cheeks weren't as red as strawberries.

"You know the other church rumor I found intriguing?" she continued. "Folks think Kate was sleeping with you."

On hearing that, Zack did a double take. Then he grinned and slapped the bar. "This goddamned town." He shook his head. "The worst hypocrites are at the church, you know?"

Touché.

She pressed on with her questions. "Do you think Dutch treated her right?"

"Kate?" Zack narrowed his eyes. "I'm pretty damned sure he didn't beat her."

Marnie was surprised by his bluntness. "Do you think...he bullied her?"

"Dutch bullies everyone," he grumbled. "It's just his way."

"So you don't think he tried to, well, brainwash her to take her life?"

"Hell, no." Zack couldn't hold back a laugh. "Is that another juicy suggestion you heard from the ladies up at the church?"

She didn't care to admit that morsel of an idea came from her own head. "But speaking of church ladies, I did hear something that seemed extra odd." She rubbed her fingers on the bar. "I heard Dutch called the church in search of someone to help clean up the house. After..." She couldn't bring herself to finish.

Zack apparently got it. He slapped his knee. Then he reached for the bottle and poured them both another shot. She didn't stop him.

"Dutch did call Stan after the shooting," Zack said. "And Stan called me. He asked if I knew some guys from the fire department who cleaned up accident scenes as a side gig." He inhaled. "I didn't." He exhaled. "I told him I'd do it."

Marnie fought off a touch of queasiness. "So you were in the bedroom after it happened?"

Zack reached for his glass.

She put her hand over his and asked, "Is it true her wedding gown was on the bed beside where she shot herself?"

He jerked his head. "Christ. Even if it's true, it shouldn't be news for the whole town."

"I agree." Marnie played with her shot glass. "But it's sad, don't you think?"

His eyes flashed with anger now. "You know what I think, Marnie? You're just as bad as the rest of those biddies, trying to make more of what happened than did."

She should probably be offended. Except she *had* set herself up for some possible humiliation with this inane line of questioning. She was getting nowhere. But there was little sense in trying to back down now.

"I hardly think I'm making too much of this," she said. "Kate died." Taking her hand off his, she reached for her shot glass. "So was the gown on the bed?" She raised her eyebrows in a question and her glass in an offering.

He studied her, his brown eyes narrowed. "Yes." He reached for his glass and held it mid-air. "There were several boxes from the closet strewn around the room. Dutch figured Kate had to pull them all out to get to the safe where the gun was stored." His left eye twitched. "Maybe her gown was in one of them, and she pulled it out for one last look."

Marnie's facial muscles went slack. He'd summed it all up with such disregard.

She was done matching him shot for shot, and she steeled herself for his goading. But he didn't take his own shot, let alone deride her for not taking hers. Instead, he set his tumbler back on the bar.

"I have a question for you," he said.

"Fair enough."

She didn't like him turning the tables like this. His eyes were inebriated slits, but he spoke without slurring.

"You seem all concerned about Kate, about how Dutch bullied her or didn't treat her right. But what about your buddy Willow? Why didn't she get Kate the help she needed?" He leaned in, closer than she liked. "Why did Willow treat Kate with oils and spells instead of sending her to an authentic shrink who could help her?"

Marnie blinked fiercely but refused to break eye contact. "You'd have to ask her."

He picked up his tumbler and chugged his whisky. As he rose to leave, he let out a loud belch.

At the door, he turned back to her. "One more question." He spoke a bit more softly now than before. "Did you know Kate drew up a deed, leaving The Diana to Willow instead of to Dutch?"

Her stomach knotted. She didn't trust herself to respond.

He smirked. "So who stood to gain most by brainwashing Kate to take her own life? Her husband? Or her wannabe shrink, Willow? The woman who now owns The Diana?"

Chapter 31

Setting her shot glass back on the bar, Marnie watched Zack leave the restaurant. A frown tugged at her lips, contemplating what he'd just said. *Kate had deeded The Diana to Willow.*

Was it true, and, if it was, how would Zack know? From Dutch?

"What do I owe you?" she asked Andre, who stood nearby.

"Nothing." He grinned. "Josh got you lunch. Zack got you drinks."

"I'm not sure Zack would be pleased about treating."

She wasn't sure how much Andre had overheard, but his eyes gleamed.

"You listen to his bullshit? He gotta treat." He laughed heartily as he poured her a coffee. "But you gotta wait a little before you drive. Deal?"

She honored Andre's request, breathing in a final whiff of Reggie's smoke when she finally left the chop house a half hour later. The first thing she did driving back to the lodge was place a call to Willow. No need to fret over Zack's proclamation. She would ask Willow directly herself. But Willow didn't answer.

Back in the room, Marnie rubbed at the tension behind her eyebrows and dug into Plan B, trying to confirm Kate had inherited The Diana after Roxy's death.

She scanned her Diana Homestead folder, clicking open one she'd named "Remingtons - Diana." It contained a news clip titled "Local Family Preserves Lake Gardner History." An inset picture showed Kate and Dutch, flashing thumbs-up in front of The Diana. Skimming the clip, Marnie found no mention of the Tripp women's deaths or of how the house was acquired.

Her attention snagged another file named "Coven Trial." She opened it to find a picture of a man and two women identified as members of Andromeda's Coven. Finn and Josh were right. They appeared pretty normal.

The three posed on the steps of the county courthouse. Granted, one of the women wore a cape and witch's hat and flashed a "V" sign with her fingers. But the man—the head priest who supposedly had a big ego—wore a simple dark suit, probably purchased off the rack. The other woman, like the man, dressed in conventional fashion, other than a somewhat flamboyant hat. Squinting at the screen, Marnie realized the woman's hat was actually her hair, which snaked around her head in Medusa-like curls. Unique? Yes. But in an attractive way, not a witchy one.

Her phone rang. She jumped on the call.

"Hey, Willow. Quick question. Did Kate deed The Diana to you?"

Willow made a little noise with her throat. "Hello to you, too, Marnie." But, to her credit, she didn't dodge Marnie's blunt question. "How did you know?"

"Zack Lightner."

Willow sighed. "I found out Halloween morning. She gave me the paperwork, gift deeding ownership to me in the case of..."

Marnie winced as her mind flashed back to what she'd witnessed that morning. Kate and Willow had visited out behind The Diana. Kate handed something to Willow, who, at first refused to take it. Finally, she accepted it.

Sweat prickled Marnie's forehead. "I asked you about it when you came in, and you just said Kate was troubled."

"She *was* troubled." Willow said. "She said she wanted me to have The Diana if something happened to her."

"Why?" It was the question Marnie kept coming back to as her mind raced.

Willow made the throat noise again. "Oh, my God," she murmured. "Because she was planning to die. She so much as told me she was checking out, and I completely missed it."

Marnie meant, why had Kate left The Diana to Willow? But there was so much sorrow in the older woman's voice, she couldn't press it.

"It wasn't your fault," she said firmly, hoping to exude comfort the way RJ had done with her back at the orchard when he'd explained that she wasn't to blame for their mother's death.

Willow's breath faltered. "But I should've seen it." Her voice quivered. "I should have sensed how bad things had gotten for her."

Marnie remembered something Zack had said back at Andre's. Who would have the most to gain by brainwashing Kate to take her own life? Not her husband, he'd said. Willow.

When the silence on the line grew awkward, Marnie broke it by changing the subject.

"I'm coming back to The Diana."

"When?"

"Tomorrow, late afternoon or evening."

Willow let out a huge breath. "You're sure you want to do this?"

"Yes." Then Marnie thought of something else. "But before I do, could you reach out to Xander and see if we could schedule some phone time. Mid-afternoon tomorrow?"

"Okay," Willow promised. Then she added, "But Marnie, you don't have to do this."

"I know."

But she was going. Back to The Diana Homestead.

As the call ended, Marnie caught a whiff of sulfur. Jerking her head, she sought out a black blob of shadow and listened for flustering wings. Nothing. She tried to tell herself the smell might indicate a chemical leak. That was most likely bullshit. But maybe…

Dusk floated in the air as she strode her way to the lobby. A woman stood behind the desk. She appeared to be in her forties, dressed in a black shirt and pants, professional but not flashy.

Marnie took a cleansing breath and approached her.

"You're Carly?" she confirmed, noting the woman's name tag.

"Yes, ma'am." Carly's brown eyes warmed. "How can I help you?"

By telling me all you know about the Andromeda Coven! Marnie wanted to shout.

She held back, though. For all she knew, Carly practiced as a solitary. Or perhaps Finn was mistaken, and Carly wasn't a practicing Wiccan. Plus, Marnie didn't need more theories about who did what on the night of the Blue Moon of 2012. She needed facts.

"I'm in room 14," she told Carly. "But I was wondering if I might be able to switch rooms?"

The woman flinched. Unless Marnie imagined it. It had been subtle.

"I'm sorry, we're booked full. I hope there's nothing wrong?"

"Nothing big." Marnie didn't mean to say it so quickly. She added, "I worried a little I might have smelled gas. And the sounds from the road... Well, they probably wouldn't be any different from another room."

"Probably not," Carly agreed. "Those are just the downsides of being on the highway and next to a gas station. But the upside is the proximity to the highway *and* town."

"True." Marnie introduced herself and added, "I've been commissioned to work on a book about the town's economic resurgence."

Carly's eyes flickered. "The ghost book."

"Yeah." In spite of herself, Marnie laughed.

"So tell me, Marnie Putnam," the woman said. "Are you a believer? In ghosts?"

This was a new reaction to the book, and Marnie was like a deer caught in headlights.

Carly pushed onward. "Road noise isn't the actual reason you asked to change rooms, is it?"

Marnie's eye muscle twitched. "No."

Carly never broke eye contact. "A number of guests have reported paranormal activity in that room. Do you want to know what happened?"

"If I say yes, can you find me another room?" Marnie tried to laugh.

"No." Carly's lips turned up a smidge. "But it probably wouldn't make a difference anyway. Spirits seek out intuits when they need to communicate."

Holy hell, this lady sounded a lot like Willow. Or maybe Willow sounded like her.

"A spirit may have spoken to me," Marnie admitted. "A woman, floating above the bathtub. She asked, 'Why won't you help them?'"

Carly leaned in. "A teenaged girl was killed in room 14 in 2010. Probably a runaway. She was never identified." Carly scowled. "A lot was happening around Lake Gardner back then. As sometimes happens, the girl's case went cold almost as quickly as she did."

Gray noise filled Marnie's head.

"But how am I supposed to help?" she asked Carly. "And who's them? Why does some random spirit care whether I help them or not?"

"I have no idea," Carly said. "But you might help open her up if you tell her you're listening. That what she has to say matters."

There was the Carly-Willow parallelism again. Willow had hung the picture of Roxy and CeCe in her hallway for much the same reason. To let them know they had not been forgotten.

"I just don't understand," Marnie said. In a big way, she didn't *want* to understand, but she left that part unsaid.

"This spirit is reaching out to you for a reason." Carly wasn't letting her off the hook. "And you're able to hear her for a reason, too."

Marnie inhaled loudly, tired of hearing about her so-called gift.

Carly's brown eyes bore into Marnie's for a beat more. "You can lean into your abilities and use them. Or not. It's your call. Now"—she picked up some papers from her desk and stacked them to straighten them—"if you'll excuse me, I have some tasks I need to tend to. I hope you have a good evening."

Carly turned her back on Marnie, who, like it or not, didn't have any more business here in the lobby. Deflated, she slunk back outside.

The shadows loomed long as Marnie followed the walkway back to her room. The rally across the road continued, but the outbursts were now more like benign chants rather than hot, angry cries. She was retrieving her key from her purse, debating between dinner and bed, when she felt a presence.

Her heart stopped.

There, lurking in the shadows by her door, stood Pastor Stan.

Chapter 32

Pastor Stan shot her a feral grin from the shadows. Chest still tingling, she gripped the strap of her purse. She could hurl it at him. But it wasn't heavy enough to scare him off.

"Hey, Marnie." The pastor's tone was anything but ominous. In fact, on closer examination, his expression was more boyish than frightening. "Hope I didn't scare you."

She loosened her clutch on the strap. A gentle wind scattered the air, raising the hair on her arms. "Were you looking for me?"

"Not exactly." He didn't step toward her, perhaps realizing he *had* frightened her. "When you passed the church yesterday, you wore a lost expression, like you might want to talk."

She fought the dirty look she felt forming. "How did you know you could find me here?"

He chuckled. "Would you believe me if I said it was a God thing?"

"My mom used to use that phrase," she murmured, still not letting down her guard.

He motioned with his head toward the gathering across the road. "The police got called in to make sure things remained peaceful. And they contacted me. Sometimes they do that if they think I can provide a soothing influence. But things had settled down by the time I arrived."

Marnie suddenly became aware the din from the MAGA rally had dissipated.

Pastor Stan's eyes crinkled into a smile. "I got lucky, because I don't think anybody would have cared to listen to me. But the God thing came afterward when I spotted your car in the lot." His eye twinkled. "He does work in mysterious ways."

"So I've heard." She shifted the strap of her purse.

"Could I buy you a cup of coffee? At the Waffle House?"

At the thought of food—even Waffle House food—Marnie perked up. She was famished.

Minutes later, she sat across from Pastor Stan, scarfing down scrambled eggs and bacon, raisin toast and hash browns, scattered and covered in perfect Waffle House fashion. With decaf.

"So you decided not to stay at The Diana any longer?" Pastor Stan sipped his own decaf.

"I didn't figure I should stay there if I wasn't going to finish the project. But I've decided to go back and complete it." She paused. "Much to Dutch's delight, I'm sure."

Pastor Stan laughed. "Granted, Dutch can come across as gruff. But deep down, he's a good soul."

"You have a talent for seeing the best in people."

But perhaps he had a point. Dutch had seemed awfully good working with the church youth in the days leading up to Halloween.

"I try not to judge, Marnie."

"Then you're a better soul than I am." She took a sip of decaf. "I'm not proud of myself, but I can't help feeling a little judgmental toward some of the folks in your church about now."

Pastor Stan's dark eyes studied her. "You know," he said, "the church is not a museum for saints. It's more like a clinic where people come to heal wounds."

"Touché." She picked up a forkful of hash browns. "The thing is, I'm not getting much comfort from my faith these days."

She blurted it out, then wished she hadn't. Something about Pastor Stan reminded her of her father, who used to get under her skin, the way he could tell what she was thinking. At the same time, the pastor had a soothing effect, like she could tell him anything and he truly wouldn't judge her.

"Sorry," she said. "I guess it weighs on me more heavily than I realized."

"It's natural to question our faith after an unexpected tragedy."

Marnie spread apple butter on her toast. "I had my doubts way before this," she said. "And Kate's service brought them into focus. Like, right there in your church, people were talking trash about her...who she was mixed up with...how those things could've influenced her decision to..." She finished the sentence in her mind.

One corner of Pastor Stan's mouth inched upward. "In case you haven't heard, the devil has to work harder inside the church."

"I've heard all the things." Her cheeks burned. "Like God never hands us more than we can handle. Well, I call bullshit on that."

He broke eye contact to focus on something outside the window. "I call bullshit on that one, too." Turning back to her, he added, "I mean, look at Kate."

His words cooled Marnie down.

"I appreciate what you said at her service." Her voice quivered. "About suicide."

"I spoke from the heart."

Marnie's mind flashed to the sign at the church: *Death with Dignity or Life with Hope?*

"So...from your heart, what do you have to say on the death with dignity issue?"

The pastor's eyes gleamed. "If you come to church Sunday, you can hear all about that."

She glanced at him sideways. "In case I don't make it Sunday, where do you stand?"

Pastor Stan put his cup down without drinking. "As a Christian, I believe only God can take a life."

There was a sudden lump in her stomach, and she didn't think it was the food.

"You say that, but you're also all-forgiving toward Kate? I mean, she took her own life on her own terms, right? Not on God's." She couldn't read him. When he didn't respond, she dipped her chin. "I'm just curious, if someone helped her do it, would you forgive them, too?"

"I would. But I'm not the final judge, am I?"

Her skin prickled. She found herself liking this man and wanting to ask him so much more. Not so much about death and the afterlife. More about our lives in the here and now. About making and breaking vows. About forgiveness...of the people we love. Of ourselves.

"Sorry." Her face flushed, trying to slow her thoughts and not get ahead of herself. "I don't mean any disrespect. I just have so many questions."

"Marnie." His eyes were thoughtful. "Our faith doesn't die when we question it. To the contrary, it dies if we stop asking questions."

She let out a steady stream of air. She must be one freaking monument of faith.

"May I make a confession?" The words popped out of her mouth before she could weigh them.

"I'm not a priest."

"I know. But..."

He waited, expectantly.

Suddenly Marnie didn't know what to say. She had intended to confess how she overheard him and Kate talking in his office. By accident. She'd heard Kate's frustrations with Dutch for keeping secrets from her.

But what did Marnie hope to gain from sharing that? She supposed she wouldn't mind his forgiveness for her snooping. But it wasn't like Pastor Stan could betray Kate's confidence and say something like, "Yes, Kate and Dutch were having problems."

If he did, it would *really* feed her frustrations about hypocrisy in the church.

"What did you want to tell me?" He prodded, his brow still furrowed.

She settled for something true but benign. "I wanted to say I appreciate you." She suddenly felt shy. "I'm not sure I'll be coming to church, to be honest. But I appreciate how you reached out to me." She hesitated. "How you listened. How you seem to care."

"I do care, Marnie." He reached for the check, but she beat him to it. "I wish you God's blessings whether you come to my service on Sunday or not." He grinned widely then. "But I *do* hope you'll come to the service."

He waited for her to pay the bill, and when he insisted on walking her back to her room, she didn't argue.

As they neared the lodge, he said, "Faith is what makes life bearable, with all its tragedies and ambiguities and sudden, startling joys."

"I believe that." She did. "I'm just having trouble trying to live it."

"I can't take credit for the words. They came from Madeleine L'Engle."

"The author?"

His expression turned childlike, so filled with hope she wanted to scoop some up for herself.

"Thanks, Pastor Stan," she said, bidding him a good night.

Inside her room, she reminisced on their visit, grateful for how it had taken her mind off tomorrow, which would begin the official end of her marriage. Her gut twisted. Was it a sign her faith was doomed if she couldn't even honor her vows to stay with Lee forever?

Maybe she *should have* asked Pastor Stan about that.

When she washed her face, an opal-like glow flashed in her peripheral vision. By the time she dried her face, it was gone. But the knot in her stomach had eased.

Ready or not, the time was ripe to move forward.

Chapter 33

Her phone shone in the dark stillness: 4:37 a.m. *Shit.* Waking up in these pre-dawn hours was becoming a habit. It was as though this time when the moon still kissed the sky had become her personal witching hour.

She lay in the quiet, thinking about random things. Pastor Stan. Lee. Her mother's ghost. God. She tried to figure out how they all wove together. Failing that, she rolled onto her back.

"I am here," she recited. "I am now. I am safe. I am well."

Her eyes adjusted to the dark just enough to lock in on the shadows on the wall.

"Slut!" A harsh male voice sliced into the still of the room.

Jolting upright, she forgot her meditation. She lurched around, trying to better make out her surroundings, remember where the nearest lamp was. But her mind was a fog.

She clutched her chest, holding her breath in the icy cold that enveloped the room. She listened intently, picking up on a rhythmic droning sound. But it came from outside the room. Probably someone snoring next door.

A low-frequency hum pulsed nearby. Slowly, she exhaled, trying to make out shadows in the black room, absent of light except for the red dot from her computer charger. Eventually, she grew accustomed to the dark around it.

A huge dark blob hovered in the doorway to the bathroom. She stared at it, breathing intently, trying to figure out whether it was moving or she was hallucinating.

"Ahhh." The male voice boomed from the shadow. "Don't think you can hide from me."

Marnie clutched at her covers. She didn't think he was talking to her.

An ugly, guttural laugh snaked through the air, lifting the hair on her arms.

"A second slut?" His tone had lightened, grown almost sing-songy. "Two for the price of one?"

He *was* talking to her. Or at least about her.

The sound of wings slapped the wall, a stark contrast to external sounds from the lot and neighboring rooms she'd grown used to hearing. The air whistled, and there was a reverberating power from what had to be a massive wingspan.

Her heart thrashed in her ears. "What are you?" It was all she could get out.

The outline of the crow shadow grew crisper, now perched on the dresser.

She couldn't move her legs. Blood rushed through her veins with such a force she feared her carotids might burst. She squinted to make out the crow's size, which *was* considerable, its wings spanning at least three feet across. But its voice—deep and baleful, void of emotion—its voice is what plagued her most.

The crow cocked its head. Marnie froze under the lifelike power of its stare. It poised for flight, and she squeezed her eyes shut. Its thunderous wings whooshed the air. She lifted her arms to cover her face.

A hard thud echoed off the wall. She jumped at the sounds of a heavy weight slapping the floor, the bone-chilling sound of a crow's cries, the eerie voice of the man now a memory.

Gradually, she opened her eyes as the room closed in all around her. Through trembling fingers, she made out the crow shadow, lying in a heap, wings twitching, legs convulsing, its stomach pulsating in desperate efforts to breathe. Its beak moved like rusty shears as if it was trying to speak. Its eyes stared up at her, dull and full of hate.

Marnie forced herself to swallow.

How had this monstrous creature missed hitting her?

She held stone still, ultra-aware of everything around her. The distant sounds of traffic from the road, the snoring next door, the hum in her own room. The air still carried the hint of stale spoiling cabbage, but as the wing slaps lessened, so did the stench. The shadow of the crow seemed to shrink as it faded.

Suddenly, a warmth washed over her as she understood. The crow spirit was like Roxy's flame, frightening to the ears and the eyes, but unable to make physical contact. These spheres of energy, which appeared strong beyond human understanding, couldn't channel their power to touch or be touched by living souls in this earthly world.

With a flush of confidence, Marnie pointed at the shadow. "You have no power here."

It emitted an eerie chortle, struggling to regain its balance and come to a stand.

She leaned over, closer. "Go away." She spoke slowly, deliberately.

The spirit sniggered. It emitted a potent whish of black smoke that reeked of sulfur. But the smoke faded quickly, as did the laughter. It weakened into a spitting mechanical sound and then down to nothing. It was gone.

Marnie pressed a palm to her heart and bowed her head.

"That was amazing," a female voice said.

Marnie jerked up, recognizing the voice. It belonged to the spirit who'd come to her last night and came from atop the dresser now, where a shadowy figure began to take shape. A blur of female curves, dressed for a night on the town, sat cross-legged on the dresser. She faded in and out of focus. Short red dress, spaghetti straps, lots of skin.

Marnie's chest tightened. "Holy shit."

"Now there's a way to make a girl feel welcome," the girl-woman replied.

Marnie's head swam. "Is the crow gone for sure?"

The woman in red cocked her head, her forehead wrinkled with confusion.

"The crow shadow that spoke like a man?" Marnie clarified. "Is he gone?"

The woman leaned forward. "He appeared to you as the shadow of a crow?" She started to laugh so hard she had to clutch at the dresser for balance.

"What's so funny?" Marnie glowered.

When the woman stopped laughing, she recrossed her legs. "That old crow is the man who killed me. Years ago. But he still haunts me." Her eyes widened. "And you scared him off."

Marnie glanced furtively around the room. "What if he comes back?"

"He might. But then you can scare him off again."

"What if I can't?" Marnie sat up straight, tossing her covers aside. "I don't understand all this otherworldly shit, and I'm sick of it." Her neck hurt from all the tension she carried there.

"I'm Fiona."

"Oh." Marnie jerked on hearing the spirit's name. Somehow knowing it made her seem more real. Fiona emitted a strong scent of sweet cherries on seeing Marnie's reaction.

"I've been trying forever to get someone to see me," she murmured. "To hear me and recognize me." Her scent waned and she wrinkled her forehead. "But I guess it's hard to care about a runaway skank who met a stranger—an old crow who doctored her drink, dragged her to a sleazy motor lodge, and strangled her, stuffing her in the tub when things didn't go his way." Fiona grew quiet. "Some ghost story, huh?"

Marnie tried not to squirm. "They never caught your killer?"

"No. And why should they care? I was just trash, you know?"

"Don't say that."

Marnie was queasy, trying not to think how she'd lingered in the shower that morning. In the same tub where Fiona had been stashed out of sight, indeed, like unwanted trash. She pushed all that from her mind.

She studied Fiona more closely, suddenly puzzled. "Why do I see you as a person? I see the others as shapes or animals or elements."

"Hell if I know." Fiona's gaze wandered. "I'm just trying to escape the killer who haunts me so I can move on."

Marnie leaned in. "And you think I can help?"

"Actually, no." Fiona ran fingers through her hair. "Your mama sent me."

Marnie inhaled sharply. "I don't believe you." She crossed her arms. "Why wouldn't she just come talk to me herself?"

"What do you think she's been trying to do?" Fiona exhaled dramatically, arms spread, palms out. "Your mama thinks you're blocking her messages for some reason."

"Why would I do that?"

"I don't know." Fiona waved a hand. "It happens. Anyway, Patsy hoped I could get through to you—even though she warned me you could be a strong-willed little shit."

Marnie's fingers fluttered to her lips. Her mother just *might* have said something along those lines. Narrowing her eyes, she asked, "Did you and my mom meet in heaven?"

"It's a little more complicated."

Oh, c'mon. Marnie wanted to pull a succinct explanation from Fiona this instant.

Tell her you're listening, Carly had said. Let her know she matters.

So Marnie slowed down, rested her hands atop her crisscrossed legs, and tried to gain some rapport. And answers.

"I'm okay with complicated," she said.

Fiona resettled herself on the dresser. "There's this holding area we go to when we die."

"So you're saying my mother isn't in heaven?" Marnie sat up.

"I'm getting there." Fiona narrowed her eyes, a warning she wouldn't be rushed. "When we first die, we go to the same place, only everyone experiences it differently. For me, it was like my favorite beach in

Alabama. A place of comfort, but also a place of reckoning. A place to review my life."

"And from there?"

"From there, we go to this big ol' Shoney's breakfast buffet so to speak." Fiona chuckled lightly. "Not really, of course. I just call it that because it has so many choices. Like at the buffet, some folks choose to go straight to heaven. Others pick reincarnation. Still others don't get to choose so much as they get stuck on an earthly plane, having to repeat what haunts them until they learn their lesson and can move on."

"What about my mother?" Marnie asked. "Why wouldn't she choose heaven?"

"She did. After your daddy died." Fiona's lips turned up at the corners. "But sometimes she sneaks back to this plane to check on you."

Marnie warmed at that. But then she soured. "Why doesn't she talk to me then?"

"Remember the message at the graveyard?"

Marnie had been so certain the Cozy-Remington orphans had written it.

"If that was from my mom, what did she mean? Who is *them*?"

"The women back at The Diana Homestead."

The heater motor purred on, and Marnie startled. Her stomach twinged.

"I've caught glimpses of my mom and my babies at The Diana. Do they need help?"

"Nah." Fiona waved reassuringly. "Loving on those babies makes Patsy happier than a pig in sunshine. It's the ladies who died there who need you. Them." She dipped her chin and eyed Marnie sideways. "Plus me."

Marnie studied her. "You visit there, too?"

"I can." Fiona's essence became completely clear now. "We have nowhere else to go, the ladies at The Diana and me. Until our stories get closure, we're stuck here. Along with our ghosts."

A smidge of fear crept up Marnie's back. "If I go back to The Diana tomorrow, what if the old crow follows me?"

"If he does, just remember, you have more power than him."

"But he *does* have power."

There was a thick moment of silence between them.

Fiona pursed her lips. "His greatest power comes from fucking with your mind. So don't let him get to you. If you need me, just call for me. I'll be there."

Her words sounded like song lyrics. Still, Marnie wasn't completely convinced.

"Hey." Fiona cocked her head. "You said I'm the only spirit that appears to you in human form. So how does your mama appear to you?"

Marnie felt her eyes come alive. "She's a brilliant floating opal. Light as a bubble."

"Ahhhh. Perfect choice for a roamer, someone who flits between heaven and earth, providing guidance to the ones they love."

Marnie's shoulders sagged. "These days she doesn't provide a whole lot of guidance."

"Maybe she thinks you're handling things pretty well on your own."

"That must be it." Marnie's words dripped sarcasm.

Fiona ignored the tone. "Listen, we both need to get some rest. We've got a lot of business to tend to tomorrow." Her figure faded to a shadow in red.

"Wait!" Marnie cried.

"You'll be fine," Fiona told her, fading away and leaving behind the scent of clean linens. And fresh cherries.

"Remember," her voice echoed after she'd left, "if you need me, just holler."

Chapter 34

Later that morning, Marnie pulled into the driveway of the Buckhead townhouse she shared with Lee. The front entryway was as she'd left it, framed in mums and autumn décor. On closer examination, Lee had pitched the uncarved pumpkins. Her jaw tightened. He knew she loved to keep the pumpkins all the way to Thanksgiving.

Shrugging off irritation, she disabled the alarm system and let herself into their home. It smelled of Pine-Sol and lemon oil. A cleaning woman came on Wednesdays. So, did the smell of clean always linger through the weekend like this? Or had Lee been eating his meals out in her absence? That seemed likely, given the immaculate state of their stainless steel kitchen.

Marnie wandered into the living room. Examining the place after a few days' absence, she felt like a stranger in her own house. From the sterile kitchen to this room, where even the bookcases were arranged sparsely, she had acquiesced to Lee's minimalist décor preferences.

Why?

On the way to her office, she stopped by the open door to their bedroom. Raw emotion ripped at her heart as repressed memories surfaced, clear as though she were watching them in movie form.

It had taken over a year of trying, but when Marnie had found out she was pregnant, Lee teared up. He kissed her belly and got kind of giddy.

He started spoiling her even more, like telling her the nursery decorating budget was high as the sky.

At eight weeks, Marnie lost the pregnancy. They'd both been broken, especially Lee. He worked longer hours and withdrew from her physically, adding to her sense of loss and emptiness. A teaching position opened closer to home, and she hoped a new start would do her good. This was pre-COVID, a time when last-hired-first-fired hadn't crossed her mind.

Another rush of sadness hit when she entered her office. Marnie had started making more solid plans to convert it to a nursery when she learned she was pregnant the second time. The room's shelves still spilled over with texts and teaching supplies, but baby fabric swatches and paint samples dotted its walls. Happy but cautious, she'd contemplated colors. When she made it past the eight-week milestone, she allowed herself to ponder a woodland or elephant theme. She lost her second pregnancy two weeks later, at the ten-week mark.

Toward the bottom right corner of one shelf, she found what she sought. Her journals from the years between the time her mom died and then her dad. There were two of them. As she bent to pull them from the shelf, something behind her stirred.

"Marnie?"

She jumped and turned. "Lee?" She held her hand to her beating heart.

"What are you doing here?" His eyes narrowed.

"Just pulling a couple old journals." She held them up toward him. "Wanted to check a few things against my current project." He didn't need to know she planned to review her previous ghostly encounters compared to her current ones.

"Well, it's good to see you." He came into the room and gave her an awkward hug.

She hugged him back, her heart still thumping.

"This means we can ride together to the lawyer's office." He clasped his hands together, pleased. "And then stop for lunch somewhere afterward."

"I'm not sure, Lee." Her throat ached, being here in this room with him. "I have an appointment in the late afternoon back in Lake Gardner."

He dropped his hands to his sides. "You can't even give me a day? Especially after how patient I've been with you?"

Her eyes widened. "*You've* been patient? With *me*?"

"Yes. This past year hasn't been tough for just you, you know?"

Her chest tightened. It was true.

"It's been difficult all around," she agreed. "We both lost those babies." She clenched her fists. "And I know there's no comparison here, but I lost a job, too."

"I'm aware," Lee said, dryly now.

She dipped her head, remembering how she had cried for two full weeks when that happened. No matter how much Lee tried to comfort her, it didn't help. Then again, he had offered comfort as one would to a child. Something inside Marnie flinched as she suddenly understood something. Her job held less value to Lee, not only because it paid less. Her work was simple and youth focused. His was big money and world intensive.

"You negated my work. You said losing my job might have been a hidden blessing."

His eyes blazed. "We were happy before...before all this fuss about babies and job loss and things beyond our control."

His words sucked the air out of her. She sat on the edge of her desk and crossed her arms at her chest. "Tell me something, Lee. If you lost your job, would you just shake it off and move on?"

"Don't be absurd." The muscles around his mouth tensed. "My work?" He made himself stop.

"Your work is important." She narrowed her eyes. "But mine wasn't?"

"You're being fucking ridiculous." He rubbed the back of his neck. "First you're blue because you can't have children. Then you think a new job as a writer will fix things. Which is it, Marnie? What do you want?"

SECRETS OF THE BLUE MOON

She narrowed her eyes, truly seeing him. "I want it all. I want to do work that matters—to me, if not to you." She took a breath. "And I want a baby, too. In fact, I want three."

His shoulders slumped. "I've told you, babe, I just can't do the fertility thing. Why can't you get that?"

"I do get it, Lee." She stood. "I'm not asking you to do it."

He cocked his head, not understanding.

She wouldn't cry, dammit. She wouldn't. "You *have* been patient, I get that now. You've tried to give me time and space when I asked. You set up this mediation today, which was thoughtful. But ultimately, it's not going to work. Because you want me to come around to the way *you* want things to be."

His eyes darkened. "You make me sound like a monster."

"No." She moved to touch his hand, but he flinched. "We've given it a pretty good shot, trying to build a life. Considering we're people who want different things."

"What the hell does that mean?"

She picked up her journals and purse. "I want a divorce."

His lips parted, but no words came out. Her tears tried to creep up again.

"I'd like it to be fair. And amicable." She wouldn't cry. "I'll have my attorney contact you."

She turned to walk away. As she did, he grabbed her arm.

"What the hell, Marnie? You're not even going to try? What's gotten into you?"

What's gotten into me?

She pulled out of his grasp. "I don't want to hurt you, Lee. But this is for the best. For both of us." She walked toward the door.

"Hurt *me*?" His voice was cold, but the anger simmered, threatening to break the surface. "You were nothing before you met me," he shouted. "Walk out on me and you won't see a dime."

But she did walk out. With her head held high.

Clutching her journals to her chest, she made it to the Outback. Her ankles wobbled only once. Her hands trembled as she opened the door, got in, and backed out of the driveway. She still shuddered after driving a block, so she pulled over and shut off the engine. Only then did she allow herself to cry.

She cried for a long time, so hard she hyperventilated. Cupping her hands, she breathed into them, alternately holding her breath, then exhaling slowly. Finally her tears dried, and her breathing returned to normal.

She checked the visor mirror as she dried her smudged, puffy eyes. Yowch, what a fright.

But she wasn't frightened. Not anymore.

Her lips twitched at her blotchy reflection. She closed the mirror and retrieved her phone. In the contact list, she searched for *Pit Bull*. That was what RJ had said she would need if she divorced Lee. She'd entered the term beneath the name of the attorney he'd shared. In case she forgot his name but wanted to find him.

Her trick worked. She found what she needed.

Taking a deep breath, she pressed *Connect*.

Chapter 35

The rain started as soon as Marnie got on the interstate headed back to Lake Gardner. At first, droplets zigzagged across the windshield, agitating her mood more than causing actual difficulties on the road. An hour in, the rain grew angrier, pelting down in menacing sheets, hindering her visibility. She spotted an exit with a Cracker Barrel and pulled over.

She put in her name for a table and accepted the pager the hostess handed her that would buzz when a space opened up. Her phone rang. Correction. It wasn't her phone but rather her FaceTime app.

"Hey, Willow. Vanita." She stared into the women's faces on her screen.

"You were right," Vanita said, pale as a ghost. "The Diana *is* haunted."

Her loud, odd exclamation drew a shooting glance from the hostess.

"Whoa," Marnie said, slinking away from the hostess's area into the store's Christmas section. "Slow down."

Willow forged forward. "Roxy and CeCe have become unsettled by all the energy being stirred up here."

"Let's get real," Vanita said. "They're pissed."

A customer, eying a sparkly white star ornament, glowered, possibly at Vanita's language.

Marnie moved to a corner of the store overwrought with mugs and T-shirts and signs bearing slogans like *Butter My Butt and Call Me A Biscuit*.

She glanced about to ensure it was less crowded. "What happened?"

"Similar things to what I told you about before," Willow said. "Spilled flour and cinnamon in the kitchen. Sugar and cookie cutters splayed about, too."

"Someone tried to clean things up," Vanita said. "Then someone else messed it all up again." She used air quotes every time she uttered the word *someone.*

Marnie's mind raced. The older women had been spooked, but they hadn't fled. They were still at The Diana, obviously okay, FaceTiming in front of the antiqued kitchen cupboards.

"Listen, Marnie." Willow rocked slightly as she spoke. "We wanted to fill you in on what's happening. But I also wanted to wait to call until...after the appointment with your husband this morning."

If there was a hint of curiosity in Willow's tone about how the meeting went, it was eclipsed by a muffled buzz droning over the line.

"Ah," Willow said. "It's Xander patching in."

"Xander?" Marnie's voice rose in pitch. "*Now?*"

The customer she'd irritated earlier glowered nearby, fondling a coffee mug emblazoned with *Bless Your Heart.*

Marnie shot her an extra sweet smile and exited the restaurant. She marched over to the row of ubiquitous Cracker Barrel rocking chairs, chose one, and sat.

"Remember?" Willow said. "You wanted me to arrange some FaceTime?"

"Hey, Marnie." Xander's dimples popped. "Pleased to meet you."

"Likewise." She cleared her throat.

Xander's eyes probed hers through the screen. "Willow's told me about some of your experiences at The Diana. You have extremely rare abilities, and I'd like to help."

"Can you help me get rid of them?" Marnie's attempt to laugh was weak.

"I'd rather help you embrace them." His eyes gleamed. "I know it's tough, especially at first. All the diverse visions, sounds, and smells as the spirits reach out in different ways."

A woman, engaged with a man in a game of checkers nearby, widened her eyes. Apparently, her game in progress offered less entertainment than listening in on Marnie, the deranged lady engrossed in a FaceTime call with a couple of eccentric women and a medium.

Marnie rose to put distance between them. She took a cleansing breath and told Xander, "I'm pretty sure I saw a spirit that looked like a person last night. Is that a sign of progress?" She gulped back a small laugh. "Or a mental health crisis?"

"That's excellent." He shot her a thumbs-up, then grew more somber. "The work of a medium can be lonely. I had my mom to run things by, and I want to be a similar resource to you. But it's not a one-way-only skillset. It's incredibly intuitive."

In other words, she was on her own.

A lone clap of thunder made her jump. The storm may not be over.

"Xander." Willow pressed her lips into a fine line. "I'm not sure Marnie should come back right now. I mean, Vanita and I are probably heading to her place. Until things settle. *Again.*"

Vanita corrected her. "You mean before the spirits go full-on batshit nuts."

Marnie's skin tingled, touched by their reluctance for her to return. But Willow's reticence nagged at her. Where was the woman who said the dead don't haunt us unless they think we can help?

She locked eyes with Willow through the screen. "It isn't up to you two, is it? Whether or not I come back to The Diana."

Willow narrowed her eyes. "I *could* forbid you to come back. To *my* house."

Rain spilled from the sky again, in sudden gushing torrents.

Xander broke the stalemate.

"Marnie's right," he said. "It should be her choice. Because it does carry some risks. People who were evil in life are also likely to be evil in the afterlife."

"But Roxy and CeCe and Kate weren't evil," Marnie argued.

"I get that sense as well," Xander agreed. "But something or someone there very well could be. Not to mention, even when benevolent spirits stir, they *can* cause damage. If they get riled up enough."

"Comforting," Marnie deadpanned.

"Remember, the spirits are energy," Xander reminded her. "Most of the time, as a medium—and that's what you are, Marnie, you don't get to choose—you hold the power to channel that energy if you put your mind to it."

"Don't you mean if I know how?" Marnie asked.

An alarm went off in Xander's office. He glanced down for an instant, then it stopped.

"Sorry, I have another appointment," he muttered, returning to their conversation. "You're right, Marnie. There *is* a learning curve involved here. But it sounds like you're learning quite quickly."

Marnie tightened her jaw. This was not a prime time to learn through trial and error. The stakes—her safety, at the very least—were too high.

Then again, what kind of life was she living if she kept letting fear rule her actions?

"Tell you what, Xander." She squared her shoulders. "Give me your best tips. Fast."

His eyes warmed. "For starters, trust your instincts. And for good measure, ask God and your spirit angels to join in protecting you from negative forces."

Ah, the God thing again. Marnie wondered if he might be pulling her leg, but no one laughed.

"Amen." Even Vanita seemed to be leaning in. "But let's pray for a shitload more angels than we think you need," she added.

The rain eased back to a light spittle. Xander's grin widened.

"Willow," he said, "you'll be sure Marnie has my contact information?" To Marnie, he added, "I'm only a phone call away."

After Xander disconnected, Marnie studied Willow on the screen. The older woman was uncharacteristically quiet.

"You seem unnerved," Marnie said.

"I *am* unsettled," Willow admitted. "Kate's gone. We can't bring her back. I'd love to ease my guilt; I think you know that. But in the end, does it *truly* matter why she did what she did? Would we honor her better just to let her memory rest?"

Vanita shook her head. "I can't believe I'm saying this, but don't we honor her best by finding out what caused her to snap and do this horrible thing?"

Willow opened her mouth, about to counter, but Marnie's pager went off, alerting her her table was ready. Relief washed over her. She didn't have the energy for these two right now with their ongoing, wavering debates.

"Listen," she said, "my table's ready. How 'bout I call you once I'm back on the road?"

When they didn't answer, Marnie peered at the screen. "Hello?"

Willow and Vanita stood rigid, like they'd been caught red-handed trying to stack a deck of Tarot cards. Around them, dishes flew from the cupboards and smashed to the floor. Onyx shrieked. And then things went deafeningly still.

Marnie's pulse quickened.

Willow and Vanita remained frozen in The Diana's kitchen. Here at the Cracker Barrel, the couple playing checkers studied Marnie carefully through narrowed eyes.

"Sorry," she said quickly, struggling to articulate. "My cat...got a little excited."

The man tilted his head, as if weighing the evidence. Marnie moved farther away, turning her back to them.

"Are you okay?" she whispered into the screen.

After a beat, Vanita said, "Yes." Her voice was breathy, her face pale.

"We are," Willow added, the color washed from her face as well. "But after we clean this place up, we're getting the fuck out of here." Her steely eyes widened. "And honestly, Marnie, I think you'd be wise to stay away, too."

Chapter 36

By the time Marnie reached Lake Gardner, it was dark. When she pulled into The Diana's lot, her headlights washed over Josh, leaning against his jeep. Her heart lurched, but she reminded herself again this was business.

She retrieved her laptop and bag. Josh grabbed his backpack from his jeep and wrestled the bag from her hand. She picked up the picnic basket Willow had said she'd find on one of the Adirondack chairs. They entered the kitchen, and she placed the basket on the table.

"You want me to put our bags on the stairwell to take up later?" Josh asked.

She nodded, noting the mix of sugar and cinnamon, the flour and cookie cutters, swept to the side but left by Willow and Vanita in their urge to flee. Ignoring a shiver, she swept the dry baking mix into a dustpan and placed the cookie cutters in the sink.

By the time Josh returned, Marnie was grinning over the picnic basket.

"What's so funny?"

She held the note Willow had tucked in the basket atop a folded jute table runner. "M," she read. "Since you insist on staying...don't forget to sprinkle your prayers with a little moon magic and alchemy. Hugs, W.'"

"Okay?" Josh's expression was hard to interpret.

"Salt." Marnie lifted a shaker for Josh to see. Returning her attention to the note, she read, "Its purity will repel and protect you from evil spirits."

"Hmmmm."

She couldn't read his reaction, so she placed the next item, a small silver stone, on the table. "Silver," she read. "It's reflective like the moon and deflects negative energies."

When she held up the third and final element from the basket, he chuckled.

"A horseshoe?"

"An *iron* horseshoe," she corrected, examining the charm-sized horseshoe between her thumb and forefinger. "Iron wards off bad spirits, preventing them from lingering in your home."

She glanced at him sideways. "You find her a bit wacky, don't you?"

He shook his head. "She works with the dying. That can prompt different rituals and reactions. Sometimes more from the families left behind than the ones who are dying. And sometimes from staff, too." He gestured toward the front of the house. "So...you want to do a walkthrough now?"

"Hold on."

"What for?"

She pulled a loaf of baked bread from the basket. "Are you hungry?"

"Are you?"

"Always." They said it in unison, laughing at their old joke about her healthy appetite.

In truth, she *wasn't* all that hungry. It just felt so good to be doing something close to lighthearted and normal for a change.

She spread the jute cloth on the table and continued to pull items from the basket. Disposable plates, napkins, and utensils. Homemade jam and hummus. An ornately decorated bento box. A bottle of Pinot Noir.

Josh tapped the wine bottle. "Nothing wacky about *these* provisions."

Marnie chuckled. "Can you get us real glasses? From the cabinet above the sink?"

She opened the bento box, filled with meats and cheeses, crackers and olives, crudités and dip. Josh returned with the glasses and an opener, and they set up their meal without words. She held up her glass as a gesture but refrained from making a toast. They both drank.

After they ate and drank for a bit, Marnie said, "I'm sorry about you and Bree." When his eyes widened, she added, "I got a vibe from Zack that the two of you broke up."

"Oh." He looked down and focused on rolling a slice of salami between his fingers. She figured the discussion was over until he re-established eye contact and said, "We were never really right for each other. But my heart hurts for her. She's carrying around so much anger."

Marnie thought back to Bree's behavior on the Remingtons' porch. And how she refused Kate's offer to drive her home when the officer ordered her not to drive.

"It seems like she blames the Remingtons for her dad's death?"

"She's had a rough go of things. The whole family has." He paused. "But at a certain point, we have to grow up and own our own behavior. You know."

It was her turn to look down, Josh's reference to so much anger tasted like sour wine. Or perhaps it was the memory of Lee, twisting her wrist, making ugly threats, that carried the bitter flavor. Dragging a carrot through hummus, she tried to push thoughts of Lee from her mind.

"What does your husband think?" Josh broke the silence. "Of you coming back to The Diana?"

Marnie's stomach twinged. "Not much."

She started to pack up the bento box, hoping to divert the subject. Almost absently, she thought to ask, "Do you want more?"

"Nah, I'm good."

He rose and started to take their glasses to the sink.

"What if I'd like another glass?" she asked, bristling a little that he hadn't offered.

He stopped mid-tracks and turned back toward her, grinning sheepishly. "Sorry."

"Oh, who am I kidding?" She tucked the bento box in the fridge. "Probably better to move things along and bring on the fun."

"So you want to tell me the game plan?" he asked, placing the glasses by the sink. "For tonight?"

"Sure." She motioned for him to follow her.

In the front room, she stopped. "By the way, I appreciate your helping me out here," she said. "Willow wouldn't let me come back if I didn't bring someone with me."

"I'm flattered," Josh deadpanned.

She laughed. "That came out so wrong. Because honestly, there's no one else I'd rather go ghost-hunting with."

Her cheeks warmed, and she felt the need to turn away.

"Anyway"—she got back on track—"the spirits started their visits upstairs in my room."

He ambled toward the staircase. "So it's plural?"

"Yes. Roxy visited me down here, too." She pointed toward Willow's office, then she gestured in the other direction, toward the front porch. "CeCe and the Cozy-Remington orphans sometimes like to hang out, here or up at the Remingtons. But for the most part, the ghosts seem to visit me upstairs." She hesitated. "My mom's come back, too."

Josh's jaw muscle twitched. He knew her mother's ghost stopped visiting her after her dad died. At the time, he suggested it might be a good thing, a sign her parents were reunited and happy again in the afterlife.

"Her spirit came back again after my miscarriages," Marnie said.

Josh's eyebrows drew together. Her heart hurt to talk about this. But it also felt good to have someone listen.

"I've lost two pregnancies." She continued cautiously toward the stairs. "When my mom visits now, she carries two little sparks of light. One's pink. The other's blue."

They were close enough now she could hear the heaviness of his breath, even though he didn't respond. She could read him now, too. He was taking in her pain.

He started ascending the stairs but stopped two steps up. "Do you see any other spirits?"

She wiped her damp palms against her jeans. "Down here." She pointed toward the front door. "Something—someone—didn't want me to leave. Roxy or CeCe, perhaps?" She dabbed at her cheeks, now damp. "I don't know. Maybe Kate?"

He frowned at that, and she struggled to swallow. Her knees buckled. She couldn't tell what was happening, except suddenly Josh was beside her, holding her up.

"You're okay." He pulled her in close. His beating heart soothed her.

She worked to match her breath to his. She knew what he was doing, trying to break her panic with slow breaths to keep her from hyperventilating. The problem was his touch stirred her to the point she still had trouble catching her breath.

"We don't have to stay here, Marn." His eyes were so kind.

She tried to focus. But he was so close. She wanted to inhale his citrusy scent and taste the wine still fresh on his lips. Mostly, she wanted to feel him inside her.

Oh, my God. She broke away, mortified. This was all so wrong.

"Marnie?" His eyes widened. They were still kind, but they now carried questions.

"It's not the ghosts." She crossed her arms over her stomach. "At least not The Diana's ghosts. It's just..." She moved her hands to her heart and exhaled hard. "I'm getting a divorce."

He didn't say anything at first. When he did, his voice was soft. "I'm sorry."

"I am, too." She started to cry.

Who would've guessed she'd have this many tears for Lee? But Josh didn't press her to wrap it up. He just let her blubber on.

Finally, he touched her arm lightly. "Do you want to leave? Do you want *me* to leave?"

"No," she answered too quickly. "I'm glad you're here."

They climbed the stairs without words. She stopped at the top landing, outside the door to her room. "Thank you. I know you switched around your schedule for me."

"It's okay." He cleared his throat and pointed down the hall. "My room?"

She nodded. He shot her a crooked grin and then ambled down the hall.

Marnie jerked awake, her pulse ticking wild, a metronome on speed. Her gaze swept the room for signs of anything other than darkness, but she was alone. Breathing in deeply, she willed herself to calm down. It was almost funny, the frequency of her dreams in Lake Gardner. She wasn't laughing, though. This dream started out as though she'd been floating. Until her chest went heavy, her body cold.

In the dream, Josh stood beside her outside her bedroom. He cleared his throat and pointed down the hall. "My room?"

But instead of nodding, she touched her icy fingers to his warm cheek. His crooked grin indicated he was puzzled, but it also stirred something deep inside her.

Wrapping her hands around his neck, she pulled his face toward hers. Her heart pounded, and she felt the warmth of his mouth even before she kissed him. When he didn't pull away, she ran her tongue slowly along his lower lip. He tasted sweet, like a mix of exotic-but-familiar spices. He drew her in closer. His hardness made her knees quake, her stomach quiver. It was like she was finding her way home after years of being lost.

Suddenly, she pulled away from him, ultra-aware of everything happening.

"I'm sorry." She held herself at arm's length. Holy shit. She bowed her head, catching her breath to say it again. "Truly, Josh. I'm sorry."

Gently, he placed his hands on the back of her head, drawing her face close to his.

"You don't need to be." His voice was husky. "Not on my account."

His eyes locked on hers. It was a moment of no return, but she didn't look away. She knew he'd stop if she gave him the sign, but she didn't do that either. He bent, brushing his lips along her neck the way she'd remember until the day she died.

If she died right now—oh, my God—she'd be in heaven. Never mind she'd likely be hell-bound later. She'd be happy in this instant, for as long as it lasted.

She reached for his hands and coaxed him into her room. Beside the bed, she undid the buttons of his shirt and his belt buckle with trembling hands. He groaned when she reached for his zipper and helped him pull off his jeans. Sitting on the bed, he undressed her now, his fingers tender, his movements slow. He pulled her onto the bed, gentle, whispering her name.

In the dark, their bodies moved in a slow dance of foreplay. Later, she might have regrets. But when he entered her now, she gasped and gave in to the present.

And when she felt that final flush of warmth and pleasure, she pressed against him.

This.

This was home.

Chapter 37

J osh sat on the side of her bed, the sun casting shadowy slits of light on him through the blinds. He gazed down at her the way he used to, all those mornings ago, back when they were happy. She sat up, confused, trying to wake herself up.

Had they been together last night for real?

She accepted the mug of coffee he offered. Black. He remembered.

"I can probably get someone to cover my shift today," he offered.

She took a sip of coffee, but it didn't sit well. Last evening was coming back to her slow and steady. They hadn't been together. It had just been a dream.

Struggling, she tried to find the right words. "About last night..."

"Kind of anticlimactic, I know." He shot her an impish grin. "How the ghosts didn't visit."

A half-smile tickled the edge of her lips. But then she grew somber again.

"I'm sorry for bringing you into my mess. I shouldn't have."

"Hey," he said, "I offered, remember?"

She looked away. Gently, he guided her chin with his hand, forcing her to make eye contact, but dropping his hand once she had.

"What's going on, Marn? Talk to me."

His touch on her face had been platonic. Still, it made her shiver.

"I think I have feelings for you still," she murmured. "Feelings I maybe shouldn't have."

He stiffened but said nothing.

She sucked in a breath. "Your turn to say something back."

He rose and started to pace.

"Josh?"

"What do you want me to say?" He stopped pacing to study her.

She settled on being direct. "Tell me you share those feelings. Or, if you don't, just say so."

"God, you make it sound so simple." He scrubbed a hand over his face. "If we were coming together with clean slates, that would be one thing. But we carry baggage. Everything's complicated."

Marnie tried not to squirm. "Well, yes. I *am* still married."

"Yeah, about that..." He clenched his jaw. "What happened to us, Marn?"

"I think you know." She squeezed her mug and had to turn away.

"I'm not sure I do."

His voice cracked, just enough to make her glance up. Her stomach fluttered to see how serious he was. She didn't want to revisit this. Again. But she leaned over, setting her mug on the nightstand.

"For starters, there was Panama City Beach."

He cocked his head, his eyes homing in on hers.

"You know," she said, "when you almost drowned."

He moaned. "You're being a little dramatic, don't you think?"

"Am I?"

The memories came rushing back. They'd rented a boat for a day on the intercoastal with friends. After a couple hours, the captain idled it at a sandbar. They jumped in to swim, but the current was strong, and he hollered for them to get back on the boat.

While climbing onboard, Marnie dropped her sunglasses. Her chintzy Dollar Tree glasses. And behind her, Josh instinctively dove back into the water to grab them.

"No!" the captain yelled. "Y'all need to stay on the boat." He barked at the others. "And toss him a buoy."

Her chest tightened, watching the water's force tug Josh farther from the boat, wrenching him under the water. Every time he reached for the buoy the water overtook him. She was nauseous, even after she saw him finally grasp the buoy.

A flush crept across his cheeks now. "Well, on the upside, I learned how to swim with a rip current that day."

She got out of bed. More memories of his daredevil shit barreled through her mind as she shrugged on her robe.

"And then you had that off-roading accident with your buddies up in Tennessee. You know, the one where you broke your neck."

"My fifth cervical vertebra," he clarified.

"Yeah. Your neck." She hated the hard edge she still heard in her tone. "The doctors said it was a miracle you walked away from that without needing surgery." Her brows came together. "I'm glad you did, but it scared the hell out of me."

"Okay. I've done some stupid things at times." He met her eyes. "I'm sorry."

She, too, had been sorry. Sorry and devastated, especially since her dad had died just weeks earlier. While Marnie was trying to heal as her world crashed down all around her, Josh was...well, being Josh.

The weight of it all hit her hard as she tied the sash of her robe.

"After my dad died, I told you I couldn't deal with losing someone else I loved. Remember?"

He bowed his head. "I remember you pushing me away. I tried to give you the space you said you needed. But..."

When he broke off, she rubbed her lips, waiting.

"The next thing I knew"—he was looking at her again—"you were dating some financial whiz down in Buckhead. And then you were getting married...less than two years later. To *him*." He raked his fingers through his hair. "Help me understand *that*."

She studied him now, pondering just how to do that.

"I was terrified of losing you," she murmured.

He drew his lips together and turned away again. She recognized his heated frustration, the way his shoulders tensed and then relaxed as he breathed his way through it. When he turned his attention back to her again, his eyes were an ocean of sadness.

"I don't buy it," he said. "We risk losing people we love all the time. That isn't a reason to give up on loving them."

Trembling, she tugged at her sash some more.

"I don't think you get how raw I was," she said. "I was still mourning my mom. And then my dad wanted to die with some dignity, which I supported—against RJ's wishes."

It was quiet between them now, except for her breath, which came out ragged.

"Do you love him?" Josh's question broke the stillness.

She jerked. "My brother?"

He huffed out a silent laugh. "Your husband."

"Oh." She paused, her voice sad. "I thought I did."

"You looked pretty happy, you know."

She turned her head quickly, trying to grasp what he'd said.

"Your social media posts." He shot her that crooked grin she'd always loved, but it seemed sad now. "I tried not to stalk you, but..."

Her heart swelled. But then it sank, and she had to turn away.

"Lee's not a bad man." Taken aback, she realized she meant it. "I wanted to love him because..."

When her voice trailed off, Josh prompted, "Because?"

"He didn't thrive on adrenaline sports like you did." Her eyes bore into his. "He would never put me in a spot where I might have to..."

I might have to choose whether to pull the life switch again.

She found other words, but her voice still trembled.

"Lee was the safe choice."

Josh's eyes—those kind, beautiful eyes—pooled with confusion. He drew in a breath and tapped a fist against his lips. "Why didn't you hit me over the head to help me understand?"

The tightness in her chest eased, and she asked, "Why didn't you fight harder for me?"

She waited for a glint to touch his eyes. Instead, they clouded.

"Is that what you want? Someone to strong-arm you and take charge of your life?" He looked away. "That's not me, Marnie."

Her stomach tightened. "I know," she whispered.

She reached for his hand, but he didn't reach back. Instead, he glanced around as if searching for answers.

A sob threatened to escape. His face twitched. Could he be close to tears, too? But then he regrouped, hitching his shoulders and raising his hands in surrender.

"I don't know what to say." He stared right through her, his beautiful face void of emotion. "You gave up on us. So you could feel safe."

He walked toward the door.

Was he leaving?

"And now"—he lingered—"I don't have a clue what to say. I can't even…"

He said that last part so quietly she barely heard him.

Then he turned from her and walked out the door.

Chapter 38

Marnie's eyelids were hot and gritty. Her throat itched. Like a robot, she showered, then dressed and opened the shutters. The bright light blinded her, but instinctively, she glanced up toward the attic portal.

"Where did y'all go?" she muttered.

In truth, she was angrier with herself than with the spirits.

Josh had once been her love and her joy. He'd been her special person—the one who valued her opinions and feelings as much as his own. In a time of intense grief, she'd pushed him away. In a place where he'd come back to her, she'd pushed him away again.

Grabbing the mug he had brought her, she huffed out of the room and down the stairs. A draft nipped at her toes near the front door, and she wasted no time moving into the kitchen.

She brewed another K-cup and toasted some of the bread Willow sent. And fumed. It's not like she thought of herself as a damsel in distress. But how could Josh have left her, knowing she might not be safe? It didn't seem like something he'd do.

Then again, neither did getting involved with a married woman.

She flushed at that thought and forced down a last bite of toast. The floorboard creaked. The hair on her arms bristled. When something touched her leg, she screamed.

Looking down, Marnie realized it was Onyx. Oh, my God. Between the cat's purring and her own racing pulse, they had a complete percussion section going.

Meowwww.

Marnie bent closer. This wasn't Onyx's hunger cry, but not knowing what else to do, she dished out some food and poured fresh water into the bowl. When she sat it down on the floor, the cat's tail flicked and she squalled.

The sound, a cross between a screech and a howl, sent shivers up Marnie's spine.

Onyx stared up, jade-green eyes unblinking, taking a couple steps in the direction of Willow's office. She moved in short, strutting starts, then stopped, turning back toward Marnie.

"You trying to show me something?"

Marnie trailed Onyx down the hall. The cat stopped at Willow's makeshift altar. The picture of Roxy and CeCe stared down from the wall. Marnie felt a chill, similar to the one she'd picked up earlier near the front door.

Why had Onyx led her here? Marnie stared into the picture, seeking answers. But Onyx moved onward, stopping again at a door at the end of the hall. She waited, almost expectantly.

With a trembling hand, Marnie reached for the doorknob. When she pulled the door open, a gust of air puffed in her face. She blinked and inhaled sharply. She hadn't opened a closet, as she'd expected. Instead, the open door exposed a stairway, leading downward into the darkness.

She'd had no clue The Diana had a basement.

"Whatchy'all waiting for?" From the bottom of the stairway, Fiona's voice taunted, husky and familiar,

Marnie squinted, feeling weighed down, arms slack by her side. "I can't see you."

"There's a light switch on your right," Fiona said. "C'mon."

Marnie inched forward, flipping the switch. A dim uncovered bulb flickered from an overhead socket. She squinted in the light until Fiona came into focus, smoking a cigarette at the bottom of the stairwell. Marnie breathed in only a hint of tobacco. Fiona actually smelled more of clean laundry and cherries.

Starting down the steps, Marnie's skin tingled, wondering what lay ahead.

Halfway down the stairs, Onyx yowled. Marnie slipped, landing on her backside. And the smell of overcooked eggs slammed her senses.

"No!" she stammered, trying to stand. The old crow. That was his smell.

"It's okay." Fiona stood at the foot of the stairs, crystal clear now.

"But he's back," Marnie said. "Your killer."

"His energy force is petering out." Fiona smirked. "Kind of like what happened to another part of him that night long ago." Her eyes glimmered, then she laughed out loud. "Made him mad as a three-legged dog trying to bury a turd on an icy pond."

Marnie's fingers flitted to her lips. "So does he still have power?"

"Yes." Fiona took another drag. "But the good spirits here...we've been learning new ways to channel our energy. Like, how to band together to fight off evil."

Marnie's mouth was dry. She swallowed and made herself ask, "What is this place?"

"I think it's the basement of The Diana Homestead," Fiona said, poker-faced.

Damn Fiona. Marnie knew that much, even if she hadn't yet seen it.

Fiona dropped the cigarette and crushed it with her black stiletto.

Marnie's eyes widened. "How did you do that?"

"Do what?"

"You smoked a cigarette and then put it out on the floor with your shoe. I thought spirits couldn't touch animate objects."

Fiona wrinkled her forehead. "For one thing, I wouldn't call a cigarette an animate object." She waved her hand dismissively. "All I can say is, things are not black and white here. It's not like they promised it would be back in Sunday school."

Marnie swallowed a laugh, trying to picture Fiona in a Sunday school classroom. But then her cheeks warmed. Little girls, whether they go to Sunday school or not, grow up with dreams of becoming princesses, not runaways forced to turn tricks in cheap motel rooms.

Fiona reached into her purse to retrieve a tube of glossy red lip balm that matched her dress. She appeared so vivid, so young and full of promise. She was only a ghost, though, one who dabbed her lips with care before tucking her makeup back in her purse.

"The others you mention?" Marnie narrowed her eyes. "Is there a woman named Kate?"

Fiona shifted her hands to her hips. "You gotta understand something, lady. I just got here myself. To this way station. So I'm just starting to learn who everybody hanging around here is, let alone why they're here." She reached into her purse for a stick of gum. "Your mama was easy. She can come and go as she pleases, like I said."

There was a tightness in Marnie's throat. "I still don't understand why she doesn't talk to me anymore. Directly? Like she used to."

Fiona chewed on her gum and stared off, as if contemplating one of life's most profound questions.

"You know," she finally said, "getting messages to loved ones is complicated as all get out. What if she *is* talking to you and you're just not hearing?"

Marnie scratched the scruff of Onyx's neck, pondering that.

"Or did you ever consider your mama doesn't want to be, um, present at times when a mama isn't needed *or* wanted?" Fiona smoothed the bodice of her dress around her ample curves. "You know?"

Marnie's face grew warm again, thinking about her dream. Definitely, it *was* better for mothers and daughters to have established boundaries. Even if one *was* a ghost.

Fiona reached into her purse for another cigarette.

"Do you *really* need to do that?" Marnie asked, pointing to the cigarette.

"I'm dead already, you know?" Fiona and her deadpan tone again.

Touché. Onyx shifted, hinting for more attention.

"But what the hell?" Fiona said. "I could still cut back."

She put the cigarette back in her purse, then bent to examine a snag in her stockings.

"Damn." She rubbed at her hose, sulking.

Marnie started back down the stairs. As she neared Fiona, the air grew distorted, the way it does when it rises off the sidewalk in waves during the heat of summer. A humming sound whipped on and off, like a breeze. As it grew steady, she recognized the song.

"*Oh, sister, come on down...*"

Marnie squinted, trying to see what she heard. "Who's singing?"

"The ladies who live here."

Fiona said it like it was a no-brainer, while the scent of cinnamon beckoned Marnie farther into the way station.

"But why *that* song?"

"It's a pretty common song. Plenty of churches have sung it for years, especially after that George Clooney movie used it."

But it's my mother's song. The song we sang together.

Then Marnie saw them. The spirits of Roxy and CeCe. They hovered over Fiona, both still part flame, but with more human qualities now, especially in their faces. They wafted in the curled air, their voices clear. Well, at least Roxy was trilling sweetly. CeCe's lips seemed to move to different lyrics, but still, she participated with a blush of delight.

"Did you hear that?" Fiona asked. "The little one's trying to tell you something."

As Marnie leaned in, desperate to get past the song, an aura hit CeCe just so. It highlighted her features, the golden hair, the almond-shaped eyes that slanted upward. She looked like the sweetest of cherubs, lifting her hands, holding up an offering.

Marnie peered in closer, trying to make out what CeCe carried.

"Did you hear her?" Fiona asked again.

Goose bumps crept up Marnie's arms, focusing less on CeCe's words than on what she carried. It was a fabric scrap, the rich blend of coppers and purples from the outfit Kate had worn the night of the Remingtons' porch party. CeCe clutched the matching mask Kate had looped from her neck that night.

"I can't tell what she's saying." Marnie's gaze shifted from CeCe to Fiona.

"Something about an accident," Fiona replied.

"What?" Marnie tried to clear her confusion.

Fiona was fading, along with the ghosts of CeCe and Roxy and the beautiful haunting song. As they dissipated, they left behind the scent of fresh laundry swirled with cinnamon.

"CeCe?" Marnie felt a panicking sense of loss.

What was an accident?

Had CeCe been talking about how she and Roxy died? Based on historic accounts, that hardly looked accidental.

Surely she hadn't meant Emmett's accident? That had happened before Roxy and CeCe died, but it hardly struck her as something CeCe would be prattling on about.

Marnie's mouth was dry as she thought of another possibility. CeCe could be talking about Kate's death. Was she trying to tell Marnie that Kate had shot herself by accident?

Or was CeCe saying someone else had accidentally killed Kate?

As Marnie struggled to clear her brain, Onyx arched her back and hissed.

Marnie jumped. And then a sense of gloom whooshed through her. A shadow loomed overhead, moving closer.

"Hello, Marnie."

Her heart nearly jumped from her chest as she recognized the man's voice.

Dutch Remington was creeping down the stairway, closing in on her.

Chapter 39

Marnie covered her mouth to keep from screaming.

"Who were you talking to?" The stairs creaked as Dutch spoke. He sniffed the air. "Were you smoking in here?"

Calm down, Marnie, for God's sake.

If Onyx was cleaning herself, Marnie could surely remove her hand from her mouth.

She rose and turned to Dutch.

"I don't smoke, but I smelled something, too." She flushed a little. "And I guess I must've been talking to myself." She could hear the sound of her heart in her voice, and she smelled a hint of burned cinnamon.

Then it dawned on her. Dutch was trespassing.

Perching her hands on her hips, she demanded, "What are you doing here?"

His eyes narrowed. "I noticed you were here. Alone. At least now." The corner of his lips flickered with that last word.

Goose bumps climbed up her back. "What's *that* supposed to mean?"

"For Pete's sake, Marnie." He had the audacity to laugh. "I was just checking in to see if you were okay." He held his palms up. "Just an FYI. Small towns harbor few secrets. So if you were wanting to spend some time here without being noticed…"

Holy hell. Of course the whole town knew she'd spent the night here with Josh.

"Anyway," Dutch said, taking a step closer, "do you want me to check it out?"

She swallowed hard. "Check out what?"

"The burning smell." Dutch widened his eyes, probably figuring she was a nut job.

C'mon, Marnie, think. She wanted him out of here. But in case he didn't choose to leave—or worse, meant her harm—how could she best up her odds of survival?

"I didn't see anything down there myself," she said. It wasn't a lie. She hadn't yet been in the basement. "But you may have a better idea what to look for?"

The hair on her neck stood on end as he squeezed past her.

"Goddamned old house," he muttered.

"I'll see you back upstairs," she called after him, scampering up the steps.

No way did she plan to honor that claim. She sprinted toward the front door and grabbed the knob. It wouldn't turn. *Shit, shit, shit.* She pushed on the door. No go.

Her breath came in quick, shallow puffs.

Don't panic. Dutch might have an incredibly good reason for visiting. And if he didn't, she told herself the spirits would help her. Fiona claimed they now banded together to fight evil.

Except where in *the* hell was Fiona now?

Marnie drank in a breath and raced to the kitchen. She tried the sun porch door. Its knob was jammed, too. Of course.

Sweat dotted her forehead. She looked all around, scoping out where to make a break.

Meowwww.

Onyx leapt onto the kitchen counter. Her jade-green eyes blinked slowly. Gooseflesh tickled Marnie's arms as her gaze landed beside the cat on the kitchen knife block.

"Well, now that's disgusting." Dutch's voice cut the air like a scythe.

Onyx screeched and leapt from the counter.

Clutching her heart, Marnie turned to face Dutch. Shaking, she positioned herself to block the knives. "She's never done that before. I...I'll make sure we train her not to do it again."

Dutch stepped closer. "Hell, Marnie. It's not my concern anymore, is it?"

He scrutinized the kitchen and laughed. She didn't *think* it sounded ominous.

"You know," he said, "I still find this place pretty creepy. But Kate loved it. So I indulged her. Let her hang on to it."

Marnie chafed. *Let her.* Kate had been more on point than Marnie had wanted to admit. Lee and Dutch *did* have quite a lot in common, behaviorally speaking.

Dutch walked over to the window overlooking the gardens out back. Onyx groomed herself near the back door, keeping an eye on him the whole time.

He turned to Marnie. "By the way, there are several lightbulbs downstairs that need replacing. I'd offer to handle it for you, but, well, it's not my concern now either, is it?"

She was more uncomfortable now than frightened.

"I was pushing Kate to sell," Dutch continued. "Something about this place was starting to trouble her, too. At the same time, the more disturbed she got over it, the more she insisted we needed to hang on to it." His eyes bore into Marnie's. "She was especially troubled after the last time she visited. The night of the storm."

"That *was* quite a storm." Marnie shifted her stance. "Bad enough there was no bonfire, only candles and conversation on the porch."

"You make it sound like a tea party." Dutch took a step, moving closer to Marnie. "Which is not quite how Kate described it."

"Oh?" Marnie's breath coupled as he approached.

But then his posture, his whole façade, shifted. Instead of continuing to close in on her, he stopped by the table. And perched himself on it. The man who had squirmed about a cat pawing around on the counter had just placed his human backside on the kitchen table.

Wow.

Dutch's gaze bore in on her. "Kate said you floated around that night and things got all woo-woo. She had the feeling some spirit had possessed you." He laughed again, this time sounding embarrassed. "Of course, she presumed it was Roxy."

Marnie was about to explain the same thing she'd told Kate, that it was just adrenaline.

He didn't give her a chance. "Here's the deal, Marnie." He leaned forward, clasping his hands, resting them on his legs. "While I don't believe..." He stopped for a breath, then continued. "The thing is, if you *can* connect with Kate...."

Onyx began to purr loudly. Dutch shifted. Marnie waited.

"I told her I was sorry." He steepled his fingers. "For keeping too many secrets from her." He bowed his head. "I overreacted to everything, like Finster showing up at our house with rude questions about Emmett Lightner." He rubbed a hand over his mouth. "I don't know why it made me so nuts. But it did. And I took it out on Kate."

Marnie remembered Dutch's boorish behavior the night of the porch party. But now she saw a man filled with contrition. In spite of herself, she softened.

"Perhaps you should talk to Pastor Stan," she said. "A talk with him might be more helpful than..." She swept her arms, not knowing what she wanted to communicate.

"Stan can't help me with this." The rims of his eyes looked pink, like he'd been crying. "But I think you can."

Marnie studied him closely. Was he being sincere? Or was he manipulating her?

"Why did she do it, Marnie? Can you ask her for me?"

Marnie barely breathed, waiting for more.

His face grew void of expression. "You know, Halloween morning was one of our happiest times. We talked about how we needed to get the spark back."

He stared past Marnie toward the back door. "She even pulled her wedding dress out. Tried it on. Showed how it still fit her."

Okay. So that could be why Kate's dress was on the bed when she shot herself.

Dutch sighed. "That morning, it seemed like we stood a chance and we could move on. She forgave my fucking up our finances. I forgave her infidelity."

Whoa. Marnie felt like someone just knocked the wind out of her.

Dutch's shoulders slumped as he rose. "I didn't tell her outright, though. When she said she couldn't live with what she'd done, I said the past was past. What I should have said was that I forgave her." He stopped talking, a smaller man now than he had appeared to be minutes earlier. "Anyway," he continued, "if by some hokey chance you can connect with the dead... Tell her for me, please. I forgive her. For everything. I thought it went without saying. And it won't bring her back, I know that. Still, I want her to know."

He walked from the room toward the front door. Marnie followed, still trying to grasp all he'd said.

He muttered to himself as he opened the door, "How could she think I wouldn't forgive her?" He let himself out.

Marnie stood very still. After a minute, she went to test the door, afraid it might not work so well for her. But she, too, was able to open it without a struggle.

Rubbing her forehead, she returned to the kitchen, needing someone—spirit or human—to help her process all of this.

"Fiona?" she called out. Nothing. Just as she'd suspected.

Marnie found her phone and scanned her contacts, seeking out Xander's information. The phone rang once, then went straight to his recording. So much for Xander being only a phone call away.

Dammit. So much for trusting anyone other than herself.

Glaring in silence, she opened the back door, no longer locked. She let the door slam behind her on her way out, but not before Onyx squeezed out alongside her.

Chapter 40

The path out to The Diana's tree house lay nestled in between the Adirondack chairs and the garden squares. Marnie brushed a dead leaf from her hair as she walked, ignoring a flush of embarrassment at just how badly she wanted to know who Kate had been sleeping with.

Her mind flashed to Zack. They had been openly affectionate in front of her. Not to mention, he didn't seem like a man to let his scruples weigh him down. Then again, just because Zack was an asshole didn't automatically make him guilty.

Sitting near the tree house, watching the gray clouds hide the sun, she fought off a chill. Her stomach hardened as she remembered something else. Kate had talked about being attracted to Josh. Openly. *I'm married, not dead.* As for Josh, he'd made a pointed statement of his own. *Who knows what goes on behind closed doors?*

She squeezed her fists. *Stop it.* She had to stop with the histrionic thinking.

Bile crept up the back of her throat. What did it matter, really, who Kate had slept with? Kate was gone. Forever. Dead. Nothing Marnie discovered now could help her.

She shook out her arms and slowly stretched her neck. Being unfaithful was wrong. Marnie wouldn't deny that. Still, this was 2020. She couldn't believe Kate would have taken her life out of guilt for being unfaithful. There had to be more to the story—the story that always led back to Roxy and CeCe.

HELP THEM. Maybe that was all Marnie could do. She could find out once and for all what had happened to Roxy and CeCe. If only the spirits would stop acting so erratically.

Glancing toward the house, she sucked in a deep breath. She needed to go back in, but she also needed to clear her mind with something more real world than woo-woo.

She grabbed her phone and plugged in a number.

"Hey," RJ answered after the first ring.

"I did it." Her breath came out in little huffs now. "I have an appointment with your pit bull attorney next week."

RJ said nothing at first.

"You okay?" he finally asked.

"I am." She concentrated on quieting her breathing.

"Good." His tone turned matter-of-fact. "Maybe Lee will be more mellow about this than you're expecting."

Marnie remembered the way he'd grabbed her wrist, the undercurrent of violence she sensed he was holding back. "My guess is, probably not." She willed herself to remain calm, petting Onyx, snuggling by her feet. "But I wanted you to know what's going on."

"Okay." He exhaled a light laugh. "As long as you've tapped the keg to cover awkward subjects…are you going to be okay for money?"

"If your pit bull is as good as you say." She regretted it the second it came out of her mouth. "Sorry, that sounded crass."

"No worries. What I'm trying to say is, if you need a little help—"

She cut him off. "I should be okay." Surely, she could find work. Plus, she still had some savings she had kept in her own name although how long it would last was anyone's guess.

"But if you need anything, we're here," he said. "The kids' college accounts are—"

"No!"

She wouldn't let RJ sacrifice his and Amanda's hard-earned money or risk their kids' education to help her.

"Marnie?"

Her eyes watered. "If I need money, I'll let you know."

"We can make it a loan with interest and everything."

She wasn't sure why it suddenly mattered so much, but she made a vow to herself she wouldn't need that loan, by God.

"It's just money," he added, a playful undertone in his voice.

"I know, RJ." She smiled into the phone. "Thank you."

They disconnected, and she sat there for a while longer. It felt good to have the tensions she and her brother had carried for so long finally crumble. RJ's offer touched her, even if he was perhaps being naïve. Money *did* matter. Then again, it wasn't good to let it matter too much. Buying more clothes than she needed, redecorating their townhome, yet again... Money had allowed her so, so much, but it hadn't filled the emotional voids in her marriage.

Around her, the sky grew darker, the air gusty. She leaned into Onyx for warmth and asked, "What do you say? Have we given the spirits enough time to settle?"

The cat purred, oblivious in her happy place. Marnie wished she could feel so relaxed. Being at The Diana alone unnerved her more than she'd expected. Nudging Onyx gently off her lap, she told herself to get a grip, that she was being overly dramatic.

Inside, the kitchen rested in shadows, making it seem later in the day than it was. The picnic basket she'd foraged the night before sat on the table, the jute table runner once nestled inside it now akimbo on top. There was a sting at this subtle reminder of her evening with Josh.

She glanced up at the whiteboard, trying to chase away lingering regrets—about this morning, her recent decisions, her life in general. In the place where she used to see Willow's scribbled notes and daily menus, the board loomed empty. On closer examination, someone had started to write the letter "M" but stopped midway through, interrupted or deciding they had better things to do than leave messages that may not be read.

Her skin prickled. Were the spirits in hiding now and trying to leave her a message? Or was she just playing mind games with herself?

The old floorboards groaned under her feet as she walked down the hallway toward Willow's office. The faint scent of sandalwood still lingered. Or perhaps she just thought it did. Imagination and reality were melding at a pace that made her uneasy.

But the sound of voices was real. They were coming from the basement, and she once again opened the door to a flush of cold air. She flipped on the light switch. The bare bulb flickered to life as Onyx scampered down the stairs in front of her, lithe, on an adventure. Marnie inched her way down the stairs, pushing fear and reason aside, focused on learning what lay ahead.

The din of voices grew stronger. So did the smells—the mix of cinnamon and whisky, the blend of clean laundry and cherries. How Fiona and her cigarettes could emit such a pleasant scent was beyond Marnie.

When she reached the bottom of the stairs, a new smell caught her breath. At first it registered as pear, the scent of her mother's favorite perfume. But that wasn't right.

As she rounded the corner into the gut of the basement and her eyes adjusted from light to semi-darkness, Fiona's outline became clearer. The spirits of Roxy and CeCe hovered across the room.

Marnie honestly couldn't tell if she was frightened. She didn't think so. Had this peek-a-boo game with the spirits become so commonplace she forgot to be scared?

She shuffled behind Fiona, running her hand along the cold wall for balance. The dry sticky feel of cobwebs sent a chill up her spine. Fiona led her past musty boxes stacked atop saggy old furniture and rolls of linoleum. Marnie followed, shutting out the scratching noises that echoed from behind the walls. Never mind threats from the spirits. If she encountered a rat down here, she'd die of a heart attack right on the spot.

As they moved forward, CeCe's spirit took on more and more human qualities, peering into a nook in the wall as though she was playing hide-and-seek. A strong familiar scent tickled Marnie's nose, and she, too, bent to make out the figure who hid in the alcove beneath the ledge.

CeCe spoke with the voice of a sweet little girl. "It's okay, Ms. Kate."

Marnie's knees buckled, hearing Kate's name said aloud, and she suddenly recognized the essence she'd been unable to identify earlier. It wasn't Patsy's pear cologne but a blend of pineapple and wood-like spices—the scent of CK One, Kate's self-proclaimed signature scent.

"Please come out, Ms. Kate," CeCe pleaded.

Marnie watched, barely breathing, afraid to mess with the energy flow.

CeCe's features were so real, her baby-fine blond hair, the almond-shaped smiling eyes. She held up the copper-and-purple boho mask Kate had once worn as if offering a puppy a treat. As Kate's spirit took on its human form, a mournful sob lurched through her body.

"She's not mad at you, Ms. Kate." CeCe sounded so sweet, trying to provide comfort.

As she spoke, a strong whisky-like scent caused Marnie to cough.

Oblivious—to Marnie or to the scent of her mother's spirit—CeCe looked at Kate in a wistful way. "You messed up my insulin," she said. "But you didn't mean to."

"I know." Kate wept harder.

Marnie's heart started to race. Her mind sprinted back to the night Kate shot herself.

It was an accident. That was what Willow said Kate uttered as she lay dying. And Marnie had thought Kate meant she'd shot herself by accident.

But now, Marnie squeezed her palms and told herself to focus on just one question. One question at a time.

"Kate," she asked, "why were you giving CeCe shots?"

"For my diabetes." CeCe cast her hands upward, like the answer was obvious.

And Marnie supposed it was—in CeCe's mind, at least. If she'd had insulin-dependent diabetes, she likely needed help with injections.

But why from Kate?

"Where was Roxy?" Marnie asked, glancing toward the Roxy flame. Why did it remain silent?

Kate wiped her eyes and timidly crept from beneath the ledge. She rolled her neck as if needing to stretch it. It seemed odd for a spirit to need to stretch her muscles even in death.

"Roxy was sick." Kate spoke softly. "Terminal. She passed at almost the same time as CeCe did. But not before making sure CeCe'd be cared for."

Marnie started to piece things together. Josh had told her Roxy left The Diana to Kate. Not to the Remingtons as a couple. Just to Kate. It hadn't made sense then, but it might now.

She tested her theory aloud with Kate's spirit. "Roxy promised to leave you The Diana if you took care of CeCe?"

Kate nodded glumly.

"Mama said the Lord wanted her to go live with him," CeCe said. She beamed, at peace talking about the Lord's wishes for her mama.

Meanwhile, Kate's eyes grew shiny. She dropped to her knees, starting to cry again. Marnie's heart hurt for them all. For Roxy, who'd been too sick to care for her daughter much longer. And for Kate, who'd given CeCe a fatal overdose of insulin.

It was an accident.

An accident set up to look like an intentional act, one so heinous it stirred up stories of Satanic ritual. How could Kate have been part of that? Knowing the truth, how could she remain silent when an innocent man almost stood trial for something he didn't do?

Marnie tried to formulate in her mind just how to ask about all of that. But before she could, a horrible screeching peeled through the air, and the spirits of Kate, Roxy, and CeCe disappeared.

Chapter 41

The gut-wrenching shriek came from the kitchen, making her blood curdle. Onyx arched her back and yowled a reply, then darted up the stairs. Marnie followed, her steps shaky.

Stumbling into the kitchen, she tried to shut out the horrible squalls still piercing her eardrums. Near the back door, Fiona raged, stabbing in vain at Zack Lightner, who was trying to get out of the house.

Marnie went cold as Fiona scratched at Zack's face and bit at his cheek. Zack, meanwhile, grew red in the face, struggling with the door, which wouldn't budge.

The spirits are merely energy.

She watched in horror. Zack may not be suffering from the impact of Fiona's attacks, but the swirl of energy they created sent out a lethal vibe.

His face, still splayed against the inside window, had lost its ruddy color. His eyes flickered, and his guttural cries of dismay and horror turned to words.

"Help me, Marnie!"

Even if she wanted to, how could she?

"Don't even think it!" Fiona snarled at Marnie while grazing at Zack's face. "This fucker killed me. Now *I'm* going to kill *him*."

Fiona swiped at Zack again.

"For the love of God, Marnie!" Zack cried. "Help me."

Marnie's heart raced, her instincts telling her she should try to save Zack.

"Stop, Fiona!" she said. "Listen to me."

"Fiona?" Zack jerked, not able to hide his fear.

Fiona flinched.

Marnie hoped Zack saying her name might gain him a brief reprieve from her ire. He obviously sensed her presence, even if he didn't know who she was or what was happening. And Marnie had no time to explain things to him.

"This man is alive," she said to Fiona, desperate to get through to her. "Your killer is already dead. So this guy can't be your killer."

Zack's face paled. "Holy shit, lady. I may be no Boy Scout, but I am not a killer."

Fiona raised her arms mid-air, enraged, ready to pounce again.

Marnie was desperate to get her to back off Zack. "This man is not your killer." Her tone was firm. "The old crow is. Or at least how your killer appears in the afterlife."

As she spoke, a burning chemical smell puffed up around them. Sulfur. Zack coughed. Fiona shrunk away from him, cussing. A crow—it looked like an honest-to-God *live* one—flew into the room and lingered over Fiona's shoulder.

"Get away from me, you asshole," she hissed.

The bird flapped wildly, hovering above Fiona's head, seemingly confused. When it took a dive at her, she screamed and tried to bat away its wings with her hands. Her wide-eyed terror didn't lessen, even though the crow didn't make contact.

Zack continued to cough, pounding on the kitchen door, confined by the spirit's energy, which seethed around him like a tornado. His clothes, his hair—even his beard—rippled against their force as he tried to escape the chaos. Fiona's head butted up against his now, and the crow's nonstop screeches and swoops created even more commotion.

Panic washed over Marnie. She feared for Fiona's life—which was ludicrous, as she was already dead.

The crow escalated its attacks, emitting an eddy of smoke. It billowed around Zack and Fiona, trapped near the door. Marnie squeezed her eyes and pressed her hands against her ears, begging for the screams to cease before her eardrums burst.

The chaotic shrieks didn't stop. They changed, as did the energy in the room. Marnie forced herself to open her eyes. Fiona stood at her side now. Marnie wished they could physically touch, to squeeze each other's hands against the awfulness in front of them.

The crow was growing in size, transforming from bird to hulking shadow, emitting a crackling noise that made Marnie's teeth hurt.

Her fright turned to horror as the crow continued to alter. When the crackling stopped, the air froze still, and Marnie stared at a man—a man who could be Zack Lightner's clone.

She did a double take. This man wasn't Zack, of course. He was still choking and coughing, leaned against the door.

Onyx hissed. Zack—the original—struggled to stop hacking, his shoulders slumped. Zack—the clone—stood closer, staring Marnie down. She took a jerky step back from him, trying to look away but too freaked out to make herself do that.

The clone cocked his head, his eyes flickering, curious.

"How do you keep coming back?" he asked.

Marnie quaked, waiting for an attack, praying the wild quantum energy filling the room wouldn't do her in. But the clone wasn't talking to her. He was addressing Fiona, who stood beside her, wearing her own mask of terror.

Suddenly, Marnie's mind flashed back to the night of the Remingtons' party and seeing the photo of Emmett Lightner.

"Oh, my God," she murmured to Fiona. "Zack's father killed you."

"What—?" Zack's face paled, his back stiffened. "What the hell, Marnie?"

Fiona's eyes turned into furious slits as she swiped at the clone. When she didn't make contact, she spluttered with anger. Turning to Zack, the live version, she jabbed a livid finger into his arm. When he cried out in pain and confusion, she lit up and struck him again.

Marnie blinked, unsure of what she saw. Fiona was making physical contact with Zack.

How was that possible?

With an unstable hand, Zack rubbed at the welt flowering on his arm. "What's happening?" He shrank back in terror. "Who else is here?"

Fiona glowered. "What's his name?" she asked Marnie.

Marnie stumbled, trying to keep up with both conversations while dodging the electrifying spiritual currents that filled the air.

"Someone else is here," Zack snapped at her.

Fiona ignored him. Excited by something else. "Marnie, don't you see? You empower us when you fill in gaps, when you give us information we need." Her eyes took on a diabolical sheen. "Tell me my killer's name."

"Marnie?" Zack pressed her to acknowledge him.

"Emmett," Marnie said boldly, ignoring Zack. "The man's name is Emmett Lightner."

Zack sputtered. "What the fuck?"

Fiona addressed Zack's father directly. "Emmett Lightner," she said, raising an arm slowly to point at him. "You go to hell."

The room went stone cold. Emmett began to shrink. He cried out in anguish, his voice dwindling to a weak caw. As he sniveled and shriveled in size, he spewed out small black feathery shards. Fiona turned away so as not to breathe them in. Marnie took heed and did likewise.

Zack was not so lucky.

Bug-eyed, Marnie winced as he inhaled satanic debris, his coughs coming back, more violent. She didn't dare move, waiting for his struggle to subside. It seemed like an eon before he stopped choking, the black shards of evil inside him now at rest.

A brief quiet followed. Then the crackling noise returned, along with the giant black wings. They scooped up remaining specks of debris and Emmett's decimated spirit, closed in around it all, and hovered mid-air. Then a force suctioned the wings slowly upward. Transparent again, they floated through the ceiling and into the mysterious abyss beyond.

When Marnie finally remembered to breathe, the air smelled of linen and cherries and shimmered in a rainbow of colors.

Fiona clapped. "Oh, hell yes!" she cried. "Marnie, we did it!"

As Fiona cheered, a glistening rainbow of lights converted into wings, lovely and life-filled. They enveloped Fiona like a tender lover, and a gentle force tugged them upward. They ascended much like the crow's wings had, up through the ceiling and beyond.

Eventually, calm returned. But something stirred in Marnie's stomach. Unease. Confusion.

Why had the good and bad energies gone to the same place?

That was not the way she'd learned it would be.

The room sat still now, void of all spirits, good or evil. Zack stared at her, his eyes radiating a sense of confusion. Marnie stared back, weighed down by her own fears and uncertainties.

"You're a fucking witch, aren't you?" Zack said.

Jolting at this, she wanted to tell him not to be ridiculous. But that would be too kind. Better to let him stew in his fears. He had never struck her as a standup guy anyway.

She turned the tables, asking her own question. "What are you doing here, Zack?"

He opened his mouth to speak, but he hesitated. Then, drawing himself tall, he said, "I came to apologize. For being an ass at the bar."

She couldn't hide her doubt. "You came here to apologize?" If she wasn't so scared from everything that had just happened, she might have laughed out loud.

He scowled and ran his fingers through his beard. "Fuck you if you don't believe me." He shifted from one foot to the other. "In fact, fuck you, whatever you think. I'm outta here."

Relief consumed her. He was leaving. Hope returned.

Zack grabbed for the door, but he was shut in. He jiggled the knob, smacked at the door.

"Dammit all!"

He huffed around at Marnie, who expected him to yell, to berate her for having a jammed door. Instead, his eyes grew wide, filled with fear. She could sense he wasn't focused on her. He was fixated on something, or someone, beyond her.

Slowly, she turned in the direction of his gaze.

Chapter 42

In the hallway where Willow's office met the kitchen, Kate's wraith shimmered, her caramel hair cascading over the coppers and purples of her dress, her peep-toe booties showcasing perfectly pedicured toes. Kate's essence shone whole and lovely, not the broken, smashed-up version that still haunted Marnie from Halloween night.

"Kate?" Zack's voice cracked.

Marnie whipped around to study his face. "Can you see her?"

His eyes narrowed. "I can smell her."

Marnie breathed in her woodsy pineapple fragrance. Her signature scent.

"I wasn't done telling my story," Kate said, stepping closer.

CeCe's spirit flanked Kate on her right, appearing in full mortal form. On her left, Roxy still flickered back and forth between flame and human.

"I've done some unforgivable things," Kate said.

Zack's eyes bulged wider. "She's here, isn't she?"

Marnie ignored him as Roxy's spirit came into focus next to Kate. The room began to swirl, a slow mix of neutral shades and rich scents.

"I did Emmett wrong," Kate murmured.

Marnie's breath hitched. She waited a beat before asking, "What happened with Emmett?"

"She's talking to you now, isn't she?" Zack's words came out in a blur of panic. "What's she saying about my dad?"

"Shhhhh," Marnie hissed at him, struggling to fit everything together.

"I didn't do right by Zack either," Kate continued. "I shouldn't have reached out to him after CeCe OD'ed." She closed her eyes. "But I did. And he said I'd do time if I confessed...and then he promised to help." Her voice cracked on that last part.

Marnie still floundered to know how Emmett fit in, but she understood the part about Zack. "You and Zack worked together to cover up the way CeCe died?" she said to clarify.

"Jesus, Marnie." Zack stepped toward her. "If that's what she's telling you, it's a lie."

Marnie believed Kate. Except...

Why had they not just staged a murder-suicide scene between a mother and daughter?

She was sick to her stomach, hating how her mind had gone there. But a murder-suicide would have raised fewer questions. Then again, what better way to point the finger as far from themselves as possible than to stage a ritualistic killing? Under the light of a Blue Moon.

"She's lying, Marnie," Zack sputtered, fists balled.

Marnie ignored him. All these years, Kate had carried the burden of grief and guilt until the light of another Blue Moon more than eight years later. Marnie had to know.

"Why now, Kate?" she asked gently. "What made you break after all this time?"

Kate's spirit slumped. "Finster was digging up history that needed to stay buried."

Marnie thought back to the night on the Remingtons' porch. Finster had asked prying questions about Emmett Lightner.

"Do you think Zack would've helped me back then if he knew?" Kate's lips drew thin. "Do you think he'd stay quiet now if it all came out?"

Marnie still struggled with the pieces. Had Kate and Lightner been involved in ways that went beyond business?

She had to ask. "You and Emmett?" she stammered. "You were—"

"—fucking?" The word came out loud and ugly. Zack's face puckered as he said it, like he'd just tasted a bitter berry.

"No!" Kate's eyes flickered, as though repulsed by the sound of the word.

"It's okay, Kate," Marnie said softly. "Dutch knew. And he forgave you."

Kate shook her head. "I was never unfaithful to Dutch. What I did was worse."

Marnie couldn't fathom what could be worse. She waited.

Kate's ghost glanced at Zack, then back at Marnie. "The night Emmett died…." She spoke in a whisper. "I'm to blame."

The weight of Kate's tone reminded Marnie of her own onetime burden, the one she'd carried for years surrounding her mother's death. Eyes gleaming, she tested her theory aloud.

"You're saying you're the one who gave Emmett the keys to Dutch's car?"

"What?" Zack muttered, his face flushed.

"That doesn't make his death your fault, Kate," Marnie murmured.

"Bullshit!" Zack lunged at the place Kate's spirit lingered. "She's a conniving bitch and liar who deserved to die."

Breathless, Marnie watched Zack stab at the air, eyes ablaze, as he tried to attack Kate. He never made contact. Her essence was merely energy, after all. Translucent. Untouchable.

"I did die," she whispered, not so much to Zack as to herself. "I died inside a long time ago."

Her wraith started to fade into a twirl of neutral hues and fruity, earthy scents.

"I forgive you, Kate." A woman's voice broke the air, weak but certain.

"Roxy?" Marnie gasped.

Zack perked up, extra alert, maybe even fearful.

"The overdose was a tragic accident. But"—Roxy pointed to Zack—"the cover-up was an abomination. And I will never forgive that man for what he did."

Only Marnie heard the spirits speak. Only she saw Kate's eyes spark, her soul finally at peace after coming clean. Marnie watched as The Diana's remaining spirits basked in truth and redemption before being swooped up by the rainbow-colored wings of forgiveness.

She wanted to chase after the serenity and beauty she felt coming from the beyond. Of course, she couldn't. She remained in the kitchen, where the air hung dark and foreboding.

Zack peered at her with a sinister gaze. "I think we're alone now, Marnie." He stumbled, then grinned, lurching toward her.

A jolt of panic shot through her. She wasn't safe. She ran for the knife block. But Zack moved faster. He tackled her, pinning her to the ground.

She jerked her head to escape the whisky on his breath. He was out of control. But she wouldn't give in to her fear.

"C'mon, Zack," she mewled. "You're not a killer."

His fingers tightened around her neck. "I'm not sure a judge or jury would be all forgiving to a guy who staged a Satanic cover-up."

"They'll never have to know."

Her words came out in a squeak, which only made him laugh. She closed her eyes and tried to knee him in the groin, but that only made him angrier. He clutched his hand over her mouth, turning her to face him again.

"Look at me, bitch."

No. Staring into the eyes of this horrible man would only empower him.

He leaned in closer. "You're going to die today, Marnie."

She squeezed her eyes tighter now, wishing she could float away like the spirits had done just moments ago. Zack was losing it, cracking under pressure like an overcooked egg. Or maybe he had taken in Emmett's evil essence. Marnie didn't understand any of it. All she knew is, Zack was becoming more monster than man.

She didn't for one minute doubt his threat.

Her stomach roiled at his wretched breath and the stench of tobacco on his fingers, clamped over her mouth. Rage coursed through her veins, jolting her with renewed energy.

This asshole wasn't going to take her down without a fight.

Chapter 43

She opened her eyes and bit down hard on his fingers. He screamed as her teeth sank into his skin. She loosened her bite and tried to twist from under him, sickened by the sound of his breaking skin, the sour taste of his bloodied fingers.

He yanked his injured hand to his chest, but just for an instant.

"Stupid move, Marnie." He returned his fingers back to her neck, warm, ready to close in. She felt she might drown in the stench of his whisky. His eyes were afire. She jerked to get her face away from his.

"No!" He had her where he wanted her. "You look at me!"

Her head throbbed like a dam threatening to break. She tried to scream, but she could barely breathe. No one would hear her anyway.

The room darkened. Rain pelted against the windows. A lightning strike lit up Zack's face, contorting his sneer. Small horns seemed to spike from his hair.

As thunder clapped, Marnie squeezed her eyes shut against her delirium.

Zack rammed her head against the floor. "Open your eyes!"

She opened them to see his smile fade, which scared her even more than his lunatic grin. She longed to disappear into the smoky pallor now swallowing the room.

There was a yowl. Peering into the mist, she feared losing consciousness. She focused on Onyx, whose jade-green eyes stared down from the counter. The cat was flashing a message. *Be ready.*

When Onyx landed on Zack's head, he screamed and lurched up, struggling to free himself from the cat's claws. Gulping for breath, Marnie wriggled out from beneath him. Her hand grazed a knife on the floor. Onyx must have knocked it off the counter when she pounced on Zack. Marnie stood, wobbling, unsteady. Her knees locked, but not before snatching up the knife.

Trembling, she squeezed her fingers around the handle as Zack clutched at Onyx.

He tugged at the cat with both hands. "Get. Off. Me."

With a grunt of pain, he pulled the cat from his head and flung her into the air. Onyx slammed against the door with a mournful yowl and then went still. Marnie froze for an instant, waiting to see if the cat was okay. But it was all the time Zack needed.

Marnie fell to the ground when he tackled her. Her head felt like it hit bricks as the air wheezed out of her. Suddenly, she saw herself from above, arms outstretched, knife still in hand. Zack gripped her neck as she flailed, choking out any last bit of energy she might have left.

The air around her took on a dreamlike quality, frosted with comforting spices and creamy hues. An incredible sense of lightness flushed through her as she floated upward, the neutral whirls turning from tan to pale blue to deep aqua. She passed stars and planets. And clouds. Beautiful clouds.

No, not clouds. More like waves on an ocean. Waves that rolled in a surf that smelled of cherries and fresh linens. A hint of sulfur quickly snuffed out by the scent of cinnamon, whisky, and fresh-baked cookies.

It all churned together now, the earth and the heavens, the oceans and beyond. Wherever she was, she was not alone. She floated past Kate and Fiona, then Emmett and Roxy and CeCe. She passed the Cozy-Remington orphans. They giggled and waved, floating through the air as if on an invisible glider.

And then Marnie's breath caught. There was her father, Putt, smoking his pipe, wrapped in a puff of black Cavendish tobacco that reminded her of how much she'd loved him.

Longing prickled at her heart. Everything about this place pulled her away from the life she knew, inviting her to ride into a beautiful brand-new dimension. She was more than ready to move on to this place where dark became light...where people became angels. It was peaceful here. She felt no pain, no sense of sadness.

"It's not your time, Marnie."

Marnie inhaled the pear scent at the same time the voice, sweet and throaty, snapped her from her reverie.

"Mom?" At the sight of Patsy, the person, not the orb, tears filled her eyes. "What if it *is* my time? What if I'm ready?"

For an instant, her mom's lips turned down in sadness. "I miss you so," she said. Then a spark returned to her eyes. "But you still have work to do. So many good things await you."

Patsy's eyes filled with love and longing. Then she turned away from Marnie and started to fade.

"Please, don't go," Marnie called after her.

Just when she felt as though she might collapse from grief, her mom turned to face her once more.

"It's not your time," she called out again. "Keep the faith, marshmallow. It'll get you through."

She blew her a kiss before fading away.

Marnie's heart sank as she floated slowly back down into darkness. She squeezed her eyes tight to shut off the tears. As she opened them again, she gazed down at herself, still splayed out on the floor. Zack still loomed over her, squeezing her throat. But the black around her began to fade to gray. The room felt lighter.

A surge of energy engulfed her. Kate had let her fear win. Marnie would not.

Back on the floor again, she stared up at a madman. She clutched the knife handle poised in her hand, knowing exactly what she had to do. Flinching, she plunged the blade into the side of his neck.

Writhing in pain, Zack lurched up. She lay there, too scared to think, as he struggled to remove the blade. The gurgling sound he made trying to breathe made her gag. It seemed like forever he struggled. And bled.

When he fell back on top of her, she fought the urge to vomit. Exhaustion overwhelmed her. If he jumped back to life that instant, she had no more fight in her. He'd win.

She sought out Onyx. Knowing the cat was okay might calm her, ease her panic. As if telepathic, Onyx came to her, nuzzled at her hand. Marnie tried to pattern her breathing to match the cat's purr. If she could just hold on a little longer.

The air grew still. And white. It smelled fresh and clean as it swirled into ribbons of aquas and blues, purples and hombres. She panicked, having lost sight of Onyx. *Come back to me, Onyx.* She struggled to see those green eyes again. They helped her feel hope. Or maybe it was the glints of pink and blue light she thought she saw.

She was tired. Like she was fading. But that was okay. Feelings of love and faith and contentment coursed through her. She felt weightless.

And then she felt nothing at all.

Chapter 44

The swirls of energy were gone. So were the delicate hints of pear and the scent of cinnamon whisky and pipe tobacco. She sensed she was no longer in The Diana's kitchen, but when she opened her eyes, a stomach-churning dizziness swept over her. She squeezed them shut again.

Zack's body no longer weighed her down, but she still couldn't move. Or perhaps she just didn't want to. The sensation of disconnecting, of entering another dimension, was gone. Her throat closed on her, and she fought a strong urge to cry. If she'd arrived at a plane on the other side, Fiona had failed to tell her about this one.

She turned her head, hearing the echo-like sounds of—what?—children running and laughing…a piano playing some ragtime jazz? Men and women's voices wafted in and out of her consciousness. Murmuring voices punctuated by clinking glasses.

Was she at a party?

No. The air smelled of antiseptics and cleaning products, not wine and flowers. The erratic clink of glasses grew more rhythmic, more like the steady beeps from a machine than the chink of champagne flutes during a toast.

A hand rubbed hers in a way her mother used to do. She twitched.

"Butterfly," Willow said, patting her hand. "It's me."

Marnie's eyes shot open, trying to comprehend. Maybe Willow was here as her death doula. "Am I dying?"

"No." Willow clasped her hand in both of hers. "You're very much alive. But you did give us quite a scare."

Marnie lay half reclined in a hospital bed. The beeping sound that filled her head came from a monitoring machine. Oxygen tubes burned her nostrils.

She struggled to sit up. "What happened?"

"I was hoping you could tell me," Willow said.

Marnie sat back, trying to recall the last few hours of her life, which stuck in her mind as a big, blurred blob. She made herself think.

"The spirits were there," she said. "First in your basement. Then in the kitchen. Roxy and CeCe. And a ghost named Fiona."

Willow blanched. "I should've been there for you."

"I doubt they would have showed themselves if you were. They vanished when Dutch arrived."

"Dutch was there?" Willow's shoulders sagged. "Vanita and I were watching over The Diana. From a distance. We must have missed his visit. But when Zack came to call, I knew in my bones you were in danger."

Marnie struggled some, patching together her memories like a mosaic.

"Vanita insisted we call for help," Willow continued. "And we did. But I also said screw waiting, and she didn't argue. Thank God." Willow squeezed Marnie's hand. "You were unconscious when we got to you. We weren't sure you'd make it."

It was all coming back now. The jade-green stare that led to the knife block. The stench of tobacco and whisky. The weight of evil on top of her. The emptiness that followed.

"Zack?"

"He was gone when we got there."

"Gone as in dead?"

When Willow bobbed her head yes, Marnie fought back a wave of nausea. She still couldn't grasp the speed and power of evil, the way Zack distorted into a murderous monster. But what about her? Was she any less evil, given what she had done?

She cocked her head, afraid to ask her next question. "Am I going to be charged—"

"Oh, Marnie, no." Willow's gray eyes pooled. "You two had quite a battle." She pantomimed patting her neck. "It's obvious you had no choice."

Marnie reached with a hand to check out her neck but stopped just short of touching it. The ache in her throat wasn't just from emotions. Zack had squeezed her neck, intending to kill her. The horrors were all coming back.

A nurse popped her head into the room. "You have another visitor," she told Marnie.

"I was just leaving," Willow said, blowing a kiss and exiting the room.

Marnie wrinkled her forehead, about to say she was too tired for more visitors when Josh walked into the room.

"Oh." Marnie spoke quickly and tried to sit upright.

He perched onto a stool near the bed and touched her face with light fingers.

His eyes shone with concern. "I should have been there with you."

She didn't bother telling him the same thing she'd told Willow. Instead, she surprised herself, sharing something she hadn't even told her.

"I'm pretty sure I went to the other side…"

She hoped he'd know what she meant.

"What was it like?"

"Pretty wonderful." She couldn't describe it.

His jaw muscle flicked. "I've heard that."

"My mom sent me back."

She stared at the beeping machine beside her, still not convinced this was where she was meant to be. Her mom had told her otherwise. And seeing Josh here gave her hope they maybe could be together again. But if they couldn't, she'd find someone like him, someone who listened without judging, who never stopped trying to understand.

"Thanks for…" She stopped, afraid she might choke up. When she regained control, she said, "Thanks for always believing in me." She dipped her chin, wishing she had never doubted him either. "And I'm sorry I was so obnoxious this morning."

"You? I'm trying to remember." He shifted on the stool. "What were you obnoxious about?"

"You know. I was frustrated you were so hung up by our—"

"Baggage?" he finished for her.

"Ouch." She paused. "But yeah."

He rubbed his chin. "What if we try not to let it get in our way?"

A warmth washed over her, the kind she'd missed for way too long.

"Do you think that's possible?"

"I've got to admit, I don't like the idea of a having a girlfriend who's married."

She flushed and opened her mouth to reply. But he kept on talking.

"And even after you're no longer married, I'm pretty sure you'll still be hanging out with ghosts." He leaned in closer. "I don't suppose you might find a quieter hobby?"

Her lips curved upward, just a tad. "Like maybe off-roading?" But what she just said sank in, and she sat up straighter. "Do you still like riding your buggy? And pushing the limits?"

Josh sat up, too, his expression neutral. "Sometimes."

She sighed. "So we come back to this impasse again."

They both sat quiet for a moment. But then, careful to avoid the tubes and monitors, he picked up her hand and cradled it to his face. He widened his eyes and raised his brows.

"What?" she asked.

He kissed her hand and rubbed it to his cheek.

"What do you say we figure things out one step at a time? Deal?"

Chapter 45

September 2022 – Twenty Months Later

Marnie checked her image in the mirror. No smudged lipstick. No spinach stuck in her teeth. Now, if she could just keep smiling and navigate these heels without tripping. She shook out her hands. This was what she had wanted. Everything was good.

She walked back into the main room of the historic mill—heel-first, she reminded herself—and remembered how Zack Lightner had once plied her with cranberry sangria while showing off this 150-year-old space. She pushed him from her mind, determined not to let him dominate her thoughts too often.

A waiter carrying a tray of bacon-wrapped artichokes offered one to Marnie. She declined but asked for a water. She was too on edge to eat just yet.

"Marnie!" Vanita approached, Willow by her side.

"Oh, my gosh." Marnie hugged one, then the other. "I'm so glad you all could be in town for this."

"We wouldn't miss it." Willow winked.

After Vanita retired, she began traveling the country, advocating for safer gun laws and firearm education. Willow joined her when her schedule allowed, but she still maintained her practice as a death doula.

She also volunteered in the community, which continued to warm to her, albeit slowly.

Speaking of the community—or, more specifically, the church—Pastor Stan approached.

"Marnie." He hugged her. "I'm so happy for you." He turned to Willow. "And I'm pleased you've decided you're ready to team-teach that class we talked about."

Marnie couldn't resist. "What class?"

"The Ethics of Dying," Willow said.

Pastor Stan patted Marnie on the arm.

"Maybe that'll bring you to church?" He chuckled. "No?"

"You never know." And she meant it. She admired the pastor's passion and persistence.

Laughter and chatter continued to fill the room as waiters shared trays of hors d'oeuvres and served drinks. Marnie ignored the pinch of her shoes. Her eyes widened as Andre approached with a vase of fresh flowers.

"From a special fan." His voice boomed as he placed the vase on a nearby table.

"Oh?"

"Dutch Remington." Andre's contagious laugh echoed around them.

Ah, Dutch. Marnie didn't expect to see him tonight. No longer in local government, he now advised other small towns undergoing historic preservation and revitalization projects. He remained one of the town's biggest fans, having spearheaded a drive to erect a special pavilion by the lake in Kate's memory. More surprising still, he led a public movement to exonerate Jackson Mott posthumously of any wrongdoing in the deaths of Roxy and CeCe Tripp.

Andre touched Marnie lightly on the shoulder. "You ready, ghost lady?"

Returning to the present, she nodded. "Ready as I'll ever be."

Andre grinned, then strode onto the small stage in front of an exposed brick wall. He grabbed a water glass and began clinking his spoon against it. The laughter and chatter quieted, replaced by the scrape of chairs on the floor as people were seated.

"Good evening." The mic reverberated from Andre's big voice.

Marnie glimpsed out at the audience, less nervous than she expected, but still grateful to see familiar faces. Her brother and his family sat close to the front. She chuckled outright when she spotted Uma, now five going on fifteen, her little hands plastered to her ears to fight the squelching noises coming from the sound system.

"Sorry, sorry." Andre grinned sheepishly as he adjusted the mic. "Listen, you're gonna love tonight's event—a special tribute to our town and many of the folks who've helped it become such a delight. And you're really gonna love this talented lady here to tell us about her new book."

Andre flashed Marnie a knock-'em-dead look.

"Ladies and gentlemen, a warm welcome, please, for Marnie Putnam, here to talk about *Secrets of the Blue Moon*."

Marnie took the stage, warmed by the enthusiastic applause.

"Thank you all." She waited for feedback from the microphone, but even the sound system was working in her favor this evening.

"In 2020 I was hired by the Remington family to write a book about this small town they so loved. Kate Remington was quite generous about crediting her husband, Dutch, then the mayor, with the town's growth. But the Remingtons were also especially fond of sharing stories of the town's purported spirits, and they asked me to incorporate some of those tales." Marnie paused for effect. "I won't lie. I wasn't sure I stood a ghost of a chance at pulling it off."

The audience chuckled, and Marnie continued.

"Shortly after I accepted the assignment, Kate Remington died."

An uncomfortable hum buzzed the room, but Marnie continued.

"This book is, indeed, about the towns' ghosts, including Kate's. It's dedicated to her memory, and it honors her without distorting the truth.

It details what actually happened behind the Blue Moon murders at The Diana Homestead back in 2012. It pays tribute to Roxy and CeCe Tripp by remembering them and sharing their stories."

Her cheeks flushed, suddenly embarrassed by what felt like so much self-promotion. "Obviously, I hope you'll buy my book."

The audience laughed again. She scanned the crowd, missing the face she wanted to see most. Drawing in a breath, she finished with this. "It sounds a little off to say I hope you'll enjoy this book. Perhaps a better thing is to hope it will open you up to looking at life from different perspectives. To realizing things are not always as they seem."

A hand went up, and a woman asked, "Will you be writing about more of the ghosts?"

"I don't think so," Marnie said. "This book came out in a whirlwind, and, frankly, I look forward to a little breather. But...I'm learning to never say never. So we'll see."

From the back of the room, a man stood. "You've been pretty coy avoiding the question of whether or not you see ghosts. Or believe in them. Would you care to answer?"

"Fair question." She'd anticipated this, and in truth, she'd prefer *not* to answer. "Let me just say, while I'm not sure I believe in ghosts, I definitely respect them."

She peeked down at her notes, partly to stall, partly to help articulate her thoughts.

Looking back up, she continued. "I truly believe the most haunting stories are the ones of lives forgotten before their tales can be shared. So, I encourage you to seek out those stories. Whether they belong to strangers, or to neighbors, or to you and your family."

She caught RJ studying her closely and locked eyes with him.

"Stories matter. They are what make us think and feel and understand. They're what connect us and help us make sense of the world."

Overwhelmed by generous applause, she thanked everyone and then spent a chunk of time signing books, answering questions, and posing for pictures. When most of the guests had left, she slipped off her shoes and said a silent prayer of thanks. She hadn't fallen after all.

"Hey."

Startled, she glanced up to find Josh standing over her. He grinned down, their four-month-old son Oliver nestled in a carrier against his chest. She beamed back at them both.

"Sorry I missed a huge part of your talk." He joggled to not disturb the baby when he leaned down to kiss her, then bowed his head toward Oliver, now asleep. "Someone was a little vocal, not wanting to give you the floor. So we spent some time out on the patio."

"A dad's gotta do what a dad's gotta do." She rose and kissed the baby's head, then shot a flirty grin Josh's way. "Could I interest you in an amazing trade?"

Gently, she tugged Oliver from the carrier and nodded for Josh to grab her shoes and purse, his part of the trade.

"Amazing," Josh murmured as Marnie looped an arm through his and padded alongside him to The Mill's entrance.

"You two wait here," he told her. "I'll go get the car."

As she waited, she breathed in Oliver's lovely scent—baby lotion, goodness, and love. She drank it in, along with the warmth of the moon, which cast a magical light through the trees.

Sometimes at night, voices from those who had passed still came to call, begging her to unbury their mysteries and share their stories.

Last night, she dreamed of Fiona.

"Fiona, when we die, why do we all go to the same place?" She'd been quite metaphysical *and* loquacious in her dream. "What about God and faith, good works and grace? Do none of those things matter?"

"Of course they do." Fiona waved off the notion. "Remember, we go to the same place at first, but that's just for starters."

Marnie wasn't sure she was up to a never-ending journey.

"I just want to know what's out there," she said.

Fiona emitted a snorting laugh. "Hey, I don't even know everything yet. It's really that vast." Her eyes shimmered. "Just know there's something out here, an incredible source of goodness and love, for anyone willing to move past their stubbornness and fears to seek it."

Marnie pondered that. "But what about those who don't care to seek it?"

"I reckon that's their choice. In the end, it's what's in here that counts."

Fiona tapped on her chest, then lifted her eyes upward with contentment. Her dress flashed in the light before getting swallowed into a smoky red swirl.

Oliver let out a little burp. Marnie shifted him off her shoulder and into the crook of her arm. Leaning down, she kissed his forehead.

As she rose from the kiss, he stared at her, extra alert, wearing a mini version of his dad's crooked grin. Slowly, his gaze moved from her to lock on an opal bubble floating above them. As the orb shone stronger, flecks of pink and blue reflected off Oliver's eyes.

Marnie's breath caught, and the scent of pear tickled her nostrils. For a time, she remained transfixed by the light. She strongly suspected Oliver saw it, too.

If he did, so be it. She'd help him lean into his gifts and love without fear. She'd teach him what she had to learn the hard way—that despite its risks, love was the only true way home.

Author's Notes

So many folks have helped me along the journey to create this book and put it out in the world. For starters, my ongoing critique partners, writers themselves, have provided invaluable guidance and free therapy. Thank you, Kimberly Hays de Muga and Katherine Caldwell, for your unwavering support. Also, thank you, Lindsey P. Brackett, Karen Kirkpatrick, and Marcy Lane for your valuable first reads.

Thank you, sister members of the Women's Fiction Writers Association, for your ongoing support. I'm especially grateful for guidance shared by Leanne Pike Treese, Kelly Elizabeth Huston, Sheila Athens, J. Marie Rundquist, Kathryn Dodson, Paulette Stout, Catherine Matthews, and Pamela Kelley (who has no clue how much I stalked her helpful online publishing tips every step of the way).

A very special shout-out goes to author and marketing whiz Lainey Cameron, who taught me the value of a writing community and helped me develop a book launch plan that kept me almost sane. Thank you, also, to my cover artist, Elizabeth Mackey, my editor, Misha Carlstedt, and my proofreader, Cynthia Houston.

Sincere gratitude goes to my wonderful Pub Buds for bellying up to the (virtual) bar, reading advanced copy, and cheering me on as I hobbled my way to the publishing finish line.

Much love and eternal thanks to my family—my kiddos, who always make sure I know they believe in me; my grandkids, who remind me that writing, awesome as it is, isn't everything; and to Rice, for all the cooking and cleaning and shopping and laundry he does so that I can keep my cheeks in the chair in order to feed my need to write. I love you for all that and more.

Finally, thank you, dear reader, for taking the time to read. I am honored for the opportunity to try to connect with you through story.

About the Author

Jan Heidrich-Rice writes contemporary women's fiction laced with what-ifs. Sometimes haunting, often funny, her work is always spiked with hope and heart. In addition to fiction, she writes creative nonfiction that reflects on family and the wonder and humor of everyday life. She lives with her husband near Atlanta and enjoys spending time with friends and family, made up of three adult children and their partners, a grandson and a granddaughter, three grandpups, and four grandkits.

Interested in having Jan join you for a book club meeting? Check out her website for discussion questions as well as how to reach out to her to join you for your meeting:

https://www.janheidrichrice.com